THE GIFT OF LIFE, PLUS ONE

By

James J Hill III

This story is a work of fiction. The characters were all created using the author's imagination. Any similarities in the characters to anyone are purely coincidental.

James has also published other novels, including "When the Dandelions Sing," and "Phoebe's Heart of Stone".

Dedicated to those who never doubted that I would be able to tell these stories. Also to anyone that may be experiencing life in a way they never planned to, but still giving it all they have.

Special thanks to the following people who helped with the editing:

Flora Poloway

Amy McCormick

CONTENTS

The Gift of Life, Plus One

"My favorite thing to do is to stand outside on a warm summer day, barefoot on the silky grass, in a perfect rainbow-colored, fairy princess dress with a sparkling silver tiara on the top of my head, stretching up to the endless sky, as the sun pours its warmth onto my face," she said.

Not a day goes by that I don't hear her say that. It's music to my ears, and it warms my fragile heart like nothing else. I've learned to appreciate the simple things in life more than ever. The summer rays dancing across my own face as I watch her. I imagine those simple, yet elegantly impactful words my Agnes speaks time after time, and I smile. I hear them so clearly and know those same playful words will be heard many more times over the remainder of the summer. At least that is my hope.

Agnes is twelve, and although at that age most girls have graduated on from fluffy princess dresses, Agnes clearly knows that they are something truly special to behold. As her father, I finally see past the fact that most parents would have an issue with this. It's not their decision, nor is it mine. It's Agnes'. But that did take me time to accept.

So, for this summer, while the leaves are dancing in beat with the whirly wind, and the warm, gentle sun is slowly turning her pale skin a shade of scarlet, I shall watch my sweet Agnes twirl in the mid-afternoon warmth, singing as only she can, and forgetting all she should be able to. For this summer, I can do that for her.

My wife, Amanda, sits on the back porch that overlooks our yard, and stares. She peers out to where our Agnes is dancing away, and just stares. She doesn't say a word, nor does she have an expression on her face. It's been a tough year for her and I. Things are not going as we planned. They seldom do, but this year, well, it's just noticeably different. I understand though, although I miss having my wife next to me, smiling as she always had. Perhaps after this summer, it'll be different than it is in this moment. Perhaps she will be back to the woman she was, enjoying the laughter of our children that we have together brought into this world, and she will smile again.

Our plans changed. I've forgotten some of what we decided we would do. We had married at twenty-three for me, and nineteen for her. Amanda's parents were firmly against it from the start. We were both so young that it made sense for them to oppose us marrying at that time, but they did not know what we did. That nothing, literally not a single thing, could change how we felt for each other.

Just last summer we celebrated our thirteenth wedding anniversary in this very yard and grew even stronger than we had ever been. We leaned on one another for more than we ever expected to need to, and somehow, we learned more than we knew we needed to, or wanted to.

Strength beyond any measure of strength was surely needed, and so we pushed all our crazy fears and doubts as far away as possible, even though we knew that fear was a real part of this. There was no getting around that, but if we could stomach a little at a time, and then find an absolute hope that would help ease us past the remainder of that doubt, we could survive.

Life was going well, until, well… not every year is going to be just as the last one. With the changing seasons, comes a change in the seasons of our lives. We all go through that at some point. A change in seasons. It's just part of the process. If we did not, life would be utterly predictable, and what fun would that be.

Marriage is hard. It's not for the faint of heart, and it's not something you should ever do because you want to grow up a little faster than you need to. It's sacred, and full of commitment that you may not be ready for until you are faced with having to be. It's not just for love. It's also full of frustration, and weakness, and despair. You experience regret, and doubt, and you either learn to push through together, or you don't.

It's a struggle of two completely different mindsets that must merge together to form one silly, yet completely understood pattern from which you will base decisions on, and those decisions sometimes need to be made, even if you aren't quite ready. Sometimes, life forces you to alter your dreams and desires, and sadly shows you that you are not in as much control of this life as you think.

But for now, I am just going to watch Agnes. I'm going to give my wife some space she needs, but assure her that when she's ready to talk, I am here for her. I'm willing to listen to whatever she needs to tell me. There is no rush for that though. I know she just needs to run through the phase she is experiencing, and I accept that. I don't enjoy it, but I accept it. It's the promise I made to her thirteen summers ago, and it's the promise I have kept.

"Agnes, honey, you look so fancy in your dress and tiara! Don't get dizzy, or you will fall. You know how you fall all the time," I say with a goofy smile on my face. She does fall a lot, but it's not her fault. It's really not her fault. I just wish I could fix it for her. So she would never fall, ever again.

"Amanda, do you need anything? It's hot out, sweetheart. Let me get you a drink. I'll just be another minute, okay?" I tell my wife.

She doesn't say a word. She just sits there. I smile and shake my head as if I understand. But I just wish she would talk to me. Because as much as I understand, I also do not.

Just another minute of watching Agnes, and I will go in and fetch her a cool glass of lemonade, and she can do with it as she pleases. Hopefully she will drink some. It's hot, and she's lost weight over the past 12 months. It's noticeable enough that people are genuinely concerned she's going to get herself put in the hospital, but she just won't listen to anyone.

God, I just want to go back to last summer. I want to be exactly where I am now, dancing with my beautiful wife, while the kids run and laugh through the sprinklers that we set up the night before. The yard was wet and got incredibly muddy, but who cares. It was our celebration. Now, it's our thirteenth wedding anniversary and we are meant to be happy. Life is exactly where we need it to be, or perhaps it's where it is meant to be.

Chapter 1

While Young

* * *

The summer of 2016 is approaching, and Amanda, my wife, is planning an outdoor party for us. It's our anniversary. Our thirteenth to be exact. She's really good at planning these things, and I am not. I take directions well, so it compliments her perfectly. She points, and I do. I like it like that.

Her mind is so creative, and when she envisions something, it always seems to come out exactly as she has it in her heart. You know how most people watch a video of a cake being made by some middle-aged woman and then they attempt to make it just as they saw it, because it looks amazing and so easy? Then when the time comes to remove it from the oven and decorate it, it looks nothing like the video said it was supposed to. It's horrible. The smooth lines you saw on the video are crooked. They don't match up in color, size, or location. Nothing looks the same at

1

all. It's a total disaster.

But not for Amanda. She watches those videos, gets all the ingredients together to make what she had just looked at, and then when it comes time to reveal it, it looks as if the person in the video made it and dropped it off on our porch for us to enjoy. She has a real talent for that sort of thing. It's something I cannot begin to understand. I do not possess that talent at all.

She can take an entire list, know exactly what is needed, and then like a pro, she can put that all together like magic. Effortlessly it seems, but I know she puts a lot of work into it. I don't want to take that away from her. She may make it look easy, but I know how hard my wife works at everything she does.

That's why when she gives me a list of items to pick up, I don't hesitate. The list goes with me, folded in my back pocket, and I wander around the local grocery store like a lost child, trying to figure out what cumin is and where to find it. There are so many different types of honey mustard, that I sometimes need to check in with her to ensure I am picking up the right one.

Amanda laughs at me, but it's because she knows I am trying. She knows I want to make this special for her, but I don't know how to, other than to follow her explicit instructions. That, I can do. Even if I need to check in with her once or twice, because she didn't tell me if she wanted red seedless grapes, or the ones with seeds. I'm sure she knows exactly which ones are best for whatever she is making.

Sometimes Agnes, who recently turned eleven, will tag along. She has a lot of her mother in her, but she also has the balance of me. She's very creative, like Amanda, but she also has trouble with being confident about certain things. She strives to make everyone around her happy, and sometimes that can take a toll on her.

She's great with her siblings. Both Erik and Dot, (Dorothy really but Dot just stuck), love their older sister. They look up to her and trust her. She would never steer them in the wrong direction, so when she tells them something, they listen to her. Most of the time they do, anyway. There are those rare occasions when they test the waters.

Erik is turning nine this year, and Dot just had her sixth birthday.

Erik is a fairly typical boy. He plays video games most of the time, but when some of the neighborhood boys come over to play in the yard, Erik throws on some shorts and a t-shirt and is outside with just a second's notice. They play a version of baseball in the yard that they made up themselves. Instead of using a hardball, they use a tennis ball they found in the garage, because during the spring they managed to break not one, but two windows in the garage. The tennis balls work well, and don't cause the same damage as the baseballs did.

The bases are made out of broken slate that we had lying around after we did the patio. Several pieces were piled up next to the shed, with no real plans for them. When it rains, the boys tend to slip on them, but when it's warm and the weather is dry, they are perfect substitutes for bases. I tell Amanda that eventually we will need to get him real bases, but she loves the creative side he exhibits and tells me that we should just let them go and see how they figure it out. She's right, of course. She knows our kids so well.

The boys can play for hours on end. Their parents call to check on them, but they know we are keeping an eye on the kids. Sometimes I think they are calling to make sure we are okay with all the boys hanging out in the yard. We are. It's nice knowing they are safe, and with them just yards away from where we are, it makes that so much easier.

Besides, Amanda loves to sit on the new patio. She wanted this ever since we bought this home a few years back, and I knew eventually she would find a way to talk me into it. I wanted to wait some. Saving seemed to be something on my mind a lot as the kids started to grow older, but Amanda assured me there was plenty of time for that later.

"Jon, the kids are young still. We have plenty of time to worry about all that adulting stuff later," she would say to me.

She was an adult, but I knew what she meant. Life was meant to enjoy, and while we would want to eventually retire someday, tomorrow was not the day. But if we built the patio today, tomorrow we could enjoy that. I had to hand it to her. She made a solid argument for it.

Dot is this tiny being. Her nickname fits her perfectly. When she was born, she was early by nine weeks. The doctors were worried she was going to have complications, but she managed to impress them all. She's a fighter for sure, and scrappy. I sometimes think she's more like Erik than she is Agnes. Maybe because they are closer in age, or perhaps because it's just her personality as it was meant to be.

I don't always steer my children one way or the other when it comes to them being who they are. I love that they are so unique and sure of themselves. For me, and for Amanda, we just want our children to have happy lives. Full lives. If we can provide the vehicle for which they can develop just who they are, that's enough for me. I'm learning this, anyway.

I work hard, and the money is decent. I run an accounting business from home, so I am there often. When I hear the kids running around the rooms of the house from the thin walls of my home office, I smile. I can help provide that happiness for them, and it makes me feel fulfilled. This. This is exactly the life I envisioned when Amanda and I first talked about having children of our own.

My father, Richard, is also an accountant, so I learned a lot from him. He's a good guy overall, but wasn't really as involved in my life as my mom would have liked. He's just one of those men that constantly sees a need to work and gain, but he lost the true meaning of gain.

We should work so that we can enjoy what it is we have built. Instead, he was always building, and seldom enjoying.

These days though, he's finally slowing down some. My

mother Gail wants to travel, and she's told him she will do that either with him, or without. I think he's finally understanding that it's time. I know he has regrets about the way he lived, but I don't know that he could have done any different. I had him to show me what not to do. He didn't have the same opportunity. His father died when he was young, so he had to learn this on his own. His mother never remarried, so that father role model to show him how to balance life and work, or how not to, was nonexistent.

My parents don't live too far away. Maybe a fifty-minute drive, give or take a few, depending on the traffic, but close enough that they come down once or twice a month, unless we need them a little more. They never say no, which is a huge help. The kids love having Meme and Pop-Pop over. They know whenever they are coming, so are the treats. They spoil the kids, and I guess that may be partially because me and my brothers were not. I think my dad feels bad for not spending more time with us, and not getting us simple gifts, just because.

I don't have any ill feelings towards him for that. I know he did what he felt was the best thing to do, and I turned out well because of the opportunities and lessons he did give to me. It's balance to me.

My brothers, they aren't as forgiving. One, Michael, lives in California now. He entered the Navy and did some traveling, until he met his wife while stationed out west. He's been there for six or seven years now and has only come back once to visit.

My other brother, Alex, lives in Waterbury, Vermont, not far from where we grew up, and maybe an hour and a half from where we now live. He comes by a little more often, but not as much as I would like. He's unmarried and keeps mostly to himself, working in the computer field. I can't remember exactly what it is he does, but whenever we have an issue with one of the computers, he immediately knows the fix.

I love my brothers, but they are on their own journeys. Their paths are different than they expected, I assume, so they are trying to find that happiness they felt like they missed out on.

The kids don't know them all that well. Agnes knows them more than the others, as she was the first of the kids to be born for all the brothers to dote on. She brought us together a little more than we had been for many years before, and I was happy for that. She's a special kid for sure, meant to bring people together, in spite of the reasons that we are apart in the first place. That, I know about my Agnes.

I'm not sure we are done having kids just yet, but for now, Amanda seems content. She hasn't really said much about having one more, but I know her. She loves being a mother more than anyone I know. She gives so much to all her children. She has a genuine passion for motherhood that most people can only dream of.

Who knows? Perhaps one of these days she will call me into the kitchen, while she's making one of her fantastically perfect cakes, and nonchalantly ask me what I think of having another child. We are both still fairly young, and having one more would be exciting, although we have settled into the dynamics of the current family we have. I would think about it. I think I would. I cannot be sure if I am being honest with myself.

But for now, this is the family we have, and the family I was born into. It's actually an interesting mix. I see my brothers and I as so different from how I see my kids. My kids are close and enjoy each other, even if they are so incredibly different. I like to believe I have had something to do with that, and of course my Amanda. She truly spends the most amazing quality time with them, and it's made a massive impact on how they see the world.

I am in awe of my wife for who she is, what she creates, and just how much love she gives to this world. She is my angel here on earth for certain.

Chapter 2

The List

* * *

"Dad, did mom tell you which of the grapes she needed for her recipe?" Agnes asks.

"Oh, yes, honey, she wants the red seedless. She said she must have forgotten that little detail," I respond back.

Agnes laughs, because she knows her mother rarely forgets details. Even the smaller ones. She remembers to jot everything down in such a straightforward way, that it's hard to mess this up, even for me.

"I think your mother is losing her gift," I say, laughing with my Agnes.

Agnes walks over to the fresh fruit section, grabs a few bags of seedless grapes, and holds them up high in the air to look them over. She playfully examines them as if she is searching for the perfect bunch out of them all. One by one, she drops them down, until she has looked over just about the entire bunch of them.

"Here. These are the grapes Mom wants," Agnes says confidently.

She places them in the cart I am pushing through the aisles, and without a glance in my direction, continues to the next item on the list. She's graceful yet clumsy at the same time. It's cute, really. She's trying to be an adult, but she's holding on to that shred of childhood that she pretends is gone. But I see it. She's a big kid at heart, who sometimes forgets she is, and I don't think she's truly ready to let that go just yet.

Once we are through the store and have grabbed all the ingredients we were sent to get, I tell Agnes our mission is complete. She teases me about how I talk. I'm just trying to be funny, but I guess my dad jokes are a bit corny, but I can't help myself. They just roll off my tongue as if it's a necessity to get them out. Like we go to a class when we first become expecting fathers, and they teach us how to be this way.

"Okay, yes. I know. Not funny dad. I know. But one day, you will miss these old dad jokes," I say.

"Nope, I won't, because you are always going to tell me them. You are always going to be here and always going to be my dad. So, I am stuck with hearing them," Agnes replies.

I know that is not true, but I also know there is no need in talking about what we cannot change. One day I will not be here with Agnes, or my other children. I will grow old, as we are meant to, and my time will be left for someone else to use. But my children don't need to worry about that now. I have plans to be here for many more years, even with my lame dad jokes.

We place the items on the conveyor belt so that we can pay for them and get back home. It's a small local grocery store, and someone must be out sick today, because the owner is running the register. He knows us by name. He knows everyone by name. It's a great gift he possesses, and I am always amazed at how much he retains. I'm not sure, but I think he is from Poland. I always mean to ask him, but never seem to find a way to without offending him if I am wrong. Like when people from Ireland get offended if you ask them if they're from Scotland.

"Well, hello there dear princess Agnes," he says in his thick accent and deep soothing voice.

"What have you here today? Is your mom making something sweet and delicious for you today with all these wonderful ingredients you have picked out?"

"Yes, she is Mr. Z. We are having a grand party for my parents' anniversary. They were married today, but long ago," Agnes replies.

Mr. Z is really Roman Zalinski. The kids always have trouble remembering his last name. I believe many adults do as well, so he has always told everyone to call him Mr. Z. He's a portly man, standing no more than 5'5", and has a round face with darker skin. He's always smiling and telling us stories. Not the kind that make you want to rush out to get away, but small, little ones that make you appreciate life.

"Ah, I see! What a wonderful reason to celebrate. Marvelous really. I do hope they have many more to celebrate. My wife and I? We have been married for forty-three years now!" Mr. Z tells her.

Agnes seems shocked that anyone could be married for so long. She can't fathom what forty-three years is like. For a child, that seems like a lifetime. Maybe in a sense it is, depending on how old someone may be when they marry, but as you grow older, you understand that forty-three years is a blink of an eye.

"Forty-three years! Holy cow! That makes you..." Agnes begins to count in her head.

"Old as a dinosaur! That is what it makes him," Mrs. Z shouts from behind the customer service area.

We all get a laugh out of that. There are many larger grocery stores in the area that have sprung up, with a much larger selection, but I would not trade this experience for anything. I come here for many reasons, and one is because they make us feel like part of their family.

"Agnes, are you allowed to have a piece of candy?" Mr. Z asks but looking my way.

"Yes! Dad doesn't mind at all, do you dad?" she says laughing at me as she grabs the candy from his hand.

What am I to say? No? It's part of the experience for us here. That small gesture keeps me coming back to their quaint store, and I am not sure if they realize that or not. I truly believe they do it just because they are those types of people. People with big hearts, that just want to make others smile as much as they do.

As we leave, Mr. Z tells us to enjoy these early years of marriage as best we can. I thank him and we head out to where we parked the car. I think for a moment about that though. It feels like we have been married awhile now, but the truth is, we have not. Not compared to people like my parents or Mr. and Mrs. Z. They've been married for so many years, that it's hard to imagine where I will be when I hit forty-three years of anniversaries.

"Dad, I like Mr. Z. He's always smiling, isn't he?" Agnes says in between chomps of her chewy candy.

"He is, Agnes. They have figured out the secret to being happy, apparently, " I respond back.

"What is the secret?" Agnes asks.

I think for a moment. Had they figured out the secret? Or perhaps this was just another dadism; a thing dads say just because it seems like what we are supposed to say when asked a question such as this.

"Honey, I don't really know to be sure. I guess it's a combination of things. Acceptance, understanding, forgiveness, contentment. Maybe they have all of that," I respond.

Agnes just chews away at her candy and walks over to the car without responding. I figure she heard me but was busy with her own thoughts now. It didn't matter. I wasn't even sure the answer was right. It seemed right, though. I had those things for my own life, and I certainly felt happy. But was I *truly* happy?

As I load the paper grocery bags into our blue sedan,

my mind starts to wander some. I think back to my parents and now begin to wonder if they are truly happy. Did they get out of life what they expected to? Am I on the right path to end up staying with the same woman for the rest of my days, or am I going to be a statistic like so many of our friends who are getting divorced after just a decade or two of marriage?

We have these friends, Roger and Lily, who were married two years prior to us getting married. Each week we would get together on Fridays and have a few drinks and some snacks, as Lily would call the appetizers. They seemed happy and content in life, with their three small girls and two tabby cats. Amanda was always saying after they left for the night, how happy they always seemed to be. As if they were maybe *too* happy.

Too happy. Something I never really thought about until Roger and Lily split. When they told us, I thought it was a joke at first. While they weren't known for pulling jokes like this much, there was no way it was true. We had rarely seen them disagree on things or fight openly. Who knows what goes on behind closed doors, but isn't that sort of thing hard to hide?

Amanda and I are happy, but are we too happy? After talking with Roger about how he was going to handle everything, it became clear to me that what you see on the outside doesn't always reflect on what is going on inside. But I felt as if I was genuinely happy on the inside. We surely appear like the model family to the naked eye, but to me, that's because I have the model life.

Amanda told me that sadly sometimes these things happen, but not to let that question our love. We are built differently, and we have formed our family in a way that makes us strong. Just because they couldn't find the way to make it work, didn't mean we wouldn't if we experienced issues as well.

She made sense and I felt solid after that, but there are times I wonder. Will we always be this strong? Will we always find a way through tireless storms that seem to push us to give in to its mercy? I'm certain Roger and Lily felt that they could endure anything thrown at them as well, before realizing that the reality was, they could not. Or maybe they could but didn't have the vigor to fight for it hard enough.

There are just so many distractions in the world today, that it seems as if we could have an endless number of people and places to occupy us when we felt down or troubled. A quick glance at social media could make us feel loved by someone we have never met, nor thought about meeting, until we did.

I don't know why I've thought about it so much lately, but something has me wondering just how strong our bond truly is.

Our children mean so much to us and we certainly spend a great deal of time running them to friends' houses for sleepovers, or piano lessons, or whatever else they may be doing at any given moment. But do we give each other the time we need to be a married couple? We haven't gone on a date in a long time, but not because we don't wish to. More because we are always running the kids around and just can't seem to find a few hours straight to make it an enjoyable evening.

I keep telling myself I am going to plan something special for just the two of us, but it's Amanda who is always so good with the planning. I hate it. In fact, I would probably never go away if it was all left to me. Funny how Amanda is so different in that aspect, and we have made it work now over a decade so far.

Agnes is looking at me as I am seated in the car, just staring blankly in front of me, as my mind wanders through so many thoughts at one time. She tilts her head sideways and begins to poke at my nose as she likes to do. Silly thing, really. She is always poking our noses whenever we seem a bit too occupied with something. Most times it's cute. Sometimes, though, it's a little much when I am so focused.

But this time, it's fine. I come out of my trance, and shake it off, while cracking a smile from ear to ear.

"Sorry, honey. Just making sure we have everything for mom, and that I am doing things right," I say.

Agnes just sits back and stares out the window. She's a girl for sure and sometimes a bit goofy. It's cute to watch her enjoy the simple things that life has to offer. One of those things is the car rides to anywhere. She can stare out the window for as long as we drive, and ask questions along the way, like,

"Hey dad, why do some trees lose their leaves when it gets colder, but others are allowed to keep their green all year round?"

It's quite amusing to hear all the thoughts that go on inside her head at any given moment, but honestly, she does have some fantastic questions that I even need to pause on. Her curiosity is refreshing when you look at all the other children of her generation. They sit for hours in a car complaining and playing video games the entire trip, never knowing what is right outside their windows. They miss everything around them because they can only focus on the screen in front of them.

It makes me wonder about this generation of hers. Will they have no passion? Will they always want instant gratification, and because they have all the answers with a simple search on their phone, will they never develop a creative imagination with all the wonder around them?

Agnes seems to have that fascination within her, and I love how she embraces it. I don't think she much cares for what others are doing around her. She's more interested in what she is doing that makes her happy.

As we drive back home to bring all the ingredients we just grabbed from the grocer, Agnes drifts off into her curiosity once again.

"Dad, do you think animals feel love, or do you think they just find the first mate that they see?"

It's another one of her questions that I have to think about before I answer. She's young, so many times you can give a canned answer and it will stop a child from being more inquisitive, but I don't want that for my kids. I want them to ask away. So I take a moment to think about the question she has let out into the air.

"Well, Agnes, I really don't know. Love is a strange thing. Sometimes people think they are in love, when it's anything but. Then at other times, they love, and don't receive that love in return. Maybe we complicate it as humans, and animals make it easy. Growing up, I had two dogs and they would never leave the other one alone. I swear they loved each other, but maybe they were just accepting that they had one another and no one else," I explain.

Agnes doesn't look over, but that doesn't stop her curiosity.

"When they died, how did the other dog handle that? Did one die before the other?" Agnes asks.

"Well honey, funny you should mention that. I never thought about that until now. I remember Cleo, the male dog, was so different when Babs died. We had to put Babs down when her legs weren't working the same way. It was hard on me and my brothers too, but Cleo was the saddest of all. I can remember him laying around, not wanting to do much of anything. He had a sadness to her eyes that I never saw in an animal," I reply.

Agnes doesn't miss much. It's as if she knew what I never knew. That Cleo was simply heartbroken because his partner, whom he grew to love unconditionally, left his side. I saw it, but I never put much thought into it until this conversation.

"Dad, Cleo loved Babs. I bet when she was put down, he wanted to die too, so he could be by her side again. Did he ever get happy again?" She asks.

"No, Agnes, honey. He never did. I can't remember exactly how long he lived after she died, but it wasn't all that long. I thought maybe he just got old, too, and didn't move the same, but now that I think about it, he was younger than Babs by several years. Maybe he just died of a broken heart," I say.

Chapter 3

Andrew

* * *

Amanda was born an only child. Her parents, Fred and Christine, wanted to have more children after she was born, but Christine had complications and emergency surgery after Amanda's birth, and that unfortunately prevented them from having any more of their own.

When Amanda was about to turn eleven, her parents sat her down in their living room and asked her what she would think about a baby brother. She had always wanted a younger sibling, but had grown to accept she was an only child, and she settled into that role well. Plus, she was now almost a teenager and to have such a small child around, would not be what she was hoping for before.

"I don't know...wait, are you pregnant? I thought you and Dad said that you couldn't have any more children," Amanda said confused.

She was right. Her parents were not able to have any of their own after Amanda was born, but that didn't mean they couldn't have a growing family. Her parents were talking about adoption, and they had a chance to adopt an infant from overseas. In fact, they asked Amanda as a courtesy, but they had already started the process and were just awaiting the call that it had all gone through.

That call came, and Fred and Christine were thrilled, although a bit nervous at first. They knew what the agency had told them about the child, but not much more. Nothing was known about the parents of the infant. He was dropped off on someone's doorstep and those people who found him there were unable to care for the boy, so they had little choice.

Andrew. That is what they named the boy from China.

At first, Amanda was skeptical. Andrew was garnering so much of her parent's attention, that she began to grow resentful. While Andrew had nothing to do with the situation as an innocent person to the party, he was the cause of her losing the attention she had once had completely to herself.

It took her parents some time to see that Amanda was struggling with things, but eventually her father realized that in trying to help one life, he was impacting another. It wasn't that they meant to change things for Amanda so drastically, but he understood that they had, and it had changed basically overnight for all of them.

Amanda struggled for a few years, but grew to appreciate

her younger brother. Things settled down, and eventually she felt no different about how things were. I think she understood that her parents had done something great for a stranger that they loved unconditionally before they ever met him. That was impressive, Amanda reckoned. That someone could have such a fondness for a stranger from thousands of miles away, shocked and impressed her as she aged.

Andrew learned noticeably slower than those around him. His mind was there, but his reactions were not. He would look at things for long lengths of time and say very little. Both of Amanda's parents shrugged it off at first and explained it simply. Every child learns at a different pace in life, but they all eventually figure it out in due time.

While there was merit to this, it wasn't what was happening with Andrew. Something else was going on with him, and pretending all was okay, was not going to make it that way.

So when Andrew was going on seven years of age, his parents began to look for a therapist to assist. They knew they were not in a position to handle this alone, and they desperately wanted their boy to grow up like those around him, and to learn the tools he would need later on in life when they were no longer capable of helping him.

Frantically, they made call after call, trying to find someone with an opening, and someone they felt could work with Andrew well enough to understand what he truly needed, and not just do a textbook healing, as they often heard it referred to. Their boy needed someone that was patient, willing to listen, as well as they were willing to offer advice, and someone that was not looking to simply get paid for their services.

This shaped Amanda's personality and how she viewed things in life. Instead of judging people or situations at first glance, she learned to look deeper and to see a little more for what could not be seen readily. It helped her whenever she wanted to judge people and their actions, or lack of actions.

Amanda knew that people made decisions in life based on many factors, and she didn't have to understand those reasons in order to accept them. She would tell me all the time that unless she could walk a mile in someone's shoes, she had little right to pretend she could grasp how a person felt and why they reacted as they did.

I loved that about her. She didn't give opinions unless she could from experience. Her mindset was that unless it was affecting her or her family, what difference did it make?

She watched Andrew grow into a wonderful, loving young man, and although he didn't have the ability to do what others his age were readily doing, he seemed happy with life. Andrew never seemed to mind that he was different, or perhaps he never noticed. And Amanda knew, it simply didn't matter.

I like Andrew. He's shy, but funny. When I was first dating Amanda, he would pack a bag and pretend as if he were going with us. It was his "stowy bag". I first thought that term meant because he thought he was a stowaway, but later learned he meant "story bag". Andrew always had his bag with him, and inside were a few small books, some paper, crayons, and a few of his toys he liked best.

I didn't know how serious he was, or if he was just pulling my leg, but one afternoon I came by to get Amanda, and instead of laughing off Andrew's request to go, I asked him if he had his "stowy bag" packed and ready to go.

Amanda at first wasn't sure if I was teasing her little brother, or perhaps just playing along with him, but I was certainly serious. I wanted Andrew to go with us, although to be fair, I was extremely nervous. I had nothing special planned that afternoon and thought maybe I would win Amanda's heart with the gesture. But what if her parents didn't approve? What if Andrew were to realize I was serious and back down because of his shy nature? Would Amanda see this as me trying too hard?

I saw this going so many different ways, but what I least expected, was the reality of what happened.

Everyone, once they realized I was serious, seemed to be okay with it. I remember her parents having reservations once they knew I was willing to actually go through with this, but I think they were also curious. Maybe they wanted to see if this young man who had taken a liking to their daughter was really what he seemed to be, or maybe they wanted to see just how I handled Andrew on a date with his sister.

We got into the car I borrowed from my father and

headed down into town. Andrew had his bag with him, but did not open it at first. I think he may have still been shocked some that he was going on this date with us both, but Amanda talked with him the entire way. I chimed in when I felt I could say something as well, but I too, was nervous. I just had so much hope that this would go well and began to fear it was not going to.

But Andrew did open up some. He talked with Amanda about his bag, and when she asked to see what books he had chosen for this adventure, I realized that to Andrew, that is exactly what this was. A grand adventure for him. One where he did not fully understand what a date was for Amanda and me, and one where he didn't quite understand what he was doing with us. I had no real plan. Maybe because I half expected his parents to say no, or for Amanda to not want him to tag along on what was supposed to be an actual date.

Either way, we were pulling into a spot on South Main Steet, and I had to figure something out.

Amanda loved the small quaint shops that lined the downtown district. She told me that when it was December and the ground was covered in a dusting of snow, she would beg her parents to take her there just so she could see all the bright lights, as they lit up the entire street and all the store fronts. She loved this area, so I decided to take her here. I just hoped Andrew would be okay with this. I hadn't asked about how he was in particular settings.

Before I turned off the car, I looked over to Amanda.

She was so pretty sitting there. I knew she was anyway, but looking at her staring excitedly out the window at all the stores with that slight smile she had, just did something to me. I waited for a moment before interrupting her gaze.

"So Amanda, is this alright? Will he, I mean, will…"

She knew what I was trying to say. I was tripping over my words because I had no idea of how I was to act. I didn't want to offend her by acting as if he wasn't able to do normal tasks, but I honestly wasn't certain of that.

Amanda laughed, and her head went back to look at Andrew as she did.

"Hey buddy, you ready to walk around and see some stores?" she asked him.

Andrew was always smiling, so it was hard to judge his excitement. He just leaned up to look out his window to see exactly where he was before responding. His bag was clutched close to his chest, and in one of his hands were the books he was telling Amanda about on the way down here.

"Stowy bag," was his response. I wasn't sure what he meant by mentioning the bag, but Amanda knew right away.

"Yes, Andrew you can bring your story bag with you. Let's put all the books and crayons back in so you don't lose them, okay buddy?" Amanda said.

Andrew started to sit back in his seat, and he carefully placed each item in his bag, in a very calculated manner. He was ensuring he did not miss a single item, and that they were all well cared for.

I looked over at Amanda and she was just watching her little brother as if she were his guardian, protector, or even his mother. It fascinated me. Here we were, so young and innocent, yet this girl, this young woman, was handling things like someone who had years of experience under her belt. I knew in that moment that I had made the correct decision in bringing Andrew with us. It allowed me to see a side of her I had not known.

We walked with Andrew around the different stores, watching as his excitement grew from one to another. He carefully picked up items and looked them over, before placing them back exactly as they had been originally placed. It was his thing. He wanted to look at everything and study them, but then he had a strong desire to ensure they were left as he found them. It confused me at first, but then I just realized it was his thing. Just like his "stowy bag" was his thing.

So much made sense to me that day. It was eye-opening for someone that never had someone in my life like an Andrew. He was different for sure, but fascinating. Had I not had the chance to see his interactions up close for myself, I may never had known the wonderful things he brought to his own life.

One particular item kept grabbing his undivided attention. He gravitated towards this blue figurine in one of the shops. It wasn't anything shiny, or full of colors, or scary, or cool. It was a simple figure of a girl holding her father's hand, looking up to him. She was dressed in a long dress that was just a little too big for her, and her father was looking down back at her with a smile. The figurine stood about twelve inches high and was made of some type of resin.

I have no idea what about that figurine made Andrew so happy, but it didn't matter. He saw something in it that made him excited. This one, he took a little longer to put down. He studied it, held it up to the light, and turned it around and around. It was plain, yet anything but, at the same time.

Amanda had to get back home and pack for a trip she was going on the very next day, so we finished up in that store and began our way out. I had to use the restroom, so I told them I would just be a moment.

When we all arrived at the car, Andrew was smiling as usual, but he just looked as if he had a very special afternoon. He seemed to hold his head up just a little more, and that? That made my afternoon.

As we drove back to their home, Andrew opened his bag and was looking at the pictures in his story books that he brought with him. He was laughing and smiling, and Amanda was just giggling.

"This, this was good, Jon, thank you. We had a great afternoon and date," she said with a smile.

I pulled up to their home, and as much as I didn't want the afternoon to end, I knew it had to. We did have a great afternoon. It went different from how I would have pictured it if I had tried, but that was a good thing. My nerves were gone, and I felt perfectly happy with the entire day.

Andrew waited for Amanda to open his door, and I walked around to where they were to assist.

"Hey, Andrew, here," I said giving him a bag I had with me.

He didn't say anything but took the bag and walked away. I wondered if I had done something wrong. Maybe he wasn't used to getting gifts and was particular about that. I had no clue, but he just walked to the front door and into the house, as his parents were standing there waiting.

"Don't worry about that. Andrew is still very shy and doesn't always understand things. He had a wonderful day. Trust me, I know," Amanda assured me.

"No problem. I just wanted to give him a small gift to thank him for going with us. It's no big deal, really." I replied.

Before Amanda got out the question I knew was coming, Andrew yelped loud enough that we heard it outside. His excitement was overwhelming, and he was showing it how he wanted.

"Jon, did you buy him that blue figurine?" Amanda asked.

"I did. I don't know, he just looked so interested in that one over everything else. I just thought it would make him happy, that's all," I said back.

Amanda didn't have to say anything. She leaned into my arms, put her head on my shoulder, and squeezed me. I knew I had done a good thing today, and that made it all worth it.

Amanda's parents waved as Amanda let go, kissed me on the check, and told me that there was something special about me. I felt like I never had before when she told me that.

Waving back at her parents as I walked to the driver's side of my car, I heard Andrew call my name.

"Jon!" he said.

"Yea buddy?" I replied.

He held up the blue figurine to me and smiled. His head dropped low as if he was being bashful and could not come up with words to say. I didn't want to make him feel any more awkward, so I just said,

"You are welcome, Andrew. Keep it in a safe place!"

That was how my date with Amanda and Andrew ended, with a smile on my face, and a warmth in my heart. I knew then, I had plans for us in life.

Chapter 4

As Agnes Falls Ill

* * *

As parents go, I think Amanda and I have a good understanding of our children. But like any other parents, we too, make mistakes, like the time we left Erik at the bowling alley after a birthday party. I swore his friend Kyle said that his parents were going to take him home after they had the last of the pizza, but apparently not. Nope. We left Erik there alone, and the owner of the alley called us to ask if we were going to ever take our son home or if he was now employed at the alley.

That was embarrassing. Amanda and I don't really bring that one up, but Erik does. Anytime he's upset, he reminds us,

"So, are you guys just going to leave me alone, you know? Like that time at the bowling alley? Remember that? Because for some reason, you forgot me."

Yea, safe to say that's his go-to whenever he doesn't

feel like we are being fair to him. It's funny how kids can't remember to clean their rooms when we ask, but they can remember one mistake we made a year or so ago.

I don't harp too much on the past though. My dad told me to look forward because that is the direction I am going in. Although that makes sense, I still at times feel as if the past is important. If we remember something we experienced and just how we handled it, we may learn from that. Maybe we handled it correctly, or maybe we did not. Either way, it's a lesson we should carry with us and use when needed, or pass down to someone else who may gain from the insight we now have.

Andrew still lives with Amanda's parents, and we see him from time to time. The kids love Uncle Andy, but they call him Uncle Dew. He still has his old "stowy" bag and carries it wherever he goes. If her parents go away, which is a rare occurrence, he stays with us and the kids. It's nice having him here, but it is a lot of extra work. I hate saying it like that, and I never do out loud. I don't want anyone to know I struggle at times. I can get overwhelmed, especially lately. This past year has worn on me like a rainstorm on suede. I feel rough and dried out.

Last year, when we held our anniversary, Andrew slipped and fell on the table that held the beautiful cake my wife, his sister, made. It was not on purpose, and he wasn't messing around or anything. It just happened. I was afraid Amanda was going to be so upset because of all the work she put into our cake, but she brushed it off with a smile and told

Andrew it was going to be okay.

Poor Andrew was so upset. He thought he ruined the party, and his bag that he carried like a bible was covered in icing and fruit. Amanda, though, quickly took the bag from him and promised she would return it good as new. Andrew, he trusts Amanda more than anyone else, I believe, even more than his own parents. It's amazing to see that level of trust come from him. He enjoys me, and while I think he has trust for me for certain, it's not like the trust he has for his sister.

At that same party, poor Agnes caught some type of bug and was inside most of the afternoon. She was able to eat a little, but then she asked if she could go lay down for a few. A few turned into the entire afternoon. We checked on her off and on, and so did both of our parents, but she didn't have a high fever and so we just thought maybe she was a little rundown. Could be a sugar rush that brought her down. Who knows, but it was nothing to worry about because she didn't feel warm to the touch.

Erik and Dot were fine, however, so they must have missed catching whatever it was Agnes caught. They were both running a hundred miles an hour all over the yard, and my mom gets a big kick out of any time they do that. I didn't have that energy when I was a kid, so she assumes it comes from Amanda's side of the family.

"Jon, I'm going to start to clean up some. Would you mind checking on Agnes? Maybe wake her up so she's not awake all night. You know how they have trouble sleeping when they are asleep all during the day," Amanda said.

"Yea, I'll do that, then come back out and help you finish up. Leave the tables. I will take care of those later," I replied.

Amanda's parents had to head back home with Andrew, so they left before we started to clean. My parents were hanging with Erik and Dot so we could finish up things, so that helped greatly.

I walked in to check on Agnes and she was still sleeping. She looked so peaceful sleeping with her little snore. Of all our kids, she is the only one that snores. It's not an obnoxious snore. Just a slight one that you would expect from someone in a deep slumber.

"Honey, it's dad. How are you feeling?"

Agnes didn't move much. She clearly had intentions on resting much longer than we anticipated. Just earlier that day, she was spunky and excited to celebrate with us, and now she's tuckered out hard.

I was unsure I wanted to wake her more, but I did understand Amanda's point. If we had let her go for too long, she would have had a miserable night trying to fall back asleep.

Just then, though, my mom walked in to check on us both.

"Jon," she whispered to me.

"Is she feeling okay yet?"

"I don't know mom. She's not warm, but she doesn't seem to want to get up. She didn't really respond to me when I tried. Maybe she just needs more sleep?" I asked.

My mother has a good touch with these sorts of things. She had always wanted to be a nurse but having children and a husband who worked more than he didn't, kept her from achieving that dream. She didn't seem to ever complain, but I know if she could have done one thing differently in her life, it would have been that. She would have been wonderful as a nurse, too. Her understanding of what someone needs is precise. As a child, when my brothers and I would get sick, or get hurt tumbling down a steep hill near our home, she always knew how to treat us. Rarely did we ever need to go to the doctor's office.

I moved aside so my mother could sit next to Agnes and check on her. She put her gentle hands on her cheeks, then on her forehead. I watched as my mother worked her magic, knowing she would be able to make everything better for Agnes.

She told me to go get a thermometer, just to be sure she didn't have an underlying fever, and so I did. We keep that and the children's medicines and Band-Aids and an assortment of ointments just down the hall, on a high shelf, out of reach.

As I returned to the room, my mom didn't look as sure as she did when she first went in.

"Here mom," I said as I handed her the thermometer she requested.

My mother didn't say anything to me, but she was talking to Agnes.

"Baby, Agnes, it's Meme. I want to check your

temperature real fast, okay sweetie?"

Agnes slowly opened her mouth, aware of how that all worked. My mother slid it in and before she could tell Agnes to close her mouth, Agnes did. We waited, me in the doorway leaning against it, and my mother on one knee next to Agnes.

After about ten seconds or so, a beeping went off and the thermometer comes back out. Agnes still just laid there and kept her eyes closed shut. She just wanted to rest more and to be left alone.

My mother looked at the thermometer.

"Well, Jon, it's not real high. 99.5. So she just has a slight fever, but she does seem unusually tired. Have there been any big changes in her routine, or her diet or anything like that?"

I tried to think back to over the last few weeks. She ate a few too many slices of pizza the week before and had a belly ache for the night, but that wouldn't be causing an issue for her here and now. Did she eat cake before the party? She couldn't have. Andrew slipped and dropped that masterpiece onto the patio below.

No, nothing really different.

"Not that I can think of mom. She was fine earlier with me when we went to grab groceries for today. Just her typical goofy self," I replied.

I was starting to feel a little worried. Was I missing something? Did she maybe eat something the night before that didn't agree with her?

Just then, Agnes told my mother she was going to vomit. I ran into the kitchen to fetch a pot, but it was too late. She had thrown up all over the floor and the bed. My mother was there to let her know it was okay, just as she grabbed the pot from my hands.

'Here, baby. Throw up in this," mom said.

Agnes was not herself at all, and I told my mom I would go get Amanda and let her know. I don't handle this sort of thing well like they both do. If there is a question about an equation or a homework problem that the kids can't figure out? I'm their guy. That I can handle, no problem at all. But when the kids are ill, Amanda knows, just like my mother does, what's best.

I ran out to the yard and told Amanda what was going on, and that if she heads in there, I will finish cleaning up out here.

She didn't seem overly concerned, which calmed me down a lot. The kids get sick and that will never change, so I guess I was just overreacting about this. They have thrown up before and will again. I just am not used to handling that and watching It, to be honest.

"Okay, Jon, I almost finished putting the extra food away. If you can just finish that up and get the plates and napkins and cups put away, I will do the dishes after I check on Agnes and your mom, and we can relax for the remainder of the evening," Amanda added.

It's a nice balance to have someone compliment how I am. Typically I panic when it comes to handling sick children, especially ours. Or diaper changing, which I have not done in many years, since the kids are older now, thank God. When I am out of sorts, Amanda is not. She evaluates each situation quickly before coming up with a plan for what needs to be done. Just as if she were baking one of her beautiful cakes, she creates a list in her head of what steps need to be taken and when. I like that she has that ability because I clearly do not.

As I watched her close the door to the refrigerator behind her, as she placed the last of the extra food we prepared for our anniversary party, I just felt a little uneasy for some reason. I wasn't able to put my finger on it, but maybe it was just that I was a little tired. Hopefully I didn't catch whatever Agnes did, I thought to myself, because I couldn't afford to miss too much time with clients. Besides, I under-stand the true definition of a "Man Cold", because I am a big baby when it comes to that.

I once was so sick, I started to hallucinate wildly, calling out to Amanda in the middle of the night, exclaiming that I was dying and just let it be. I would feel better off dead and would no longer need to deal with this horrible pain from all the vomiting I was doing. I literally begged to die.

Amanda would roll her eyes and tell me,

"Jon, you aren't dying. You have the man flu. Just hang in there and by tomorrow you will start to feel more like yourself."

She, of course, was always right. I did start to feel a lit-tle better and having her nurse her big baby of a husband back to health was both appreciated, and a blessing, for me, at least. I hated getting sick and she knew this, but even while rolling her eyes at me, she had some sort of sympathy towards my condition.

"Jon, come here," I heard my wife call out from Agnes' room as I was just about to head out for the last of the chairs.

That didn't sit with me well. She never called me for something such as that. I am of no help when the kids aren't feeling well, unless it's to run out to the drugstore to fetch some cold medicine or another remedy she knows will do the trick. So, to hear her call me into the room gave my stomach flutters, but not the good type.

"Hey, Babe. What is it?" I replied as I breach the threshold to her room.

Her room is full of color. Agnes decided last August that she wanted a fairy room. The colors were pretty specific that she wanted to adorn her walls, so I had to check with a few paint stores to find the correct ones. I finally did, and then there were the curtains and throw rugs that, they too, were pretty specific. She knew exactly how her room should look when it was finished, and aside from the blanket she requested, the room was exactly as she planned. The blanket was on back order, and so we promised Agnes we would order that just as soon as it was back in stock.

Time went on through the end of summer and into the holiday season and we just had forgotten to check the status of the blanket, so it never got ordered. Agnes had brought it up once or twice while I was working on a client's taxes, but I was a little too busy to stop what I was doing to check to see if it was back in.

Besides, it was a blanket. Simple, just to keep someone warm. It had different color stripes along the bottom third, and a fairy princess at the top, winking, amidst a cloud of pixie dust. Cute for sure, but nothing that was needed any-time soon. Besides, this was the third time we had changed her room, and she would surely want something different when she hit her teens. They always do, I am told.

"Jon, I don't really know just yet, but she doesn't have a fever really, and she isn't vomiting, but she just doesn't look right. I've tried to get her to talk about what is bothering her, but she's not able, or willing to talk. She just wants to sleep. I'm going to take her first thing tomorrow to the doctor's office. Can you keep an eye on the other kids?" She said to me.

I had some things I had planned to do in the morning, but I was sure I could change those. If not, mom and dad were still there, and I could always ask them. We would figure something out. I was more concerned that both my own mother and Amanda seemed concerned. They rarely do, because they know children get sick, then they get better.

Always. Children get sick, and then they get better.

Chapter 5

Andrew's Excitement

* * *

I remember Amanda telling me when we first got married that she wanted to include her brother in the ceremony as something special. She thought it would mean so much to him, but also to her parents, who really tried to include Andrew in all aspects of their life, as best they could.

I told Amanda I would think about it and figure something out, but to leave it to me. I knew I couldn't have him come to the bachelor party, for obvious reasons including the fact he would only be nine, but I understood that he was extremely important to her, and that meant he was also important to me.

Andrew, while still severely shy around people, had opened up to me over those years that I and Amanda dated. He was always asking me if we were going on a date again, and each time I dropped off Amanda, he was waiting up to see if I had another gift for him. Sometimes I would just get him a small trinket if we were close to a place that sold them, while other times I would ask her if he wanted to tag along. When he did, I knew his bag was never far away, and that always made me smile. To have something you held so dearly, that high in regard, I just couldn't grasp it.

Andrew just seemed so pleased with life, even though the people around him that were the same age as he was, were able to do things he could not. I wondered if that would bother me if I was in the same position as he was. Apparently, he had realized that his life was perfect just the way it was, no matter what anyone else saw or felt.

I had seen Andrew throw a fit a few times over the years, but mostly because he wanted to do something that his parents felt was not right for him. For instance, this one time, he wanted to try out for soccer, but after doing so a few years prior, his parents were just not going to be able to handle another experience like that again.

Two years prior, in the spring of 2002, Andrew begged and begged to try out for a local township league. He wanted so desperately to fit in, and for him, he thought he did. But unfortunately, no one else seemed to get that.

When the team selections were being handed out, Andrew was placed on a team called the Black Bandits. They all received black shirts with numbers on the back, and Andrew was thrilled. He wore the shirt the night before the first practice was taken place, refusing to take it off even as he went to sleep that evening. All he wanted to do was wear that black numbered shirt and be ready. But Andrew had no idea what he was getting ready for.

He had no coordination, and no sense of the rules needed to play the game. The most he had ever done was to help organize bingo at his community church, so this was going to be a large jump from that. While he was told that by his parents, he would not, and honestly could not, truly understand that all.

The night before, his parents laid in bed, wondering how this was all going to play out. They were trying to remain as positive as possible, but deep down they feared the worst for their son, and wondered if they should have stuck to their guns and just said no.

As the morning sun touched upon their home, Andrew shot up and ran into the bedroom of his parents. He was dressed, had his sneakers with cleats on that his father had surprised him with, and a water bottle that had his name printed across the face of it. He, of course, also had his "stowy" bag as well.

His mother tried to tell him that the other boys and girls would most likely not have bags with them, and perhaps it would be best to leave that at home for safe keeping. But you could not deter Andrew from taking his bag wherever he went. That was his most treasured possession in the world, and something that made him feel whole. His nerves were getting to him some the more his mother tried to talk him out of it, so she just let it go. His father told her,

"Honey, he's not going to leave without it. It's just easier to not argue this any further. You know how he can be."

She did indeed, although it did not make accepting that any easier. She was nervous for him. What if the other children teased him about it? How would he handle that? He had not been around a large group of strange boys and girls much at all in his life, so this would be new territory for him and his bag. The thought of that all made her sweat. There were already going to be so many apparent noticeable differences between their son and the other children, that she just didn't want to add to it.

Andrew's father, Fred, just figured that his son needed to see the world for what it was and all it had to offer. If he needed his bag with him, well then, he needed his bag with him. Kids can be cruel, and he knew this because he was picked on a lot as a young child as well, but he turned out alright despite that type of thing. Andrew would as well, he told himself.

Christine rose from the bed that Andrew was practically jumping in now and put her slippers on her feet so that she could head down to start breakfast for the family. Andrew was so excited, that he did not want to eat, but his mother drew the line there. He needed nourishment and was either going to eat, or he was absolutely not attending the practice, and he could scream and kick all he wanted. That was that.

"Andrew, just listen to your mother and eat something. She's right. You don't want to burn all your energy and not be able to play with the other kids, am I right?" Fred said.

Andrew just smiled as he always did, looking away with his big brown eyes, and never directly at his father, as if he understood. He wanted to leave right away, so he probably figured if he just ate something quickly, he would be on the road shortly after.

Amanda was still asleep, but Andrew took care of that, too.

"Sissy!" he screamed through her closed door.

"It's time to eat. Now. Eat. We are going! Now!"

He started to bang loudly on the door of her bedroom, and finally, Amanda threw the blankets over her head and added a pillow for good measure, saying,

"Yes Buddy. I know. I know. Give me a minute".

She was not prepared to rise just yet, but she was well aware that if she did not, Andrew would surely be back pounding away on her door, and she would never be able to fall back asleep. She had no idea of what time it was anyway, so she just got out of bed, took a long stretch high above her head with her fingers locked tightly together, and opened her weary eyes.

As she got dressed and brushed her teeth, she began to walk down the back staircase that led right into their kitchen.

Andrew was seated at the table, sitting with his legs under his butt, as he always had. He was bouncing up and down, and back and forth as he shoveled waffles and maple bacon into his mouth. It took what seemed like a minute and a half for him to consume all that his mother had placed before him, and then with a belch, he was up and running to fetch his bag.

"Slow down partner!" his father exclaimed.

"The rest of us have to have breakfast too before we can go," he finished saying.

They were both truly happy for their boy, but the lingering concern of a disaster in the making would not leave their minds. They just wanted this day to be as Andrew would want it, but they knew it could not. He was not into sports, so the fact he begged them to play took them by surprise altogether. Maybe it was the sense of feeling a part of something that got him curious. Maybe he was just that he wanted to get out of the house and do something he never had before. Whatever it was, his shy nature, at least for the time being, was seemingly gone in the wind.

Once finished, they all piled into the car, and with his bag in his hands clutched closely to his chest, they were off to the field.

As they pulled up to the parking lot, they could see parents and children all walking to the four fields spread out along the flat acres of the township park. The park was beautiful and full of fields, walking trails, two basketball courts with real backboards and nets, and a play area full of different metal rides that the younger kids could enjoy. It was nice that they lived so close by and could visit the park pretty much any weekend they were free.

Fred parked the family car, and turned off the engine, leaning forward to look out among the sea of different colored uniforms all marching to the fields. He was amazed that so many children had signed up for this league and wondered if this would always be like this. It seemed as if more and more children found other distractions to keep them busy, like video games for instance. He was worried Andrew would want to play them nonstop, especially knowing his personality for always sticking to what made him happy. They decided not to get him a game system of his own, and so far, he had not asked. That was a big relief to his parents.

"Well, son, are you ready for your big day?" Fred asked.

Andrew just stared out the window. He froze in his seat and said nothing. Amanda tried to reassure him that it was going to be a great time, and that we would all be there to cheer him on. But he would not budge.

Fred was a little frustrated, but tried to stay relaxed.

"Buddy, this is what you wanted, remember? To come here and play with all the other nice boys and girls. Well, here we are. Let's say we get out and at least walk over to your team and see what you think. What do you think about that idea?" Fred asked.

Amanda finally was able to get Andrew moving enough that he agreed to walk out, but only if she would hold his hand the entire way. She agreed.

So, with his bag in one hand, and Amanda holding the other one firmly, they started out to the field, in search of the black uniforms that would signify his team.

As they walked down the loose gravel path that led to the main trail leading to the fields, they could see that most of the teams were assembling and kicking around soccer balls with each other. There were both boys and girls, of all different ages, sizes, and ethnicities, and this was a welcome sign for both Fred and Christine. Maybe their fears were just overblown worries that parents held no matter what the situation may have been. They always worried about their boy because he was, well, different, as they would say.

The black team was to the far side of the fields, so the walk was a bit longer. Andrew was grasping Amanda's hand firm enough that she patted the top of his head to try and relax him some and to allow the blood to circulate in the tips of her fingers.

"Look, Andrew! Some of these kids are small like you, and probably your age or even younger. This is going to be so fun for you!" she said.

The field came into view and the coach could be seen setting up bright orange cones and throwing soccer balls out from a netted nylon bag. Around him were about eight or nine other children. Only one was a girl, and the rest were boys whom all looked just as bewildered as any newbie would be.

Andrew would still not let go of Amanda's hand, and so she had to sit him down on the green grass to try and explain to him that she could not play by his side, because she was too old for this league. They would not let her on the field, and besides, he would have trouble chasing the ball down if she was slowing him down.

He did not care. His bag was clutched tightly to his chest, and his breathing was getting heavy. So heavy, in fact, it caught the attention of the other kids. Most just stared Andrew's way, but a few were laughing at his situation. This was not going how they had hoped, but was probably going as they deep down, expected it to.

"Buddy, the coach is about to start. You need to get over there and listen to what he says. He is going to give you an idea of what you need to do! Come on son, let's get this going, okay?" Fred begged.

Andrew reluctantly let go of his sister's hand finally but refused to drop the bag. He just was not willing to part with it and was just figuring he would run with the bag in his hands.

"Hello everyone. I'm coach Wilson, and this is, for most of you, your first-time playing soccer. Has anyone ever played before? With a show of hands, how many of you have played this sport before?" the coach asked.

Two boys, the ones who had been laughing and pointing at Andrew, both raised their hands emphatically. Fred kind of figured that. Those boys were athletic and coordinated for young kids, so he knew they had played either this or another sport prior to today. That was fine, as long as those boys understood that not everyone else had. It was great for them, but they needed to be patient with the ones that had not. Besides, everyone has a first day at this at some point.

The coach told the others not to worry. He would teach them all the basic fundamentals of the game, but most importantly, he would make sure they all had a good time playing.

Still, though, Andrew was reverting back to his shy self, and you could see that he was struggling with paying attention and was starting to open his bag to pull out something of comfort. They were sitting on the grass about a dozen yards from him, but did not want to draw attention to what he was doing. It was a tough spot to be in for them as parents.

"Hey, son, what's your name?" the coach said looking in the direction of Andrew. But Andrew said not a word.

"Hey, maybe we can put the bag down with mommy and daddy and you can get it after we are done. How does that sound to you?" the coach continued.

Nothing. Andrew clutched that bag as if it were the last thing he would ever own in his life. Fear was taking over, and he was in a position where things could go very wrong for him, and his parents and sister all knew it.

As this went on, the two boys kicking the ball around sent a shot over towards Andrew's direction that clearly had ill intentions. It found it's mark as the ball hit Andrew right in the pit of his stomach. Andrew dropped to his knees, and his "stowy" bag fell to the grass below, spilling all its contents onto the field.

The boys laughed through a halfhearted apology, and the coach told them to knock it off, but it was just a little too late. Things were over for Andrew that morning right there, if they had not already been a little earlier. He was holding his stomach crying and trying desperately to gather up all his items that had spilled out just a moment before.

Fred was pissed. He knew those boys had done that completely on purpose, and he let them know it. He marched over to the field in the opposite direction of his boy, while Christine and Amanda had already sprinted out to help Andrew. Once he got within a few yards, Fred screamed at the two boys, causing their fathers to march out onto the field now as well.

It was a big mess. Fred wouldn't back down from what he felt was right, and one of the boys' fathers had thrown himself into Fred's path, causing them both to stumble on the field, entangled in front of now screaming children and parents. The coach ran over along with another parent to break the two adults up who were now tussling fiercely.

So, when Andrew wanted to try out again two years later, there was just no way his parents were going to go along with that this time around. It was still too fresh in their minds. They would need to find something else for Andrew to put his time and energy into. Soccer was not going to happen now, or ever again.

Chapter 6

Live For Tomorrow

* * *

Agnes had some strikingly similar situations when she was younger, and those continued through her pre-teen years, even as we thought they would not. Amanda had watched Andrew go through bouts of bullying and teasing throughout his life, but she never expected her children to deal with the same struggles that he had experienced. Andrew was, well, he was unique, and unique brought with it an entire set of problems that were unique to him, so why would Agnes need to worry?

But Agnes was unique as well, just in a very different way. She was a little bit introverted, but a little bit extroverted as well. It depended on what she was doing specifically. She had a goofy nature about her, and truly danced as if no one was watching, and sang as if not an ear could hear her voice. Or perhaps she never cared if anyone watched or heard. That was her gift. She was like her uncle Andrew in that sense. Neither seemed to worry about what those around them thought, or their brash opinions, as much as their parents had.

There were dance classes that Agnes had signed up for, and thoroughly enjoyed, but there were cliques to those studios. Kids would pair up into groups, and Agnes seemed to be constantly on the outside of all of them, looking in. She didn't dress as the others, opting to wear colorful, beaded skirts over her dance leotard, and she wasn't as interested as everyone else was to do the dances perfectly, preferring to adapt her dance to her specific mood that afternoon.

She practiced, but if she wasn't able to remember the dance moves exactly as they were intended to be done, she would just alter the moves to make it easier on her. That was a talent entirely unto its own. She could take what was meant to be done and choreographed for the dancers and make it her own. Where this could be seen as a weakness to most, her mother and I saw it as a strength of hers. What she failed at initially, she succeeded in artistically with her unique ways and warm spirit.

But at the end of the day, the studio needed the dancers to perform, and Agnes was not going to ever grasp that well enough to stick with it. So, we decided to pull her from the classes, and instead we encouraged her to watch videos online about dances that brought an interest to her. This way she could alter as she felt a need to do, and no one would judge her or try to change her direction whatsoever.

She loves to perform shows for her family. Anytime either

my parents or Amanda's parents come over, they get a show. She tells everyone to sit back and reminds them that while the performance is going on, they are not allowed to leave their chairs, and must silence their phones. My mom always laughs at that, but not enough for Agnes to get interrupted.

As whatever song Agnes picks for the dance starts to play in the background, she dims the lights in the family room, and we wait. Sometimes you can tell Agnes has worked hard on the moves and has choreographed them well, and other times you can see that she is making the moves up as she twirls and dips in front of all of us.

Dot tends to run in the background as a backup dancer, and Agnes never seems to be bothered by that. She either is so engrossed in what it is she is doing, or she enjoys having her little sister playing a part in the presentation. It is something both Amanda and I understand more than I think Agnes does. She includes anyone who has an interest, no matter what it is they want to do. I would have thought that Dot just jumping up and down behind the star performer would frustrate Agnes, but then I am reminded of who I am talking about.

Agnes.

She understands the importance of inclusion. We are seeing such a divide in the understanding of excelling and taking part lately everywhere we turn. You have arguments for both sides, and usually those arguments come from a place of personal experience.

If you have a child who is hard-working and talented,

that has earned his or her place in something, it can be hard for those parents to understand why a child that cannot do the same gets the same recognition. I get that. It does make sense to me for certain.

But I also understand a child that has not been given the same gifts when they were born, no matter how hard they work at it, and despite the number of hours they surely try to do what others will do, those gifts will never be the same. It's just not possible for all people to do the same or have the same, period. We are all unique and where one person has a gift, another does not. So who should get to experience more than another?

I have vastly different views on this, but at the end of the day, I understand that as parents, we aren't going to raise our children the same, and we certainly are not going to agree to the same. But I have Agnes to be concerned with, so my loyalty shall focus on that.

I remember the story that Amanda shared about Andrew and the soccer fields a while back. Did he have a right to play because he lived in a free country that afforded him that right, or did the other children have a right to excel and learn at a different level because they had a better gift for that? I honestly don't know that answer, and I am unsure others do. Strong opinions are just that, opinions.

So, when Agnes was struggling with her dance classes, I saw the dance parents snickering and rolling their eyes as if I should just remove my Agnes so that their daughters had more time to focus on being the best dancers they could be. I hated that. The dance moms. There were a few that understood Agnes' and my situation, but most of them banded together in such a way that people seemed to steer clear.

At the end of the day, we decided to compromise. Agnes could dance as she pleased, but we didn't want her to feel out of place as the other children laughed and pointed, just as their parents were doing.

I learned a lot about different perspectives during those dance classes. Children learn more from us as parents than we realize. These parents have kids that fit in to a mold, and that was great for them. But give them a child that doesn't fit that mold, and has a free-spirited soul, and they may see things through a different set of glasses. I believe that to be true because I am that parent. I have a tough time seeing it from their perspective, so it's understandable why they cannot see it from mine.

But one doesn't make the other wrong. It just makes it different. So, was Andrew meant to experience soccer as the other children did, or were the other children inherently meant to? It's the same for Agnes. But it doesn't matter for now. Agnes is happy doing her own thing, and I can only hope as she grows, she knows we did that for her, and the decision we made to pull her from dance came from a place of love and not from a place of frustration or embarrassment.

Agnes doesn't seem to let much bother her, which is a massive relief to her mother and I. It most likely affects us more than the kids, but that is just how those situations go. Sometimes the kids deal with it at a higher level than we expect or understand, and sometimes it's us as parents that feel the strain of those situations more.

Erik actually gets involved, too. I know there are male dancers at the dance studios as well, so we just assume he enjoys the art of this. Maybe he does this to support his older sister in her performances she gives for us, and maybe he does because he also wants to have all eyes on him while the grandparents are watching with such interest. It doesn't matter though, because he just seems to be silly with it all. Nothing unusual with his excitement. Besides, he plays baseball and basketball with the neighborhood boys, and during the fall of 2015, he is signed up to play flag football, although that took some serious pushing on my part to convince Amanda.

Dot is still so young that we don't know what direction she is going to lean towards. She can be the serious one of the group, even though she is the youngest. Every now and then, like when she makes an appearance behind Agnes during one of her marvelous dances, she acts like a kid. But sometimes, that kid can be just as serious as a full-blown adult.

All our children are built entirely differently. It's something we have learned to love and understand. We know that God has intended for our children to have unique personalities, and capabilities throughout their lives. We may want them to grow in a particular direction, but that doesn't mean that they will, or even should. They are meant to grow as they are, but that can be a hard pill to swallow for many, including Amanda and me, at times.

Like that time when Agnes asked to dye her hair a white and purple mixture. Amanda, being the artistic one of the family, was willing to consider it in the summer months while school was out, but I was less interested in that no matter what the time of year.

I didn't want her to experience ridicule at the hands of others. Simple things like running to Mr. Z's grocery store could cause people to stare at her and could make her very uncomfortable, and me as well. I knew that I didn't want others to look at me as if I were a terrible parent for allowing my young, pre-teen daughter to dye her hair a different color than it was naturally.

I guess there were certainly boundaries to what I was okay with and what I was not okay with. I really tried to justify my argument with Amanda, and while she was on the fence about it, I was an absolute no.

Amanda understood my concerns, but I am not sure she ever agreed with me on it. She just told Agnes maybe when she got older, we would reconsider, but for now, she had plenty of color in her clothing to hold her over until such time as we decided to allow it.

Agnes was upset of course, but she got over it. She was on to the next thing within a few weeks, and I felt like we had conquered a dilemma and made our point enough that we won.

That was how I looked at things like that. Either the children were awarded points for winning a debate, or we as the parents were. It really wasn't about points per say, but more about the understanding that we were the adults and responsible for the kids in so many aspects in life, that if we just simply gave in and lost those arguments, what type of examples were we setting?

I think we are born to be that way in reality. Born to feel the need to be right and born to not always understand the mind of a child, even though we may have also been that way as a kid. Although, I never really cared to have my hair painted purple and white. The most I ever wanted to do was to get an ear pierced, because in high school, several of my friends were doing just that, and I wanted to fit in. But my father told me it was not possible. While I contemplated going against his demand that I not do so, ultimately, I chose not to, and I still stand by that decision today. I would never have an earring now.

I think girls are meant to wear those sorts of things, and boys are meant to run the bases, swing from old dusty tires, and jump into dirty rivers, while their parents are meant to enforce boundaries. I don't know. At times I feel like I need to let up some and be a little more understanding of the times, but I also feel I have.

Our kids pretty much have personalities I would not have picked, but I love those and encourage them to be who they are. I just have certain limitations on what that means to them. I don't want them regretting decisions later in life, and I also don't want to steer them in the wrong direction.

Parenting is hard. I sat down with my dad one day and told him that. He was sitting back on his porch, just smiling at me as if to tell me, "I told you so."

But he wasn't the perfect father. He missed a lot of my games and concerts that I played in. I played the trumpet, and while it wasn't the coolest instrument for me to play, I loved it. But friends teased me enough that I decided it wasn't for me. I would regret that decision, but my father never seemed all that interested in me playing that either, so I let it go, and never thought back on it.

"Jon, I don't know that there is a manual on how to do this right, but I will tell you, you are doing one hell of a job. Those kids love you and Amanda. Now I know you question things at times. God, I question a lot of what I did for you and your brothers. I worked hard, but maybe I worked too much. For that I am sorry. I wanted to be more present, but my heart was always telling me to work just a little more, and there would be plenty of time to hang out with you guys," he started.

I sat there and looked straight ahead, pretending to be understanding, but I was a little more confused by what he was saying. How could he have intended to spend more time with us, when all he had to do was to do just that. Stop working and spend more time with us. By the time he wanted to, we were grown and living away from the home we grew up in.

He continued with his thoughts,

"Son, I want to give you some advice if I can. You do with it what you will, okay? Live for tomorrow, by living for today."

I had no idea of what my father was referring to. How could you live for tomorrow by living for today? You either did one or the other. It was impossible to live for both, wasn't it?

I spent a lot of time trying to figure out what my father meant by that, but instead of asking him to elaborate, I just told him that I would try. Try. How could I begin to try when I didn't even know how or where to begin?

The rest of the time that we sat on the porch of the home we all were raised in, gazing out across the road to the neighbor's home I once played in as a young man, my father and I just sat back and talked here and there about not much, but it was interesting to sit there like that.

He was always working and so we rarely sat down to talk about nothing much. It seemed that if I didn't have an important topic to discuss, we simply never talked. I don't remember a time where we just shot the shit and had little to worry about. This may be something I need to remember when it comes to my own children. Just because they may not have anything to say, doesn't mean I shouldn't be listening regardless.

I want to be a more aware, present father, but I need to learn to do things differently than I was inherently taught. Otherwise, patterns repeat, and generations stay the same. I feel as if I do adjust, like going to the store with Agnes for our alone time to get Amanda's list of items. But is that enough to make a difference in her life and the lives of her brother and sister? I do not know that answer today.

Chapter 7

Happy Tears

* * *

June 26th, 2004, was the day Amanda and I were wed in a town called Woodstock, Vermont. It's not the famous Woodstock everyone seems to know about because of the 60's. That one is in the state of New York. This is a very different type of place.

The sun was shining on our little town, and it was blazing hot. I remember how hot it was because we all had dark suit jackets on, and all I could think about was that I would literally pass out at the altar if I didn't drink a wicked amount of water throughout the morning. I know my body well and combined with the fact that my nerves were on edge already, I had to be sure to pace myself with all I had to do that day.

Our wedding was not large by any means, but it wasn't totally small either. We had several dozen guests, a photographer, and the bridal party that consisted of three of

Amanda's first cousins and her very best friend in the world, Ashley Bevan.

Ashley was Amanda's bridesmaid, and while she was crazier than anyone I knew; she was also excited for her friend. I remember the entire time I was wondering how she was going to act at the reception, even though she was still not of legal age to drink. That had never stopped Ashley before.

For my side, I had my two brothers, Michael and Alex, and my best friend, Anthony Ciccarone, to counter her three. They were all acting a little childish all morning long. It was hard to get them focused and to take anything seriously. I spent literally all morning reminding them of what they were supposed to be doing, who they were walking down the aisle with, and what was going to happen once the ceremony was completed.

We are both Roman Catholic, so years of attending Catholic schools should have been enough for them to know they could not goof around during the ceremony, yet I was still very concerned all throughout the day.

The good news was that my father was there with us at his place, ensuring the boys all knew he would be keeping a close eye on them. He was not going to let them make utter fools of themselves in front of Father Malory. Besides, that was also something for them to remember. Father Malory was one of those priests that enjoyed boxing on the side as a recreation. He operated a boy's club on Saturday mornings, teaching young kids how to throw their hands properly.

It was important to him to teach young men what he said was a valuable skill in life. Not for fighting, but for not fighting, as he preferred to say. He knew that if you could handle yourself well with your hands, chances were, you would rarely ever need to use them.

I liked Father Malory, but he did intimidate me, so I knew for myself, I would be a perfect man during the ceremony, and probably after as well, as he was invited to the reception. To this day, I still feel as if my parents did that to keep everyone in line. My father and mother still deny it, but they do so with a true grin.

Finally, it was time to head on over to the church, and when I arrived, I saw that the pews were filled with the people that we had invited, but it somehow felt different. I felt proud to be getting married, and excited that the people I cared for most were in attendance to celebrate this day with us.

Amanda was not there yet, but I knew that was because she would arrive last. Everyone had to be seated first, and then my mother would be walked down the aisle, then her mother, and finally, the time would come for her bridesmaids and her maid of honor to make their appearance at the front of the church.

As I stood at the front of the church, I gazed around nervously and realized that the church was absolutely gorgeous. I had never really noticed that before, probably because I was too busy trying to be cool and act as if I did not care.

But here I was, at the most important part of the church, staring at all the intricate details that somehow were carved over a hundred years ago by hand, perfectly as intended. The skill those men must have possessed was insane to me. I had trouble making a wooden car for boy scouts when I was younger, and somehow these master craftsmen had created elaborate designs into plaster with nothing more than their strong, worn hands and an endless imagination. It was probably a skill handed down by their own fathers, who likely learned it from their fathers before them.

I don't know what made me think of that just then, but I was impressed, and that kept my attention off my raging nerves just long enough to not panic.

I remember my brother Michael nudging me to make sure I was okay and not going to pass out. It must have looked as if I was in a daze, and that probably appeared similar to nervousness.

I actually felt relaxed and fine after settling in, but then the organist started playing the music that we selected for the parents to walk in, and I saw my mother coming down the aisle as my other brother, Alex, escorted her. Alex was smirking and I could feel he was going to bust out laughing at any moment, but he played it cool. Not only did he not break out in laughter, but he managed to seat my mother, kiss her on her head, and walk over to where we were all standing, without making a scene. I was pretty impressed with him.

Then my best friend, who was standing with me moments

before, had walked back to escort Amanda's mother down the aisle, and seat her. He unfortunately was unable to keep a straight enough face, that he did end up laughing a bit, but I think it was more from nerves, and everyone basically ignored it as it did not create enough of a scene. So all was good thus far in my mind.

The organist abruptly changed the tone of the music, and there entered a tiny little soul by the name of Alexa. Alexa was Amanda's youngest cousin and was a perfect fit for flower girl. She was tiny, but had spunk as she wandered down the aisle towards the front of the church, dropping small rose petals here and there, giggling and being just sassy enough to make it memorable.

The three bridesmaids followed next, and then the maid of honor, which was the first time I started to feel as if I may have a panic attack. I knew once she reached the front, that once again the music was going to change, and down the red walkway would come my soon-to-be father-in-law, escorting my soon-to-be lovely bride. That was starting to hit me more than any other day leading up to this one.

My father peered over to where I was standing, and I glanced over to see what he and my mother were doing. As I did, I saw my father nod just enough to tell me without a spoken word, that I was going to be okay. It was perfect timing too because I was second guessing myself. Not the fact that I was getting married, but the sense that I could do this here and now. I was a young man still, and what did I know about having a wife, and eventually children someday? Little to nothing. I knew only what I saw in my parents. That was the extent of my experience with this all.

Then it happened. The music changed for the final time, and there in the far-off entrance to the church, was a woman being walked down the aisle by her father, and I started to cry. I didn't want to, and felt like an idiot for doing so, but my emotions took over and I couldn't control myself.

Father Malory whispered to me,

"It's okay to cry my son, I'd much rather you cry on your wedding day, than at any point in your marriage. Happy tears are accepted by God."

As she started to get closer, I could see the dress that she picked out months ago for the first time. It was stunning, and covered with tiny beads that appeared like diamonds as she passed windows that were full of the sunlight. While I had seen Amanda dressed up for other events, including some of our own dates, I had never seen her look as amazing as she did, walking down towards the front of the church.

Amanda seemed to be fine, although it was hard to tell since she still had a veil covering her face. Her father would lift that the moment she was next to me, and give her a kiss on her cheek, probably whispering a few last loving words to her, before she was no longer his alone.

Before she completed her last step, Amanda stopped in her tracks, realizing something was very different. Her father knew exactly what she saw and smiled.

Standing directly next to me, was not either one of

my brothers, nor my best friend that I grew up with. No, standing where my best man was to stand, was her brother, Andrew. He was dressed in the same suits as the other men with me, and his hair was shiny and well kempt. He had a flower on his chest, and of course, he had his stowy bag with him, but at least he kept it on his back, instead of in his hands. It was a compromise that took more than I expected it to, but somehow, we managed to come to an agreement.

It took a great deal to keep things from Amanda. First, I had to insert another friend to pretend that he was in the wedding party. Then, I had to convince my bride that my best friend would be my best man standing next to me on our wedding day. Lastly, and the most important, yet hardest step, was to somehow surprise Amanda with Andrew as my best man, but not let Andrew give it away.

His father came up with the idea for how to handle that situation. He told Andrew that he was going to be at the wedding, but that everyone was going to stand at the front. He figured if he didn't mention that he was going to be the best man, he couldn't give that secret away. There was no way he could keep that to himself and not spill it to Amanda, and his father was well aware of that.

It was something I promised Amanda I would do. Find a way to include her brother in the wedding, and I managed to do just that. It was not easy. In fact, just thinking about it now gives me anxiety.

She stood there for a moment stunned, but quickly

gathered herself because she had other things that she needed to do this day; namely marry me.

The wedding was quick, although I think that just had to do with the entire day. It is all a blur now thinking back to the day I said "I do" to Amanda. The mass went off without much affair, even though when it became time to get the rings from Andrew, he didn't want to part with the box, because he thought he should be able to keep it since it was in his bag. That took some serious negotiation and promises of ice cream, but eventually he relented.

The reception was also something I do not remember well. I know I shook hands with literally everyone who attended, and people took photos nonstop, but it was all worth it.

I was told the food we had tasted good as well, but we had so little time to eat, with having to do formal photos and all the dances we arranged, and the nonstop photos and socializing. I can't even remember what I did eat that hot afternoon, but I do remember one thing well. My Amanda agreed to be my wife that day, and it's something I wish to celebrate for all the rest of my days.

After all the hoopla, we ended up not going on a honeymoon right away. We were going to stay with my parents for a while, so Amanda and I decided the best thing to do would be to get moved in, so that when we did eventually go away, we could come home to a place already set up for us that we could call home.

My parents had a lower level in their bi-level home, with a separate entrance, and while it was nothing fancy, it was all ours. Unless, of course, someone had to do laundry. We could hear my mom humming a song she had heard earlier in the day, while she folded the sheets out of the dryer, and so we knew that she could hear us as well when she was down there. I had to remind my mom that I was a married man now and that we may not always be quiet, so to please let us know when she was going to be washing clothes. She just smiled and agreed, but there were times she clearly forgot.

Married. It took a while for me to understand what that meant. Throughout the dating we did, things always seemed simple enough for the most part, with an exception here and there. But now I felt a sense of pride, but also a sense of urgency. What did being married change for me? I was about to understand exactly what that entailed.

At first it was pure excitement. I could work during the day and then let those I worked around know that I was heading home to the wife. It didn't seem real, and at times I would catch myself smiling awkwardly as if I couldn't just say it without my face grinning from ear to ear.

I began to realize that it was still like dating at first, but that instead of walking her to the front door at the end of the evening, I was kissing her goodnight at the end of the night. And instead of texting her "good morning beautiful," at the crack of dawn, I was rolling over to see her snoring away, with her hair a mess and her makeup still not on her face. That was all strange to me, but somehow made this seem even more adult-like.

I was accepting of her and who she was at her best, and

at her worse, which meant that she was doing the same. She would need to love me through my morning breath, my belching after having soda for dinner, and my stupid man flu episodes in the coldest months of the year.

Before, I could just tell her I wasn't feeling well and that I would text her later, but now she was able to see me as the baby I truly was. I hated being sick with a passion. It's the one thing I did not handle well, and that was well known. In fact, my own mother warned Amanda about the levels of my colds.

There were the mild ones where I would just get grumpy for the most part, and then there were those that forced my body to require sleep all day and night. The highest level of my colds were those that required someone to tell me life was worth living. I would literally beg to die, and need a voice to let me know I was not dying and just needed to drink my fluids, because eventually I would get better.

I always did, but I hated those days while I was near death. I was never actually *near* death, but it felt an awful lot like I was.

I had no idea how Amanda was when she would get sick. We had spent a ton of time together, but either she never caught anything, or she hid it well. I can't understand how someone can get sick and not want to be taken care of. Being waited on hand and foot was all I required when at my worse, but she seemed to brush most things off. I assume that is why it is called the man flu.

My mother told me that because God had intended for

women to carry babies in their bodies, he had to make them that much stronger and more capable than a man. I laughed at that, but she did have a point. I honestly cannot recall a time when my own mother had laid in bed for longer than an hour or so. She seemed to push right through anything she was handed, but I do remember my father having to sleep it off for a night or so.

He didn't get sick much though. I think my father's body knew he was going to work through it all, so it didn't bother wasting time allowing him to get sick.

I look back at the tiny area of my parent's home that Amanda and I shared with a stronger fondness than I did when we were actually living there. It was the first place we had together, and the first time we slept in the same room for a full night together.

Amanda was, as I said, Roman Catholic like myself, but she took marriage seriously. I am not going to tell you we never had sex prior to being married. That would be a lie, but she wanted to honor her parents' wishes and wait to live with someone until she took their last name as hers. That is what we did, and I'm glad we did that.

Living together was exciting for the beginning of our marriage. Because we had never slept in the same room together, this was a new, exciting experience that almost felt wrong, but was anything but. We had earned this, and I was going to enjoy all of it, even Amanda's Snoring. I just never told her about that.

I can't remember the first time we discussed having

children, or if we picked out a number that we were going to aim for, but I do remember when Amanda first told me she was pregnant.

At first, I was in disbelief. We had just gotten married, and were still learning each other, but somehow, we were expected to bring a human into this equation and figure them out as well? I knew I was an adult, but somehow, I did not feel ready for all of this just yet. Thankfully, Amanda was in love with the entire idea, and I trusted her completely. When she told me this was going to be the single best thing in our world, I believed her.

I know her parents wanted her to wait some, but things happen, and this little bundle was not going to wait for anyone.

We decided to not find out the sex of the baby before-hand. At first, Amanda wanted to know and have a gender reveal party, but then she thought it would be better to be surprised and not know. She wanted my opinion, and I had never really considered what was better.

I talked it over with my mother, who told me that there would be other children on the way, and we could always do a reveal later, but this time, wouldn't it be exciting to hear the doctor tell us something we didn't previously know?

That made a lot of sense. I thought, if we know the baby was a boy or a girl already, when the baby came out of her womb, we wouldn't have that moment of excitement and nervousness, waiting for the doctor to inform us if we were the proud parents of a son or daughter.

"Let's be surprised, honey. I think not knowing will be just as much fun as knowing, but we will have this bond wondering together for the entire 9 months. What do you think?" I asked.

Chapter 8

Don't Screw This Up

* * *

There are many things that can lift a man's spirits up high into the air, but there are also those moments that can drop the strongest of men straight to their knees in seething frustration, pure sadness, and sheer agony.

I have now experienced both kinds of those moments.

When Agnes was born that early April morning, I told my wife that waiting was the perfect decision we made. Having a child born on April Fool's Day was crazy to me. At first, I was worried the doctor and nurses would tell us it was a girl, when it really was a boy. You know, just to pull the best April Fool's gag on us young parents, but they had not. Thank God, because I don't know if I could have handled being excited for one, and then having to find that same excitement once again, when I realized they had pulled a fast one on us.

Agnes Luella Fleming.

Born on April 1, 2005, at Saint Christopher Hospital.

She weighed 6 lbs., 7 ounces, and was 19 ½ inches long. My April Fool's baby.

I have never cried so much in my life, as the moment I first got to hold our daughter.

A year ago, I cried at my wedding. Those tears I was able to contain for the better part of my wife's walk down the aisle, but this was different. Agnes brought warm tears to my eyes that I could not and would not stop from falling down my cheeks. She earned all of them.

She was breech when her water broke, so Amanda had an emergency c-section performed, and needed to be stitched up prior to being allowed to hold our child for the first time. I was the first one, outside of the doctor and nurses who pulled her from her womb, of course and through the weighing and checking her vitals, to hold her in my arms. It was surreal for sure.

Here I was, this young man, barely twenty-four years of age, and I was entrusted with a child that is not even an hour old. The nurses never hesitated to hand her over and even offered guidance in just where to place my arms, and how to get comfortable with positioning. I could not get comfortable though, because my muscles were so tight from the adrenaline flowing through my veins. I just thanked them and did the best I could, but I remember this tiny package made my arms feel so incredibly heavy and awkward.

Both of our parents were present and were on their way back to the room where I was holding my world.

Amanda, the nurses told me, was fine. She would be back shortly to join us. I felt that I was taking something away from her, having this private moment with our Agnes, even before she could. But I guess I had earned a part of this rite as well. She was, after all, my daughter too. It just didn't feel that way at first. I'm sure for Amanda it did, though. She carried this tiny human in her body for months and months, and now her stomach was deprived of that feeling. I wondered how that made her feel. Did she feel relieved, or as if something was missing?

My parents came in first, but said they would wait to hold her until Amanda had been back to see her daughter. I thought that was a great gesture on their part, and I would have never thought of that on my own. But my parents knew that this was an extremely blessed moment for us, and they felt the need to let us know they were there, but would join when we were both ready.

When Amanda was finally wheeled back into the room, I felt as if I had held Agnes for hours on end, but in reality, it was only a short while. Finally, I felt as if I was going to be able to gain some feeling in my arms once more, and that was the only reason I was happy to turn her over to her mother.

Amanda was beaming brightly, even though she was thoroughly exhausted. Nothing was going to take away from this moment for her. She waited her entire life for this to happen, and it was here, now.

As she held our daughter for the first time, she touched

her cheeks, caressed her nose, and ran her small hands over the top of her head. She unwrapped her toes so that she could see how small her feet were. She was, I think, also in disbelief that this baby was here, and ours forever. It's hard to explain unless you have lived through it, but now that I have, I get it. I get it.

Amanda was in love for the second time in as many years. I couldn't help but love the way she looked at our daughter. Our daughter. I still could not believe I was a dad, and Amanda was a mother. We just had our wedding the year before, and still were searching for a place outside of my parent's house, but none of that seemed to matter in this moment. We were complete.

We would spend several days there to ensure that the stiches were holding, that Amanda had gained her feeling back, and that the baby was doing well. My wife was adamant that she was going to breast feed our child. She was certain, that no matter how many children we had, she would.

I knew very little about that all and just assumed you did for a short time until you got home and then the baby went on milk. Like regular, Vitamin D milk. But what did I know? I had not a clue of how that worked, but I know Amanda had read a few books late at night while I was trying to sleep. On more than one occasion I had asked her to turn off the light, for her to only reply,

"Just a minute, Jon, and I will. I promise just one more page."

One page turned into one chapter more nights than not. It was hard sleeping, but my own mother reminded me that it was even harder for Amanda to sleep at night. Her body was preparing itself to grow a full-grown baby inside, and she would be going through a lot of adapting.

I tried my best to understand, but it was of little use. I just ended up placing a pillow over top of my head while she promised she was almost finished.

Now? Now I am glad she read all those chapters late at night, because if you asked me to take a test on what to do with this tiny person, I would surely fail. It's not that I didn't think I would be a good father. I believed I would even before Agnes was born, but there were so many things to remember and what if I did one thing wrong? What would happen to poor Agnes? It's scary being a father for the first time, but having a good mother is perfect balance for this.

Agnes. She just sits there, not moving a muscle as her arms and legs are neatly, but tightly bunded against her tiny body. Her eyes only open for a second, but I was told they cannot see anything. Their focus isn't there when they are that young yet. But I wonder if she can hear us, and a nurse tells me that they can. So, I talk to her when Amanda is resting her eyelids, because there isn't much else to do. I rock her back and forth, trying to gain an understanding of what she needs from me.

I love that. She will need from me, and it will be my job to provide that. I make her promises as I pat her back. I promise her that I will always be there for her. That I will try to be understanding of things that she does, even if they are bad. I promise her that no matter how crazy and mad the days seem, brighter ones are ahead.

Father Malory stops by one afternoon and wants to bless Agnes. It's perfect timing because Amanda is awake and just had her dressing changed. She is sitting up a little now, and although her hair is a ragged mess of knots and tangles, she is still so beautiful.

As Father is blessing our first child, he looks over to me and smiles. I smile back and he tells me,

"Son, you have been giving a tremendous gift from God. Don't screw this up."

I laugh slightly but wonder if he knows something I do not. Maybe he says this to all young fathers that are having a child for the first time in their lives. Whatever the reason is, I take what he says to heart.

"I won't father. I promise you and Amanda that, on my heart," I say, making a cross across my chest.

"Don't promise me, son. Promise that tiny baby of yours. After all, she's going to be the one to hold you most accountable for it, shall you mess it up," Father replies.

He stares at me, then finally breaks his serious look, and smacks me hard on the back.

"You are going to do just fine. Remember to help your wife when she needs it, and more when she doesn't. It's the best advice I have for you today," Father says.

Then he blesses me, and blesses Amanda, before telling us he must be off. He has several elderly folks from church who happen to be in the same hospital that he wants to visit.

That hits me hard for some reason. He is here to visit those coming, and those going. I imagine a lot of priests have done that over the years. Blessing those souls that are finding their way into this whole new world and giving last rites to those who have completed their journey and are on their way to an eternal one.

I am Catholic. There is no doubt about that, as I was raised that way, completed all the sacraments, and I attend Sunday services ever since Amanda asked me to with her. But I struggle some with all the teachings. I have a hard time reading the bible and following along when father reads a passage at the services. It just seems old to me, and I wonder if the bible were written today, how would that book read?

My mother tells me not to think that way, but my dad is more understanding. That is when he has time to talk about it and isn't working as per his usual. He once told me that trying to understand what God meant through human writings was like trying to fit a square through a circle peg. Humans have a tendency to hear what they want to hear, and to share what they wish to share. So what he said made sense to me, but it didn't clear up my confusion much.

I have time though, because both Amanda and I are still young, and have full lives in front of us. Now, we have Agnes, who has even more life in front of her than we do.

I'm sure she will understand more than I do about religion. Amanda will take her to church, and make sure she goes to all the services she does. I know we haven't discussed schooling for our kids, but I know I will have little say in that area.

The ride home is almost scarier than the first time I held our daughter. I have to carefully strap her in a car seat, and there are so many things about this seat I don't understand. It's brand new and so you would think they would make them easier to install, but they don't.

Thankfully, I get it on tight as possible and the nurse who walks my wife out in her wheelchair gives her approval.

I now have Amanda, just a few days out from giving birth, and our three-day old child in my complete care. They both are putting all their trust in me, even if they do not realize it. I know I have an important task to do, but this actually excites me because I am proving not only to them, but to myself that I am capable of doing this all.

When we arrive home, I see lawn signs on my parents' front lawn saying, "Welcome Home," and "It's a Girl!"

Those make me smile, but I doubt Amanda even looks. She's so focused on Agnes, that I doubt she's even aware we are home.

There we are. Finally in the driveway, and my parents, Amanda's parents, and all of our siblings are there, waiting to greet us. It's weird to see them all gathered here like that, but I appreciate it. I've been in a hospital room for several days, sleeping in an uncomfortable chair, and it's nice to be out and around family.

Andrew is here. He is hiding behind his father, and I can't tell if he is scared, or playing. I would imagine it's a little of both, knowing him. New things worry him, as he truly likes routine, and this is entirely new. His sister has spent so much time working with him and being there for him, and now she has been spending all her time with me and preparing for Agnes.

I've tried to help out where I can, but I, too, have been extra busy. Trying to work, find us a place of our own, handling extra chores while Amanda was pregnant, and just everyday life, has really taken up most of my time.

Amanda sees everyone and her eyes tear up. I ask her what's wrong and she just says that she feels a little over-whelmed. She just wants to be alone with Agnes for a few days and doesn't understand why. I certainly don't. Wouldn't it be great to have some help with everything so she can rest and sleep some? I don't get it, but I hear her, and I hear Father Malory in my head telling me not to mess this up, so I tell her to let me handle it.

It's strange as I exit the car and realize I am about to tell everyone they need to go. They want to see the baby just as much as anyone, but somehow, they are just going to have to wait a bit more. How much longer is the question. I've never been through this before.

The crazy thing to me, though, is that everyone seems to understand. Well, the older ones anyway. My two brothers just walk off as if they were doing us a favor by being there, and could care less, but my parents and Amandas' parents all seem to know what she is talking about, even if I do not.

As soon as they disperse, Amanda looks at me and asks me if I think she is crazy.

"Of course I do, but not for this. I think you are crazy to even have married me," I joke.

She finally cracks a delicate smile, and I tell her that I will get her and the baby inside, then come back out for the rest of the items that we brought back with us from the hospital. Then, I will give her time to settle in, and if she needs me, I will be on the first floor and all she needs to do is scream.

"Jon, are you okay with that? I don't know what it is, but I just feel like I need this time to bond with her," Amanda asks.

I mean, I don't have a lot of options, and being okay with this seems like the path of least resistance to me, so, to avoid confrontation and her crying even more, I am going to be okay with this.

Maybe this is one of those times that my dad was talking about. When he said that understanding the bible as man wrote it was like trying to fit a square peg in a round hole, could he also have been talking about understanding women? Because it seems to fit just as well as the square peg.

Chapter 9

Balance

* * *

We planned to have a family of four, and so when Erik was born, Amanda and I talked about the things that would be next for us in our lives. Now that the two children were born, and we had both a boy and a girl, life should have felt fulfilled for at least that part, but it didn't for some reason.

Something was missing, and although we now had an apartment of our own close to where my parents lived, there just seemed to be a gap in our plan, and so we talked about the possibility of having a larger family.

I told Amanda we should wait a few more years to be sure that was what we felt was incomplete, because maybe it was more the feeling of not having that excitement we felt when she was pregnant with both Agnes and Erik. I know there are women that absolutely love the feeling of carrying a child, and when they give birth, that feeling of loneliness sets in. I can't understand it exactly, because I have never carried a baby for nine months and then in a matter of an hour, had that baby removed from my body, leaving an emptiness that only they can truly understand.

I remember when Amanda came home with our Agnes and needed some alone time to adjust. We never talked about that again, but I always felt it was her body adjusting to the realization that she had done what she set out to do, but something in her mind told her it was not over. I figured if Amanda wanted to talk more about that she would let me know, but until that day would come, I had no intentions of opening up a very personal topic for her again.

Besides, when Erik came along, she seemed completely fine with it. Perhaps her body had been reminded of what it went through the first time, and knew that its task was complete, and her mind decided to listen that time around. Whatever happened, things went a lot smoother when we came home.

Her parents were there so often, I thought they were living with us now, but it was very helpful to have family so willing to give to us when we surely needed it. I was not going to complain.

Amanda was still running around chasing after Agnes, who loved to explore everything she could get her hands on, and Erik needed constant attention, as babies often do. At first, he did not sleep through the night, and with Amanda breastfeeding once again, neither could she.

I was busy working with my father and trying to build

a book of business for myself to get my career moving forward. My father, who was still working more than not, was helpful in a lot of ways, but I still wished he took more time to enjoy life, instead of working well past when I was finished for the evening.

I felt conflicted. Was I not working enough, or working the right amount of hours, to build my business up? I saw my father become successful working long hours and sometimes every day of the week, but at what cost? My mother loves him, but she has regrets about not doing the things they talked about when they first had gotten married.

For me, I know I need to work hard, but I also know I have a wife and now two children at home waiting for me to be present. Plus, there is no way Amanda would put up with me working like my father does. She would divorce me in a second if I didn't give her some help around the house when her parents stopped coming as often.

And she would be right to. We want a fulfilling life, but what does that mean exactly? Is it one where we have the funds to do whatever we want, when we want? Or is it a life where we count our change out on the floor to see just how much we were able to save in a year and spend on Christmas gifts for the family, while we smile through all the counting? I am reminded of the word I use so often to find my answers. Balance.

Balance seems like an easy way to handle things, but let me tell you, it's anything but. Try balancing a new career where everyone wants your full attention, and if you do not give that to them, you no longer have that client. That means you don't get the referrals that come along with that client. Later in life you can turn away people for sure and survive, but you must earn that opportunity first. It can take years to realize you are at the stage in life, and by that time, you may be too old to understand how to adjust to that.

I know counting our change on the floor while stuffing our faces with sugary snacks and watching reruns of the bachelor in our pajamas, is not my idea of a healthy life either.

I am still relatively young and in the early stages of my work, so I have time to make adjustments, but I do not want to miss that cutoff time where you now haven't done enough of either, or it becomes impossible to figure it out.

As Erik grows, he seems like a typical boy, just like my brothers and I were. He plays with cars, and watches shows that have colorful dogs and cats singing songs together in sync. He loves when we take him to the park so that he can show us how he is a "big boy" and can slide down the slide all by himself. He's a daredevil at times, and Amanda worries more than I do about that.

My brothers and I would literally jump off our back deck onto a wooden table, pretending we were wrestling in front of millions of fans. We did that even after my brother, Michael, broke his collarbone. The last straw for my parents was when Michael lost two teeth on the same day at different times, jumping into a pile of chairs that we were using to hit each other in the back.

So when Erik wants to do a flip on the swing to show us how big boy he really is, I don't have a concern at all.

For Amanda, she grew up with only Andrew as a sibling, and her parents, rightfully so, always were extra protective of him. He wasn't allowed to do the typical things boys his age were doing, and that was mainly because he did not understand the probability of getting hurt. It was something Andrew never got to experience, and I often wondered if Andrew was more like the other kids, how would he have turned out?

But that is why Amanda looked at all of this differently than I did. Her brother did not get into those tooth losing moments, because he wasn't allowed to get away with the things we did, and he didn't have two other brothers pushing him, telling him to trust them, they had done this thousands of times and never got hurt.

Boys are funny in that way. Always telling you to trust them, and never telling you that those thousands of times they had done the same stunt, was really in their heads. They had never tried to do them in real life, but for a boy at that age, sometimes in your head is the same as reality.

Then there is Dot. She was a surprise. Amanda and I had not given the green light to one another yet on having a third child, but sometimes our plans are not the plans God has intended for us.

When she came home from the doctor's office to inform me that we would be having a third child, I was shocked. I thought back to the last month or so and felt as if we had done everything the same way, but apparently that hadn't mattered. She was pregnant and all the being cautious didn't amount to anything.

It wasn't that I was upset that she was pregnant again. It was more the idea of the whole balance game I played with myself. This simply didn't factor into that equation, and I would need to adjust yet again.

Amanda was a little caught off guard, too, but she was meant to carry babies, so she quickly turned her shock into excitement once again.

"Jon, it's going to be fine. Stop worrying so much about the kids and work, and just keep doing what it is you are doing. It's working," she said.

Except that each time I felt I was doing right, I would look at the finances and think of how far away I was from where we needed to be. My father was a born saver all his life, and while I didn't know his finances perse, I knew he was well off and could retire at any time and live an enjoyable life for as many years as he had left in him.

So, I probably put too much pressure on myself to do as he had done, and that always felt like I was so far behind. This is where having someone like Amanda helped me. My mother rarely told my dad that he needed to stop and slow down to appreciate the fruits of his labor. Amanda had very little issues telling me she needed me to step up and slow down working if she felt rundown.

There were times she needed simple things, like a trip to the grocery store without having kids hanging all over her, and I would have never thought to offer to watch the kids. She knew that, so when she needed time to herself for an hour or two, she made it known. My mother would just always watch us and take us everywhere, but looking back, I wish I had made those trips a little easier and not fought in the backseat the entire trip with my brothers. She deserved a break, and we didn't give her that.

It's funny when I have all the kids together. Agnes is a huge help and seems to understand that I am not cut out for this just yet on my own. She is so good when we are hanging out and helps with both Erik and Dot. Although I still must remind her that Dot is not a baby doll, and she still needs to ask me first before she decides to pick her up in her arms and carry her around the living room as if she is hers.

Erik likes to test me. He knows where his limits are with mom, but with me he is still unsure. So, we seem to go back and forth with the games of chance, where he pushes a little more and I push back just enough. It's funny how smart my children are and how they all are so different from each other.

Agnes. She continues to surprise me. I watch her develop this personality that is a little hard to put into words, and I smile. She just loves life like no one else I know. She's always smiling and excited for whatever it is we are doing that day. It doesn't matter what it is, she has this way about her that nothing is going to ruin her smile.

I promise myself that I will always allow my kids to be

who they are, even if I do not agree with it. Their choices that make them happy are not always going to make me happy, but I believe they should be in control of that particular part of their lives. Easier said than done though. If Erik wants a nose piercing at age seven, I can't see a way for me to consider accepting that. Again, limits and balance I suppose.

When Amanda returns from her trips to the store, those ones where she gets to shop in peace, I am eager to run out and help her bring things in. It's sometimes hard to handle all three kids alone when I am used to working with adults all day on their income taxes and financial decisions. Trying to pick out what Barbie dress matches with Ken's outfit, is not where I excel. I love to play dolls with the kids, but I make the dolls wrestle each other and have a hard time being serious about how they should be dressed for their night out on the town.

Erik gets it, I think. He uses Ken to jump off the top ropes and lands an elbow on his sister's Barbie that she just finished getting dressed. Agnes is not entirely amused, but I am. I just can't show it because then Agnes could have an issue with me for taking sides, and I do not want to be accused of favoritism.

Life has been interesting to this point for me. A steady stream of new adventures has satisfied my curiosity mostly, and I am content on where I have landed thus far. I care about my wife deeply. My children are everything I had hoped they would be, and I mostly enjoy my job. We aren't rich, but we aren't poor. Our finances lie somewhere in the middle for the area we live in, and each day that goes by, we seem to do just a little bit better.

My mother once asked me what was my favorite thing to do, and I had to pause to think about it. There are so many things I enjoy, like fishing with my brother, Alex, and my father, or sitting on the couch next to Amanda as we put the kids to sleep and promise ourselves that we will stay up for an entire movie, which we never make it through. But the funny thing is that my mind goes to this one time I saw Agnes dancing with her sister and brother, and she took the time to choreograph the entire dance with her siblings following as best they could. It somehow put an imprint in my mind, and I have thought about that often.

The simplest memory seems to be the one that I find the most fondness in. So, I answer my mother with that.

"The fairy princess dance that Agnes did for us all, Mom," I reply.

It comes from my mouth without any hesitation once it pops into my head. "The Dance of Agnes the Fairy," as she called it.

Chapter 10

The Pearly Gates

* * *

A manda doesn't get much sleep after the celebration of our anniversary. With Agnes not feeling her best self, she decides to lay with her to make sure she doesn't need anything throughout the night. I set up a few old blankets and pillows on the floor so that she will be somewhat comfortable as she goes to bed, but I know Amanda. She is worried more than her usual self, so sleep will escape her for most of the night.

I put Erik and Dot to bed with little trouble, after brushing their teeth and reading them two books before prayers, as they could not agree on one book collectively. I don't mind though, because the books are on the short side, and the kids seem to get really excited for what the next pages will bring to the storyline. It's fun for me, as much as it is for them.

But this night, my reading is off some, and I hear it from Erik.

"Dad, the next page. You aren't turning the pages," he says.

I'm a little lost in thought, wondering why Amanda and my mother are concerned. I just am not used to seeing that, and it makes me a little anxious. I hate that feeling, so I try my best to push it away for now, but this isn't going to be easy tonight. I know once the doctors look at her tomorrow, it'll be much different. A shot, or maybe an antibiotic to clear her troubles up, and she will be back to Agnes the Fairy. But the wait sucks.

Once the kids are fast asleep, I walk down to check on her and Amanda, and I see my wife is running her hand through Agnes' long soft hair with her fingers, while her other hand is on her own head. She looks concerned, and so I want to give her a few moments before interrupting.

As I watch, I see an amazing mother at work. She had birthed this child, raised this child, and she continues to be selfless for her. It's so easy to take for granted everything someone does for someone else. I think it often gets dismissed as, "It's her job," or "This is just what a mother does," and that type of talk takes away from the reality of what she is doing right now.

As a male, I inherited a sense of my place in a relationship, both as a husband and as a father. Work hard to provide financial stability for the family, ensure the unit of the family understands that I am alpha and there to be the protector at all costs, and be the strong type that doesn't ever feel the need to cry, or panic. That is how I view my responsibilities, just as my father has, and his father before him.

As a female, I have always viewed my wife's job as the nurturing one that educates the children, ensures the family is well fed, and is the more sensitive one that offers kindness when needed, and kisses the boo-boos to make them all better. It's the role that Amanda had wanted, and so we figured this was the only way.

Watching from the doorway, I quickly discover that I am incorrect. My wife is extremely strong, and at times, she is the alpha when she wants to, or needs to be. She is also nurturing, kind, and fixes those boo-boos as well. I think she is the combination of all I thought a male and female should be, and it can be intimidating at times, but I love that about her.

"Babe, hey. I don't want to interrupt you, but how is Agnes feeling?" I ask.

Amanda turns to look my way, and a look of concern crosses her face, but she manages a smile. I can see she is worried, but also strong and hopeful that shortly she will be back to herself again.

"I don't know. She still doesn't have a high fever, and she's not vomiting, but something just seems off to me. She told me her head is hurting, so I gave her something to hopefully help with that. I'll be happy for tomorrow to get here so I can get her to the doctor's and figure this out," she replies.

"Yea, I'm sure. Do you need anything? I put the kids to bed, and everything is cleaned and locked up for the night," I say.

"You know what I would like, Jon? A cup of hot tea with some lemon in it," Amanda says.

I smile at my wife and nod my head to let her know that I will do that.

When I get to the kitchen, I start the water on the stove, and open the cabinet above to find the tea bags. There are a few different types, as my wife enjoys a good cup of tea, so I am guessing when I choose. Hopefully it'll be one of the ones she is craving, but it most likely won't matter tonight.

Once the water comes to a steady boil, I quickly remove the black pot from the burner so that the screaming it is doing doesn't wake the entire house.

I decide that I will pour a hot cup for myself as well and sit with Agnes and Amanda before I retire to the bedroom. I'm not a tea drinker, but on occasion I have had a cup with my wife. I have no idea of which ones taste better than others, so I really don't care about which one I selected for us. I'm just going to pour milk and add sugar to my cup anyway, so they probably all taste relatively the same at that point.

On my way back in to where they are resting, I grab a few tea biscuits that we picked up for Amanda while we were out getting her list of items. She loves those, and so does Agnes. Agnes dips them in her tea whenever she is having some with her mother. It's funny to see the two of them watching a show, with tea saucers and flowery cups in front of them, along with some snack biscuits, as Agnes likes to call them.

Agnes and Amanda are more alike than I probably see most times, but when you sit and see them together watching something on TV, it's like they are the same person, only twenty years different.

When I return, I set up the tray on the floor, beneath where Agnes is resting, and I lay the tea and biscuits out in a presentation, to try and impress my wife. She just smiles, knowing that I do this to try and impress her. I know she appreciates the tiny gesture, and I also am aware that she is too kind of a person to tell me to stop because it just looks silly. I know my wife well.

She picks up her tea and smells it deep into her nostrils. At first, I thought she was maybe trying to figure out what tea I picked for her, but I think it was more about clearing her head from this evening. I can understand why she would want to.

She takes a sip and smiles at me, as her way of saying thank you without having to say the words. I smile back and drop my head as I do, in a sheepish manner. Over a decade married, and I still can get that way around Amanda. Those "flutterflies" as she calls them. She has this gift for making me nervous, and I love that about her.

We each look over to Agnes at the same time and watch her as she sleeps. Her face is showing signs of physical exhaustion, and she doesn't have that smile that graces our lives so often, but I know she doesn't feel well, so this is kind of what I would expect from her tonight.

Still, though, I can see that smile of hers through this

all. I've seen it a million times over the past 11 years, and it would be impossible to see her without it for long. It's her best quality, I think. She can smile through just about anything.

"Amanda, remember that time when Agnes came home from school and had to do that project on what she thought heaven was like?" I say.

Amanda starts to laugh quietly because she absolutely remembers that day.

Agnes ran into the front door of the house, exclaiming that she had seen heaven and knew exactly what it was like. I was at work in the home office, so I only heard it slightly, but Amanda came in to see her with a confused look on her face.

Agnes explained that while in school that day, she fell asleep at her desk and had herself a dream about what the pearly gates looked like when you arrive at the entrance to heaven.

The first thought from my wife was why our child had fallen asleep during her schooling, and second, why on earth was she talking about heaven and having dreams about them?

Agnes continued to tell her story.

"Well, you see, I was daydreaming as per my usual, and Kenzie was tapping her pencil on the desk next to me, which obviously made me tired, and the sound of the tapping just knocked me right out," she started.

"Yes, obviously," my wife responded waiting to hear

more of this elaborate tale.

"Well, the teacher was given us an assignment at just about that time, and it was on what we think heaven is really like when we first arrive. So I guess, subconsciously really, I heard her tell the class this, and drifted off into heaven, so that I could get an A on my assignment!" Agnes said.

It was funny, because she was so serious, and while she clearly had not visited heaven that morning in class, she felt as if she had and was so excited to write her report out on what it was truly like.

Amanda was laughing more now as we talked about that day, and she continues with,

"Jon, she was so thankful that she got to visit, and just knew it was to give her an A in that class. I wasn't so shocked when she got an A, because she is so creative, but the description she gave was brilliant. She had put a lot of effort into her story, remember?"

Agnes said that while she was knocked out, as she put it, in class, she heard this glorious music being played far in the distance. She said she was trying to hear where it was coming from but could not at the time. Then, she said there was this man, whom she could not describe well, reaching out his hand to her, and motioning her over to where he was standing. She said she felt completely safe with this person and began to walk over. As she got closer to him, she could see a smile on his face that reminded her of diamonds. When she got to that part of the report, she drew a silhouette of a figure with sparkles where his mouth would be.

Then she said she grabbed the man's hand, and they were moving upwards, although she could not really tell they were moving. The only reason she knew was that everything below her was getting smaller, and the music that she now knew was above the two of them, was growing increasingly louder. At the top, there was a platform made of a yellow gold, and the man stepped out onto the strip, and motioned for her to as well. So she did.

When she was showing us the report, I remember picturing everything she described, and I too, wondered for a moment what heaven was really like. It was a fun project to watch Agnes work on.

Agnes said that after she stepped towards the man again, she could see rainbow colors all around her. She said that the music was coming from behind a black colored gate, and as she approached it, she could see figures dancing in the near distance, smiling and singing this beautiful song.

The man she was with started to laugh some, and just watched as Agnes mimicked the dance she saw. It's as if he was impressed that she gets it.

The pictures she drew for her report were detailed and actually really good. You could tell that she put a lot of effort and creativity into those pages and drawings.

I can't remember all the things she mentioned just now, but I know that she said as soon as she got to the gates, she laughed so loud that everyone looked at her, and stopped what they were doing for a moment. She said, at first, she thought she was in trouble for making such a scene, but that after a moment or two, everyone knew what it was that made her laugh so hard, and they, too, all began to laugh just as loud.

When we asked her what had made her laugh so hard in her dream, she said that the gates were not pearl in color, even though we call them the Pearly Gates. She found this to be the most ironic thing of everything she witnessed. The Pearly Gates were not pearly.

"I bet you still have that report she did somewhere, don't you babe," I said to Amanda.

She lets out a giggle that confirms she does indeed still have it. I knew it. She saves so much of the kid's projects, and crafts, and report cards, that we will never forget what our children have accomplished in their youth.

It's nice to have these pleasant moments with my wife. She leans in and places her head on my chest as we sit and talk about the things Agnes does. I think it's comforting to her that we have each other and our beautiful children all together. Not everyone has that luxury.

When our friends signed the final divorce papers and officially ended their marriage, Amanda was sad. She didn't want to believe that families could split up when there was still hope. The thought of her children not having both parents around all the time was disturbing to her, and she just felt empty for Roger and Lily, and even worse for their children.

At first, I was talking with Roger, trying to give him the

best advice I could, and Amanda was talking with Lily. It caused issues for us, because I found myself defending Roger when she would tell me what Lily said about him, and Amanda would jump to the defense of Lily when I would tell her that Roger accused her of cheating.

It was not healthy for us to get in between them, as much as we were simply trying to help. It doesn't usually work that way. We felt like we were siding with someone over another friend, and it became too much for Amanda to handle at the time.

I finally had to tell Roger, in order to save my own marriage, I was going to need to step back some. The best advice I could give him was for him to seek out counseling, and to follow their recommendations. It was the last time I spoke with Roger. I don't think he appreciated that advice, and probably felt as if I had betrayed him. I had not, though. I simply was saving my marriage.

Amanda did the same, although Lily initially understood and kept in touch with Amanda for almost a year before she, too, disappeared. She had met someone soon after her divorce, and so Amanda just assumed she moved on with her life and wasn't in need of her help any longer.

I'm certain once things settle down for them both, we will once again be a part of their lives. It just won't ever be the same though.

Well, finally I can see that Agnes looks more comfortable with her resting, and she turns over to her other side facing away from us. It's a small comfort to us knowing she at least is moving. She hadn't moved a muscle all afternoon, and that was probably most troubling to Amanda. At least, I hope, now my wife can get some much-deserved rest.

I gently move the porcelain teacups out of the way and lay down next to my wife as she tires and attempts to fall asleep for a few. As she does, I sit there rubbing her head, knowing I will also be sleeping here next to her. I feel the same pull to stay with our Agnes, and ensure when she needs us, we are both here for her, as I promised I would always be.

Chapter 11

The Greatest of Moments

* * *

I think about Andrew often, and I wonder what goes on in his mind. I wonder, does he think like any normal functioning adult, but just cannot act on how he feels, or does he think more as if he never aged past a certain point in his life?

Because he doesn't speak much, it's hard to understand just where he stands with his life, but I know this. That guy is genuinely happy. I rarely see him without a fantastic, broad, curling smile, even if it's just a mundane task he is working on. Nothing seems to get in the way of his happiness, and it has my mind in a curious spot. Is it better to not know how the world works, and to have little to be responsible for? I mean, maybe having people care for you, and not having to worry about retirement and what schools your children will want to attend, if you can even afford them, and being concerned each time they catch a cold, is where it's at.

I know, though, the reality is that I am blessed to be where I am. To have the ability to do the simple things Andrew cannot...I need to stop being so damn selfish sometimes and more understanding that Andrew probably would give anything to have the ability to communicate his thoughts much clearer than he can. I'm certain there is a frustrating side to not being able to effectively communicate.

Andrew is a good uncle, although the girls see him more as a cousin than an uncle. Because he acts so much younger than his age, they find him both curious and interesting. Agnes, especially, has taken a liking to him.

She had always taken a liking to Andrew though, and since she was young, she's always called him Uncle Dew. He's never seemed to mind, and in fact when the kids do call him Uncle Dew, he laughs hysterically, and that can bring anyone within hearing distance, a massive smile. It's because that kid, well, man now, is always so happy with everything.

Dot always finds her way to him whenever he comes over. She pulls out her dolls, and Uncle Dew opens his bag to show her what he decided to bring that particular day. Sometimes it's a Hot Wheels car, and other times, he packs a Ken doll that we bought specifically so that he could play alongside the kids.

Erik is a little more standoffish, but it's not because he's afraid or anything like that. Erik just seems to keep himself occupied with things outside of what the girls and Andrew play with as he starts to get older.

For instance, he plays video games. A lot. That was something that Amanda's parents never allowed Andrew to get into. I understood the thinking behind it, but I wonder if it may have helped Andrew's coordination more. Doesn't matter though, as it was just how they decided to raise him.

Erik could spend all day playing those games if we didn't force him to go outside and let the game consoles cool down some. I get it. Kids play and communicate so often through these systems today, just as we did with riding bikes to each other's homes all day long. It's just a different world now with a different means of communicating.

I remember riding bikes as a young boy from one town to the next. Half the time, my parents didn't know just how far the group of boys and I peddled off that day. Of course, it would seem like we peddled to the other side of the state at times, but in reality, it was a town, maybe two towns away, at the most.

It reminds me a lot of the phrase I see on social media over and over again:

"You never realized growing up as a child, that one day, would be the last day you played with these kids."

It went something like that, I recall, and when you sit and think about it, it's entirely true. Yes, I still see some of the boys I hung out with at the river, fishing off the banks, or riding our Mongoose bikes over the footbridges into the next town to see if the girls there were better looking than the ones in our hometown. But I can't seem to recall the very last time the boys and I peddled far off to a new destination and made it back home just before the streetlights turned bright and our parents started to worry. I try, but I cannot picture that day in my thoughts.

When you look at the youth of today, and the fact that unless they are occupied by some extracurricular group event, they are home in their rooms, with the door shut and the lights off, playing on a computer with people they have never met, and probably never will. I wonder, what will they think in twenty years about their youth? Will they realize they missed out on so much that they should have and could have done, or will they not know the difference because they never experienced it?

Maybe I am just like my parents were, though. I know as a child my mom and dad didn't think we enjoyed enough of our youth the way they had. It's probably every generation that feels like they are the ones that had the best childhood experiences, and each one after them are wasting their youth.

Whatever it is, I just hope that our children do something that they will carry with them the rest of their lives as a time they were wicked happy. My fondest time? Riding the bikes through rain and sun, just to see pretty girls with the boys. That's my favorite one.

I remember asking my dad what his favorite memory was once. At first, he was busy and didn't seem to be interested in reliving his past, but with a little pressing, he opened a door to his childhood he had long since closed off unintentionally.

"Jon, the best time I ever had, the very best time from when I was a young boy? I was maybe, ten or eleven. Just a runt of a kid really, and probably smaller than all those around me," he started.

"My parents had sent me to summer camp. The name of the camp was, ah, let me see here. Delmont Falls. Wow, Jon, I haven't thought about that place in many years. It was a camp that catered to groups of kids so that they could explore nature at its purest, and bond with other kids their own age. We had, oh I don't know, a dozen or so kids in our cabin. The cabins weren't all that big, but we managed with all the kids. This one boy, Jeremy Scone, or Sconce, I can't really remember right now, but it doesn't matter. He and I were inseparable. We would sneak out of the cabin at night with flashlights, pretending we were detectives trying to solve a murder late at night. Him and I got caught towards the end of the summer, but those times we did not get caught? Those were the best nights I ever had as a kid for sure," my dad said.

Agnes has friends, but she's not the most popular kid around, mainly because she's quirky. I love how she is, but I think other kids her age struggle with the fact that she is so unique. They probably don't know how to take her. I will need to sit with her, as I did with my own father, and ask her what, so far anyway, is her favorite memory. I want them to understand they should be paying attention to those, because the last time they will get to do whatever it is they are most fond of, is coming to an end.

Dot and Erik are still too young to understand this, but Agnes is of the perfect age. I feel like she is going to come into her own any day now, and surprise us all by maturing overnight. I know a lot of kids seem to just flip a switch and go from playing with dolls to putting on makeup with each other as they head to a school dance in groups.

For Andrew, I bet he has a moment he loves more than any other, but I am also certain he cannot share that with us sadly. It's okay though, because for him, he has a long time in front of him to continue making more memories. He will not have to worry about paying bills and working a job, or kids that need to be at practice at one time, while another child needs to be on the complete other side of town at the same exact time.

While those times create a different set of memories, and I love being around my kids on those drives, I miss riding my bike and being a kid at times. It was just fantastically different. We thought we were older than we were, but that was part of the excitement. We were allowed to be something we weren't, but then were allowed to revert to what we actually were. It was the best of both worlds as I saw it.

Who knows, maybe the best memories all three of our children will have, will be with each other. I spent a lot of time with my friends, but less with my brothers. Those memories usually center around fishing with our dad or piling into the family station wagon to go visit a relative, or to see a park that my dad had on his bucket list. Those long drives across the state allowed us to make up our own games in the backseat to kill time. Otherwise we would have been annoyed with each other and probably choked one another the rest of the trips.

With our trips, it's usually Agnes who keeps the younger ones occupied for the drives. She is super creative and doesn't seem to mind the long hours we sometimes spend together on road trips. In fact, she rarely asks if we are almost there. You hear stories about kids asking that, and I am certain my brothers and I did on many occasions, but kids today have so many distractions that seem to make the rides go faster than they actually do.

Amanda gets in on the fun as well because she is just as creative as our Agnes is. Sometimes they bounce ideas off of each other, just to see who can create whatever it is they are trying to do, in the most unique ways.

I've mentioned before that I am not the creative one. I wish I was, but it's just not in my blood. I leave that part of raising the kids to Amanda. She and Agnes could probably create an entire story of wonderful fantasies, simply from a long road trip, and have everyone wanting to read more.

In fact, that happens to be one of the games they all play as I watch the other cars on the road in front of us as well as behind us. One of them will start to talk about the drive, and then Amanda yells,

"Next!"

She then points to the next child, and that one must pick right up where the last one left off. It's interesting, because the kids come up with the craziest stories, and they somehow seem to blend so well together as if they were meant to be that way. Amanda even shouts her "next!" and then points at me as I am driving, trying to listen to them, as I also try to look for the next exit that is approaching any moment now.

I'm not quick and inventive with the stories, so most times they just boo me in a playful manner, but every now and again, I come up with something worthy of their excitement. It's more often that I do not though, and I go back to looking for another route as the exit we were after has come and gone.

"Jon, let's pull off the next chance we get and stretch a bit. I'm getting a little restless and the kids need to use the bathroom. Besides, your legs need a good yawn I bet by now," Amanda says.

She's poetic with her words, and even if I don't always understand where it comes from, I understand the intent. I suppose that is more important. Knowing what she meant clearly mattered more than how it came about, to me anyway.

We don't always get to take these trips, but when we do, I try to soak up every last detail along the way. As a boy, we barely noticed the scenery around us, but as I grew older and wiser, I learned how important it was to pay attention to the little things. A tree with a trunk several feet around that has probably been in place for a few hundred years, or a cut through the mountain that only Mother Nature could make so perfectly, are the things I look for now.

I would tell the kids to look at the classic cars from the 40s and 50s that we would pass along the interstate, and sometimes they would show an interest, but most times it was only me who did. I loved watching cars from yesterday, still humming along the roads across the state, wondering what they had seen that I had not. It sounds silly, but I bet those old fenders have passed actors and actresses, along with countless sports figures from this generation and generations that are no longer with us.

My dad would always point out antique cars and trucks, and the pride in his excited voice was knowing what year they were, and how he knew that information. It was usually the shape of the front headlights, or the way the raised fins were just so, or possibly the color of the car, as it may have only been offered in a certain year or a limited time. He knew it all when it came to old cars, but now, everything seems to be lost. That sexiness of yesterday's metal is replaced with plastics and comfort and gadgets to push sales.

I feel that way about how the kids play today. They have lost the excitement and the appeal to go explore the muddy riverbeds or riding through an old farmer's field to discover some old glass bottles that had been left there by some old farmer who forgot to pick them back up.

Kids don't see the things we did, and I doubt that will ever return to glory. It's about the new movie with all the newest special effects, or the game that everyone must have, because they added new characters that were not in the original one. It's all computerized now. Childhood is no longer earned. Those scars, that we wore proudly like badges of honor, are a distant memory. A scraped knee once meant that you had done something crazy and gone above and beyond what the last kid had done, but now it probably means you fell while plastering your face to your iPhone. That's not earned. It's laziness.

With each day that comes, I try to remind each of the kids that one day, you will miss today. One day, you will look back and wonder how you missed ten years of your life, because they went by without your permission. Life doesn't need you to accept it's moving on. That part hurts. It goes at the pace it wishes to, even when you wish for it to slow down or speed up.

Life happens. That is the best way I can describe it. Life happens.

Chapter 12

The Arrival

* * *

We've had very little sleep. Every slight movement or small noise that we hear from where our Agnes is resting, alerts us, and we wake. For the most part, she has slept fairly well. There were a few moments where she cried, which is unlike her, and that troubles me. I hate hearing my kids cry. Not like the "he took my toy and won't give it back," type of cry. Those don't bother me in the least. They are a part of understanding your patience and it's a valuable lesson to understand as you mature. You aren't going to always get things simply because you want them in life.

This cry was one that begged us to take away whatever was hurting her. As a parent, that hurts more than anything. It's like a dagger stabbing you quickly over and over. You want to take away the fever and chills, or the pounding headache, or the sharp pain of a broken arm, and allow your kids to just be kids again. When they cry in agony, it hits you something awful.

I know that the kids have all been here before with stomach bugs, or a touch of the seasonal flu, but it doesn't make it any easier just because you have handled this all before. You hate seeing your children not feeling themselves. So, our night, while mostly uneventful, was not one of rest.

I see Amanda is up before me, and she's stroking Agnes on her arms. She's whispering to her, but it's too faint for me to hear the words she is speaking to her. I thought about moving closer to hear, but those are words Amanda wants Agnes to hear and understand, so I don't need to concern myself with those.

As I stand up to stretch out my bones, and as Amanda would say, let my legs yawn some, I look around for my phone so that I can see what time it is.

It's right where I was laying just a few moments before, and so I pick it up and realize it's still only six in the morning, so the doctor's office is not even going to be open yet to schedule an appointment for Agnes.

"Coffee?" I ask Amanda.

She just nods as she looks at our daughter. It makes me smile how loving and attentive she is to our children. When you think of a mother, who would give anything for her children, this is exactly who you should picture. She's literally the best person I have ever met, and although we have our moments, these moments trump those difficult ones we share.

The kitchen is fairly clean, with just a few things laying around from the night before. I tried to get everything in order so the morning would be easier for us, and I think I did a pretty decent job of that.

As I pull the coffee out from the top cabinet and place the filter in before adding the coffee, I look out to the back yard and remember how Agnes was dancing like a goofy child less than a full day ago. It's funny because she had rehearsed so hard as a gift to Amanda and me, and that was the best gift we received yesterday.

I could see she left her rainbow crown on the lawn when she decided to come in and lay down. I don't know how she left that there, as it may just be her most prized possession. I'll get it while the coffee is brewing, I tell myself. She will want that after her doctor's visit for certain.

The coffee is done brewing, and I pour my usual two sugars and one cream into mine. Amanda, she prefers it just as she does her tea. Black.

I don't feel hungry just yet, and I know Amanda is one of those people that can't eat when she gets up. Her body tends to need time to adjust before she can add nutrients to it.

"Here babe, your coffee is ready. How is she this morning?" I ask.

Amanda reaches her hands out, cupping the mug in both, and smells the coffee while closing her eyes. She's tired. I can tell. But she feels like she has a job to do, and she takes that very seriously. I am always the one sitting in the background telling her to just point and tell me where and what to do, and I will. She's better under pressure, and I am better at taking directions. It's why we work so well together.

"I think she's feeling a little bit better, Jon. She was talking with me a little, but she closed her eyes again to get a little more rest. I'm not sure she feels as bad as she did yesterday, but I still want to get her to the doctor's office to get checked out, just to be safe," she says.

"Of course, I'll check the hours, but I think they open at nine. I'll try to get the first available and call my parents to watch the kids while we go. They won't mind," I assure her.

My parents are always willing to give a hand. It's nice that we have such great people around us, so that when we need them to step in, they do so seamlessly, without hesitation.

The other kids are still sleeping, and I expected as much. They had a large sugar rush last night, and their bodies probably need all the rest they can get. Erik and Dot both have a sweet tooth, and I blame their mother for that, although I don't really blame her as much, as I know she loves her sweets.

"So they do open at nine, but I was thinking of just having my parents come now, and we can leave a little after eight and get there first thing. We can stop for coffee and a bagel on the way, and by then, maybe Agnes will be hungry as well. Does that sound good?" I ask as I sip on my coffee.

There is this great little bagel joint about a mile and a

half from the house, and Agnes loves to stop and get her cranberry bagel with cheddar cheese and an over-easy egg. She hasn't had any food since at least midday yesterday, so she's going to want something shortly after she wakes.

Amanda agrees that it is a good idea, and I decide to go and call my mom to let her know. Then I can go to shower and wake myself up some, and shake off the night's horrible sleep, so I am not loopy all morning. The cold rush of the water will wake me, and I'll be more alert.

Once I finish both of those tasks, I peek into both bedrooms to check on Erik and Dot. Only, Dot isn't in her room. She walked into her brother's room at some point in the middle of the night and passed out on the floor next to him with her favorite pink, softy blanket and her doll, Penelope, tightly squeezed in her tiny arms.

I pull my phone out from my pocket and snap a picture because it's adorable how she just made a little spot to sleep in next to her brother, who probably wasn't keen on her sleeping in the bed with him. Dot has gone back and forth with pull-ups to help her not pee her bed sheets, and usually she's pretty good, but every now and again, she drinks a little too much water before bedtime, and doesn't quite make it to the morning.

I don't bother to check her, because she's passed out hard, and my parents can handle this. I'm sure I have had my moments growing up, where I snuck a little juice or water before bed without my mother knowing. It's part of being a kid really.

I'm dressed now, so I decide to head back down to give Amanda time to get herself together. She isn't one of those women that needs a ton of time in the morning to get ready, but she certainly needs more than I do. Me? I throw an old t-shirt on that I've had since college, brush my teeth, put the mostly clean jeans from last night over my legs, and throw a hat on in 10 seconds flat. It's easy for me to not care as much, because, well I guess because I just don't care. There are perks to being a male at times for sure.

Amanda gets up and gets herself together while I sit next to Agnes and wait. She's resting, so I don't want to bother her now. I just scroll through my phone trying to pass the time, waiting for my dad and mom to arrive, Amanda to finish, and the kids to get up. I have no idea what order that will all happen in, but I guess it really doesn't matter.

Besides, I have time to catch up on the stock market, and to see what seems to be moving today. I try to follow my investments daily, but lately I've been so busy, that I look only here and there when I have a free moment.

Just then, I hear a strange sound from where Agnes is sleeping. Only, she's not sleeping now.

"Agnes, honey? Daddy's here. Is everything okay sweetheart?" I ask her.

She's crying and holding her head, and I drop my phone down to go check on her. She's in pain, I can tell, and I don't know what to do.

"Honey, your mother will be down any minute now, okay? I'm here though. What's wrong, honey?" I ask, trying to comfort her with my words as best I can.

"Daddy, my head hurts. Why won't it stop?" Agnes cries.

I wish I had that answer. As a father, it is my job, at least in my mind, to protect my wife and my kids more than anyone else can. It's my job to make things better and easier at all costs, and to always have the answers. Only, I don't always have those answers, and that bothers me. I wish I did, but the best I can do is guess at this point, or at least make her feel good with a little white lie, if I am not right.

"Mom and I are going to take you to the doctors as soon as they open, and they will figure this out, get you some meds, and by tonight I'm sure you will feel much better. Back to dancing around the living room for mom and me, okay?" I respond.

"Plus, we are going to Amelia's and getting you whatever you want on the way. You love their bagels, and if you don't tell your brother and sister, we can stop on the way back home and grab some ice cream cones. But keep that our little secret," I wink as I continue.

Amanda finishes up in what seems like record time for her. Whenever we are going out with friends, or on a rare date night she has planned, I know it will be "just another minute," for about a half hour more. It's never excessive like I hear my friends tell me, but it's also never in the time she claims.

Their wives don't even bother to hide it any longer. Instead of telling them it'll only be a minute more, those guys have learned to start the process of getting ready only when their wives tell them they are just putting their shoes on and will be right down. This way, they know as soon as they are showered and dressed, it truly will only be one more minute.

"Hey, Hun, I think we should get going. Maybe someone will be in the office early. She's not feeling well at all," I say to Amanda.

My parents pull into the driveway, and with only a few words spoken between us, I carry our Agnes to the car, place her in the rear seat, strap the seatbelt over her, and place a pillow against the window so that she can continue to rest her head.

Amanda gives my parents a quick rundown on things, then tells them that Erik and Dot are both still fast asleep, but when they wake, to give them anything that is easy for breakfast.

My parents nod quickly and wave us off as if to say, "We got it. You go and deal with this, and we will hold down the fort while you are gone."

Amanda decides to sit in the back seat with Agnes to comfort her, and I slowly back out of the driveway to head on down the road. The road is lined with decent sized oak trees, and they are so green and full of dance this morning. It's a little bit windy, and I know Agnes, if she felt better, would be talking non-stop, and asking questions all about the trees.

She would most likely ask me if I think the trees can hear music that we cannot, like a dog that hears high-pitched sounds that a human doesn't. Otherwise, why would they be dancing?

Or maybe she would wonder if the swirling wind was asking the tall trees for this dance, before moving on its way to a far-off land, to find yet another dancing partner.

Usually I just laugh off her questions, but this morning I miss them. She is her mother's child for sure. A full imagination with a curiosity that brings her soul alive. It's who she is, and she is clearly not herself this morning. I ponder on the idea of trying to ask her questions, but I know they won't be as perfectly thought out as hers are, so I decide to not ask. Besides, I don't think she feels much like thinking about these small things today.

As we pull up to the bagel store, there is a small line of cars wrapped around the outside, but they are usually quick with getting the orders out. I pull behind the last car in line because I think it'll still be faster than getting out, going in, and waiting in line for the order that way.

"Agnes, your usual?" I ask her.

She's now lying in her mother's lap, and Amanda is stroking her head, trying to comfort her from the headache she has had for a full day now.

"Jon, just get her that, and we can save it in case she's hungry after her appointment. She's probably not going to eat it now, but it's better to have something for when she is," Amanda responds.

I already know what to get Amanda. She gets an Everything Bagel, with just a little butter, and an orange juice. It will be good for her to eat, because it could be a little while wait, especially since we still do not have an appointment scheduled. The office is still not open for another twenty minutes or so, so we are going on blind faith that they will be able to get us in today, and the earlier the better.

As I pull up to the window, I order what the girls want, and then I just get a coffee for me. Two sugars, one cream today. I don't feel much like eating, so I decide to wait until later on.

We are back off and heading towards the doctor's office we have been going to for about five years now. The kids love to get stickers when they are finished their appointments, and at eleven years old, Agnes still loves to pick through the basket of different ones, trying to find the perfect purple or pink one in the entire lot. She usually ends up with more than one, and the nurse always laughs, knowing this.

The parking lot is still empty, so I pull into a front spot, put the car in park, and hand the food off to my wife in the back seat. She just places it next to where she is seated and doesn't even bother to ask Agnes if she wants any. She knows the answer already. She does, though, open a fresh bottle of water we had in the car, and tells Agnes that she needs to sip just a little for mommy.

Agnes sits up just enough to open her lips and allows Amanda to pour some into her mouth. She hasn't had a drink since she first complained of not feeling well and resting yesterday. We know dehydration can cause a headache and are pretty certain that because it can cause one, it probably doesn't allow you to heal from one you are already experiencing.

At exactly 8:52 AM, I see a car pulling in, and out steps the receptionist who handles all the appointments for the office. We aren't going to rush out just yet, figuring she will need a few moments to turn on the lights, and get her morning routine underway.

As she enters the office, she notices us parked there, and smiles our way. I'm sure she knows this isn't the first time someone needed to get in to see the doctor prior to them officially opening.

Other cars pull in, and a steady stream of nurses and doctors enter through the front door, about to start off their shifts.

"Well Jon, are you ready?" Amanda asks.

Chapter 13

Uncle Dew

* * *

Back when Agnes was maybe three or four, there was a time Andrew had fallen ill, and he had to be admitted to the hospital. He, of course, required his bag be with him at all times.

I had to run back to his parent's house to fetch it, because he wouldn't make it easier on the doctors unless he had old "stowy" with him.

During his stay, I distinctly remember he was either doodling or writing something in a notebook he had been given by Amanda and I before we were even married. I wasn't certain he could write, but I remember Amanda telling me that he could communicate his thoughts much better that way.

Time passed and I never thought to ask her how well his writing level was, but I know he always had that bag and notebook wherever he went. It became a part of his identity, and if I sat and tried to think of a time, other than the one where he was taken to the hospital in an ambulance, that he did not have it with him, I would probably draw a blank.

His parents had once tried to get him a new bag, but he would not allow that. His bag was soiled from the years of carrying it anywhere and everywhere, through both pounding rain showers and squalling snow, and it had seen much better days. But it was his bag, and so it did not need to be cleaned, or replaced in his mind. That was just how it was going to be, so, eventually, his parents stopped asking him.

When he came over to visit us and the kids, Agnes was always very curious about the bag, but didn't overstep when she talked to him about it. It was more of an excitement and bewilderment for her.

He didn't say much ever, but she just seemed to understand what he wanted to say, even if no words were spoken. They have a great bond, Agnes, and Uncle Dew.

Erik and Dot, they never really seemed all that interested in the bag, and instead just accepted that he always had it, and it was his most prized possessions that he kept safe in there. Sometimes he would take a few items out for them to see, and sometimes he just kept it closed entirely, preferring to keep those precious items to himself.

You grew to understand, and to expect this behavior from Andrew, so it was never a surprise. You got one or the other, and both were perfectly fine by us and those closest to him.

Andrew had developed an infection inside his lungs and

had to stay for several days so that it would clear itself up, and it eventually did. Those days were anything but easy, however.

The nurses either loved him or despised him, and both for good reason.

When Andrew wants to be playful and fun, there may not be a better soul to be around than him. He loves to play tricks and can win anyone over with both his broad smile, and his infectious laughter.

But when Andrew doesn't want to be bothered, or you need to draw blood from his veins, let's just say, there are much more pleasant sounds that come from African safari animals giving birth deep in the jungle. He can screech and raise his octaves to levels no man or woman should need to hear, ever again.

It was interesting visiting him back then. We took Agnes with us because she always asked to go visit her Uncle Dew, and I'm sure it was a welcome site for Andrew to see someone he was so fond of as well. We left Erik home with my parents because he would just fuss too much, and Amanda wanted to spend time with her brother without feeling as if she had to rush things.

For Agnes, though, it was never a worry. She's not the type of child to rush you out of whatever it is you are doing. She seems to have an ability to find pleasure in everything. Even sitting in a hospital room, with nurses coming in and out, trying to keep her uncle relaxed and calm.

Most times, she would entertain the nurses with a twirl

she had seen in a Disney movie, while other times she had a million questions for each nurse, ranging from, "Why do you need to use that needle and not another one?" to, "what are your parents like, and do you think they would enjoy my twirl as much as you did?"

She never seemed to stop asking and having a thirst for learning, and while that can grow old for some parents, it did not for me. I am one who loves to learn the ins and outs of everything. I once took my parents' bedroom, wall-mounted phone apart to see just how a caller could send their voice from hundreds of miles away to right in our home. My father was pretty upset with that one, and I never figured that out, that is until I took a book out at the local library, that explained the how and why. I guess I could have saved my parents the trouble and done that first, but live and learn I always say.

Andrew sat up anytime Agnes was speaking. Looking back, I wonder if he too, was learning the answers to questions that he could not ask and was glad that his niece was there to do that for him.

The two of them together was always going to be interesting, and even as they grew older, they never lost that beautiful connection they built when Agnes was just a tiny child with the mouth that never seemed to stop.

That hospital stay actually took a lot out of Amanda, though. She cared for her brother deeply, I knew that for certain, but seeing her there, worried more than I had ever seen her worry, was hard on me. I can only imagine how hard it was for her, though. She loved Andrew and was always so protective of her younger brother, so for her to be there, not able to do anything, and having to leave it in the hands of others? Well, it wasn't easy for her at all.

But she, as hard as it was, was also trusting of the experts. She watched them carefully as they poked her little brother, ensuring that they gave care to each step they took. It wasn't that she was looking to tell them how to do their job. She was ensuring that they gave her brother the same respect they did to anyone else.

When we would leave, she would remind her brother not to give them any further trouble or backtalk. He would laugh at her when she said that, but for a little while anyhow, it would do the trick. He would eventually revert back to his mischievous ways, but at least those nurses were able to get a little reprieve.

The younger nurses didn't seem to mind as much as some of the older ones, but maybe that was because they had not seen all that the older ones had over the years. Having a hundred patients, if not a thousand who acted as he did, could wear down anyone's patience.

Christine and Fred, Andrew's parents, were always grateful for the company as well. Fred would stay long hours sitting there with Andrew, just talking as they watched something on the television, but I know he wanted the company of other adults around too. Christine was there a lot as well, but she was volunteering at her church, and they were extremely short-staffed at this time, so she tried to commit as much of herself as possible to both.

Fred and I talked a lot while there. Andrew was often playing with something he had placed in his bag before he got sick, so he would occupy himself for hours at a time and not even notice we were sitting there.

I would pull a chair over to Fred, and we would shoot the shit about the rising stock market that week, or what was going on with global economics, and sometimes, just about local sports that we followed. I don't know that he really cared what we talked about, as long as he had someone there to help pass the time some.

Fred is a ferocious reader and can consume several books in a week's-time, so he always has something to discuss. It's great for me, too, because I love to consume data on anything and everything, and he provides that well. He's not overly opinionated for someone that has worked so many hours in his life, but he does tend to lean one way more than the other.

I'm not a very political man, so I am happy to hear his side, which is usually well thought out, and full of facts. Sometimes, I think he is stretching his opinion a little, and those facts, may not be facts at all, but he's an observant guy and knows when I may not be buying what he is selling, and he changes the subject seamlessly.

When Andrew falls asleep, and it's still visiting hours, he talks about his son. It's apparent that he has a strong pride for his son, who has overcome a great deal in his life, but he is also worried about him. Fred has learned well over the years, how to communicate with his son, but he's also worried that Andrew doesn't always mention when he's having trouble with something. Case in point, no one knew Andrew had an infection, which apparently, he had for some time, until he coughed up a little blood.

Had that not happened, who knows, and Fred knows that. It's just how Andrew is, though. He's not the easiest person to understand, and he can hide an issue that he should not, possibly for fear of what it may turn out to be. As Fred likes to say, "He's like an ostrich with its head in the sand. If it can't see you, it thinks that you cannot see it."

Andrew was happy when they started to clear the infection out, and he was feeling more like himself once again. I know he would be excited to get back home to better food, and more toys and things that he would be able to switch out in the bag. I don't know how he decided what would go in the bag and for how long, but he seemed to have a system for that. What I did notice, though, was that one item was always a staple in his bag. That notebook we gifted him. It was tattered and beaten up almost as much as the bag was, but he never seemed to mind, and always seemed to have more pages left to write or draw whatever it was he did.

When he returned home, his parents had set up balloons along the driveway for him. He remembers that with each of the two kids we had at the time, balloons lined the driveway and front porch to our homes, as a celebration of the newborns. He's always liked balloons and both times ended up filling the backseat of his parents' car up with them when they left.

So, this time, they decide that it may make him feel a little more special if they do exactly the same for him.

Andrew was giggling like a child as he drove into the driveway with his family. He instantly saw the balloons from a ways away, because he's one of those people that constantly is looking around to see what others choose not to. A simple ride up the street to the store can bless him with sites he did not see the day before. A large tree branch fallen from a storm, or a flower blooming that was ready to burst a week ago, can bring joy to his eyes each time.

It's exactly as Agnes is. Maybe she learned it from Andrew, and maybe it's just something she discovered on her own, but whatever it is, they both share that quality. I bet if the two of them could talk clearly, they would have dozens of stories to tell about things you and I would never think to look at.

Andrew was home, and life was going to go back to normal again for the time being. That was all we all wanted. Simplicity. The worry for Andrew was more than any of us wanted to deal with at that time, or ever again.

Chapter 14

The Gift of Sparkle

* * *

Carrying Agnes into the doctor's office did two things for me that morning. First, it made me realize that she was still my baby and needed me very much, and second, she was a tiny person who sometimes came up with the most creative things just as an adult would. A sense of pride took over me.

This is my job, to carry all my children whenever they need me to. I promised them each, on the day they were born, that when life got too hard, I would be there to carry each of them.

I actually wrote it down the first time I said it to Agnes, so that I could repeat it to any children we would have afterwards.

"My little child. Know this as you grow.

I am your father, and I have a hard job ahead of me, but it's one I am prepared to do.

For there will be days when you follow me, and as you watch me, I hope that I set a great example of how to live as you follow my steps.

There will be times when you walk right beside me, where I hope to treat you as my equal, no matter how you decide to live your life.

There will be times that you walk in front of me, when you are in a rush to grow faster than I want you to, and I am forced to let that happen and watch your steps as you once did mine.

Then there will be times that I carry you. When you have tried everything that you can think of, with all your strength and might, to follow, walk beside me, or in front, and simply cannot. Those days, it's time for your dad to take over.

I promise that you will always have me to carry you, no matter how old you may be, or how many times you have stayed away from me on your own path.

I will always be your father, and never will I let you walk alone.

That is my promise to you today, and every day."

This is one of those times, I carry her, because she cannot walk, and I remember that promise I made to her eleven years ago. I am keeping that promise, and it fills me with a great sense of pride.

The receptionist, Joan, sees us walk in, and the first thing she does is to put her hands over her mouth, and to let out a sigh, as she says,

"Oh Jon, what's wrong with poor little Agnes this morning?"

She knows all the kids by name, as we haven't been to any other doctors' offices since the birth of them all. Well, there was one time when the benefits we have for the children changed and the doctor's office did not take that plan, but they eventually did, and we were able to continue with the place and the people we trusted, and with the doctors who knew our children best.

"Joan, she started getting headaches yesterday and wanted to rest, but then a short rest turned into the rest of the day and into the night. She's complaining of a headache, but it seems like maybe this is more than just a headache," I say.

Amanda interjects before I can go on.

"Joan, I know we don't have an appointment, but we wouldn't have come in without one if we didn't feel like it was very important. I just feel like she needs to see the doctor sooner than later, just so she can get whatever medication they think is best. Please."

Joan nods with a slight smile, acknowledging what my wife told her. She has four of her own children who are now adults themselves and having children of their own, so she understands when a mother has her concerns raised. She can sympathize with Amanda, and I know that gives comfort to my wife.

Joan tells us to take a seat, and she will slide us in just as soon as she is able to, but that it should not be long.

There are always those that are running late, as well as the ones who come in, have nothing wrong, and need little of the doctor's time.

As we walk over to the waiting area, I sit down and place Agnes to the front of me, laying her head on my shoulder. It's been awhile since I have sat with her like this. She's growing, and barely has time to give me a hug, let alone time to sit with her dad as we had once done so many times over the passing years. While we wait for them to call us back, I am not going to let her go. Just like those times when you were a kid and you didn't realize there would be one last time playing with those friends you thought would be there forever. This, too, will be one of those times. I may never get to hold my sweet Agnes like a child again, so I will soak this up, even if the circumstances aren't ideal.

Amanda is texting with her parents to let them know we arrived, and that she will keep them posted. She tells me that Andrew was upset he didn't get a chance to say goodbye to Agnes before they left last night, and I smile at her. He's a good guy and loves his family.

It's not terribly long before one of the nurses comes out to let us know we are next. We follow her down the hall and into one of the examination rooms, where she closes the door behind us, and looks over her chart.

"Well now, Agnes. What seems to be bothering you today?" She starts.

Amanda starts up, knowing Agnes doesn't feel much like explaining how she is feeling. I'm sure she would much rather be back home not having to deal with doctors and examination rooms and nurses possibly drawing blood from her arm. I get it. I am not one to go to the doctor unless it's absolutely necessary, and even then, you might need to convince me it's truly necessary.

"Yesterday, she was running and jumping like a grasshopper around the yard, playing just as she always has, and putting on short shows for us. It was our anniversary, and she had made up a great dance she wanted to share with us all," Amanda began.

The nurse smiled as she listened, knowing that Amanda would get to the point, but that maybe she did that so that Agnes felt a little pride while there.

I remember Amanda and I talking about Andrew, and how despite his issues with communication and his lack of manners sometimes, he enjoyed whenever someone pointed out something that he had done recently. When you took him to the doctor for a routine checkup, or a follow-up to one of his appointments that required a stay, the best way for you to calm him enough to allow the good nurses and doctors to help him, was to make him full of pride.

It could be as simple as speaking about a picture of a lion that he had colored well the morning of, or perhaps a session with his speech therapist that had garnered him a star for the day, because he had worked harder than usual.

Whatever it was, he, like a child, needed that. It almost assured him, that it would all be fine while the professionals checked him over. He had little to fear, because they knew, he had done something marvelous recently.

I think that is why Amanda started off with that. In her mind, she was doing what her parents had always done for her brother, and it worked. Even though Agnes did not face the same issues that Andrew had to, she still felt pride. She still needed assurance that she was special, and Amanda was best suited to explain that. I think Agnes always appreciates when her mother speaks well of her.

I try too, but I don't have the same touch. My words seem to come out flat, or over-exaggerated if I am trying to focus on it not coming out so flat. It's not easy, and I truly believe it is something you are just born with. Some people have that gift for understanding, while others, like me, have other gifts. Mine seems to be a gift for wanting the best for my family, and finding ways to make that happen through sacrifice and patience, while my wife has what I refer to as, *the gift of sparkle.*

She can throw words together that no one else would think to group together and create a smile that was missing. She can take a sad situation and find comforting lines to help others understand that it was for the best.

I don't know why some of us are born with gifts that touch, and some of us are born with gifts that do not. I don't know. Maybe all the gifts we are given in our time here can touch, but it may be that we don't always learn how to use them properly. It's not about what you have to share, as much as it is about the way you share it.

Amanda continued to explain what happened less than 24 hours prior,

"At some point, she must have realized she wasn't feeling quite herself and went inside to sit down on a chair to catch herself some. When we went in to check on her, she was fast asleep, and you could tell she was not in a restful, peaceful sleep as much as she was in a sleep out of desperation."

Agnes was still in my arms, but I felt like I should be placing her on the table in the room on top of that waxy looking paper they lay down for you. She was moving around uncomfortably, and it was making it increasingly hard to hold her in a comfortable way, for both her and I.

As Amanda told the nurse about Agnes and her headaches she was having, and how she complained about things in an unusual way, the nurse listened to her but began to check on the vital signs of Agnes as she laid there.

Nurses always impress me. They seem to have an inept ability to multitask so well, and never seem to miss a beat. They can take your blood pressure while talking about the pain you are experiencing that brought you here in the first place. They seem to have a great understanding for symptoms you felt were strange, but they know are not. It's a tireless job, I always felt, working all those hours, with people who don't want to be around you, because they would rather be well. I don't know how they do it, but they somehow find a way.

I also always wondered about the ones who bring joyous

news of a newborn child into the world, and those that bring sobering news of the final breath a parent took while in their care. How a person can do both, if need be, and still balance their jobs and home life, I just don't know. But they are gifts to people who need help.

The nurse smiles at Agnes, probably more of a reaction, because I don't think Agnes sees it. She's still holding her head, and now is making noises out of discomfort. I am feeling uneasy, and my stomach is filling up with butterflies because, this is my first-born. I hate seeing her here like this when all she wanted to do was to dance all day for us.

"Agnes, the nurse is going to finish looking you over, and the doctor will be in, and we can figure this out, okay honey?" I say to her.

I just want to get this over with and get back in the car, drive home, and have a drink with Amanda while Agnes heals. That is all I am after here today, because I like simple. I want simple, and this? This is not simple to me. When I can't fix something by myself, it's because it is anything but simple. I want to be that dad I promised to be. The one who carries them when they need me to, but carries them for the reason of healing them. I just don't have that ability.

"Okay, Agnes, thank you sweetie. The doctor will be in shortly, and you will be able to go home," the nurse says.

When she closes the door, Amanda sits on the table next to Agnes and starts to hum a song to her. She doesn't need words because her humming is soothing and so pretty. It's funny how mothers have a gift to calm a child by humming.

I don't know that I have ever heard a father do the same, and if he did, would it be as effective? Probably not. Just another one of those times that you realize how our gifts are so unique to us.

I'm looking at my phone, just scrolling through posts people have made. I'm seeing posts that others are sharing with their kids, or what they had for breakfast that morning. Some people are complaining about a customer they ran into that wouldn't understand how the store policy works, while others are simply posting a selfie of themselves smiling. It's a tale of anything and everything each time I scroll through, but as I sit there, reading through the endless messages there, I realize something important that I had not before. We are here alone with Agnes. She's feeling this sickness alone, and all those people who seem to like our post, or who send well wishes when someone is ill, can't really do much about it.

It's strange to me. I could post a photo of Agnes on the table, with my wife sitting next to her, looking at her, wondering what she can do different to give sweet Agnes some comfort she so desperately wants, and people will offer prayers and tell us that they are thinking about us. Right after, though, they will be back to posting about what waitress at what lunch spot fouled up the order, and they swear they are never going back to that place again.

But Agnes won't be any better while they post that. Did they mean to say they are sending prayers? Do any of them stop whatever they are doing, and actually pray? Or is it because it's the "right" thing to say? It probably doesn't matter what I think, but it just crosses my mind while we are sitting there and wait for Doctor Sohn to stop in.

It's almost thirty minutes later, or so it seems to us anyway, and finally the doctor has made his way into the room where we are waiting with our Agnes.

"Hey folks. Sorry for the delay. We've been a little backed up with only me on the floor today. Now, let me just look at the notes and we will see if we can't get you on your way back home. How does that sound?" the doctor says as he looks towards our child.

Agnes is sleeping again, so she doesn't even hear what the doctor has to say, but even if she did, I don't know if she would care much. When you don't feel well, words of encouragement or positivity don't seem to do much, but for us as parents, they seem to touch us a little better.

We just want Agnes feeling better and back home, and we trust the doctor's office entirely. Plus, the doctors always seem calm and have the right words to sooth us back down from our heightened concerns.

When Erik broke his arm last fall, we were worried about how he would handle the pain for days on end. But after the doctors set it, they assured us the hardest part would be keeping him from breaking the other, as boys tend to be reckless that way. They were right. Erik, he just couldn't sit still, and while that was what the doctor had warned us about, it was comforting to know he was not complaining about any lingering pain from the break.

Doctor Sohn looks over Agnes and then the chart he still has at his fingertips. He checks the glands around her neck, and places his hands on her head, as if to tell her he knows she doesn't feel well, but he will be gentle with her. He is there to help her get back to the happy, quirky, little girl she is meant to be.

"So, I don't see anything too alarming just yet. She seems fine, other than what you were telling us about her extreme headaches. Has she been drinking a lot of water? Any change in her diet, or anything like that?" he asks us.

"No. No real change in anything she has had to eat. She doesn't always drink a lot of water, but that's not unusual for her. She's always on the go, and when she is having something to drink, it's usually some sort of juice she prefers," Amanda tells him.

"I see. Well, I am going to prescribe something for her headaches, and let's see if we can't get that under control first. Once we can relieve some of her pain, we can go from there. How does that sound?" the doctor replies.

He doesn't seem overly concerned at all, which calms my nerves down enough that I smile. I don't know that I have smiled since yesterday early afternoon when we were still enjoying the company of close family and the amazing weather we were blessed with for our party.

Amanda, who is usually calm anyways, seems to breathe a sigh of relief, knowing that this just seems like a small thing she is dealing with. But I know Amanda. She's going to continue to monitor this closely, and if she fears it's not getting better when it should, we will be right back again searching for better answers.

For now though, we are just happy that we are going to get her some meds, and then take our sweet Agnes home, so that she can get back to herself once again. We will need to heat her up some of that spiced apple crumb pie she so loves. We didn't have that until well after she had gone in to rest her head, but of course, knowing it is her favorite dessert in the entire world, we saved her plenty. With one scoop of vanilla bean ice cream on top, she will be in heaven.

Amanda finishes up with the receptionist, while I head to the car with Agnes in my arms. She's awake now, and not complaining as much as she had been throughout the night and early morning. Perhaps she is already on the mend, and this is clearing itself out. Either way, we will stop and get the prescription filled so that we have that as a sure thing.

Back at home, Amanda lays a few random blankets down on the recliner in the family room, props Agnes up with a pillow, and gets her a tall, cold glass of water for her to take her meds with.

Agnes at first doesn't want to, but when we tell her it's this or further headaches and no pie and ice cream, she reluctantly agrees. I'm sure it was the pie over the headaches that helped her make that decision.

She sure does love that pie.

Chapter 15

Breathe, Baby

* * *

"Jon!" Amanda screams from the other room. I'm working at home today and have a ton of clients that need my attention, as I have had several days of family commitments I needed to deal with, and now I fear I am not finished with them all just yet.

Amanda rarely calls me with that tone she just used, and it gives me temporary chills that keep me in my seat longer than you would expect it to.

It's a strange feeling to sit there and wonder if whomever is calling you with despair in their tone will continue with whatever it is they are in need of, or if you will just need to go and see. I am paralyzed for a moment, waiting for her to give me more, but she is not. There's an eerie silence throughout the house, as I allow my ears to roam for a sign of anything that may give me a clue as to what the urgency may be.

Eventually I find my legs beneath me, and hurriedly get myself out of my seat, and into a search for what my wife is in need of. I am not even certain as to what room she is in, but the house isn't all that large, so I find her quickly in the stairway leading to the bedrooms. She's on the floor hovering over someone and talking softly to whomever it is.

It's Agnes.

"Babe, what's wrong? Is she alright? What happened?" I ask confused.

I hear the words Amanda is now saying, but I must listen closely and with strong intent. She hasn't answered my questions yet, so it's all I can do for the moment. I don't want to ask again, for some inexplicable reason. Maybe I am scared to know why our daughter is laying on the bottom steps, while my wife is over top of her, blowing in her face, while speaking softly, words of encouragement.

"Agnes, you are okay. Agnes, breathe baby. Breathe honey. Mommy is here. Everything is fine, baby. Talk to mommy, Agnes," Amanda whispers.

If I was the calm, cool, collective type of person, I would be on the phone with 911, giving our address to the dispatcher on the other end, while explaining to him or her what exactly the emergency is. I would then relay instructions to Amanda while we wait for them to pull up, and things would go as they should from there.

But I am not that type. I am the scared, confused, and panicked type of person. It's not that I show those traits, but I have them for certain. I can hide them well enough to not worry anyone, but inside I am an absolute wreck and hate it. I just want to go back to work and have everything fine again. I literally just hung up on one of my biggest clients, and honestly cannot afford to lose anyone at this point. But of course, I also want our Agnes to feel herself. I don't even know what happened yet. Maybe she just fell and knocked the wind out of her? Or maybe she just passed out, and Amanda is just giving her some air to wake her up.

It happens all the time. I remember back as a kid, having the wind knocked out of me on a few occasions. Once, this boy who was in the same grade as I was, but clearly was large enough to be two grades north of me but still dumb enough to be three grades lower, punched me so hard in my stomach, that I couldn't catch my breath. I was buckled over, trying to just take a single deep breath in, but nothing. I still remember to this day how that boy made me feel, and I still hate it.

"Jon," Amanda finally continues, "I need you to call 911, let them know Agnes seems to be having a seizure, and then get me a wet rag, make it cold, and bring it back in here, okay?" she tells me.

Quickly I am off to my office to retrieve my phone, and I am trying to dial 911 as I run the faucet and dampen a towel I find in the kitchen. I honestly need to have a pep talk with myself when this is all over with. There is no way I should be this nervous and fumbling with such simple task. Especially at my age.

Eventually I wet the towel, and before I leave the kitchen, I settle myself down and dial 911.

Quickly I hear the woman on the other end of the phone say those words we all know so well, "911, what's your emergency?"

I'm walking back briskly into the room where Amanda is still seated with Agnes, and at the same time, answering the operator's question.

"Hi, um, yes my daughter, our daughter seems to be having trouble breathing," I reply.

Amanda interjects quickly without moving her eyes into my direction,

"Jon, tell them she's having a seizure," she says.

"Sorry, yes, my wife just said that she's having a seizure. How old is she? She's eleven years old," I reply.

A few more questions and answers are lobbied back and forth, but I guess the most important of those was when they asked where we lived. I'm certain they asked that and I'm also certain I gave her that, but I can't seem to recall. My mind is just racing way too much at the moment.

I also must have handed Amanda the damp towel because I am no longer holding it in my left hand, and she has it on top of Agnes' head. Maybe I am better at this all than I thought, but just have a hard time seeing it as it transpires. Whatever is going on around me, at least Amanda is here with me, and with Agnes of course. She is always the voice of reason, and the one that is the calmest out of the two of us. I know my role here, even if it takes me a moment to implement that.

It feels as if the waiting is taking longer than it probably is, but I've never had to summon an ambulance prior to this, so I don't know how long these things should take. All I know is, with each passing minute, I am feeling inadequate and that bothers the hell out of me.

"Amanda, what is she doing? Is she breathing? Is she, is she going to be alright?" I ask.

When you watch a movie on television, it seems as if the ambulance is always there immediately. There are several cops around first, usually performing CPR, and then as the ambulance arrives, a group of concerned people step into the house, quickly assess the situation while speaking to the officers, and jump right in, seamlessly. It all seems to take place within a few minutes, and then they are off to the hospital where nurses are at the wait.

In reality, this isn't how that happens. At least not today it's not. I don't see any cars racing up the street. I don't hear any sirens blaring, as they come within view, ready to wisp our Agnes away, and into the waiting arms of those who will nurse her back to health. I see none of that. I'm on the front porch now, looking both left and right, begging the operator on the other end of the call I am still on, to hurry up.

She's calm, and I guess that's why she is so good at her job. Getting me nervous, more than I already am, would only serve as a crutch right now. She's been asking questions the entire time, and with my analytical mind, I know she is simply trying to keep me calm and collected. She's doing well, but I am struggling to stay as focused as she would like me to be.

"Ma'am, I don't mean to be pushy, but where the hell is this ambulance and why are they taking so long to get here?" I finally muster out.

Just as those words come from my lips, I can see at the end of the road some blinking lights. They are driving slowly at first, and then I can see them picking up the pace some. I remind myself they don't know this street like I do, so they are most likely looking for the address, so they do not pass it.

The best thing for me to do now, is for me to go to the middle of the street so they have a point to which to travel to. It works. I wave them down, and the operator reminds me I am doing a great job, although I am not sure it's comforting right now. I feel I should be doing so much more inside, but outside seems to be where I am needed presently.

They see me and are coming now at a speed that makes me feel much better about this. I decide to walk back inside to check on my wife and Agnes, but I leave the front screen door propped open so they can come in with no issues. It's all about being efficient right now and not wasting time. That's what I keep reminding myself. Be efficient.

I still to this point don't really know what is going on. There are so many things happening at once around me, and I need to settle myself better so that I can figure this out. I feel useless and I hate that feeling. This is my job to handle these situations, and I feel like a complete and utter failure.

"Amanda, they are here. They just pulled up to the front. How is she?"

"She's breathing, Jon. She's breathing again. Let's just get her to the hospital so we know what is what," Amanda says.

I don't say anything because I sense my wife is frustrated. Not with me, but more with the fact our child is suffering medically and we cannot help her. We are relying on others to use all the abilities they have mastered over the years, and we feel so helpless. But I don't see it this way at all. My wife is the essence of calm. She is the one that truly is keeping Agnes safe and helping the ambulance folks before they even arrive.

I have no idea what I would do if it were just me here alone. I am certain I would have called 911 just as fast, but I am more concerned with what I would do with Agnes while they were trying to locate our home. Amanda talked with her the entire time, in such a calming voice and manner, that I am positive it relaxed Agnes, even during her seizure. She blew air into her face, which is something I would have never thought to do, so that Agnes could get air into her nostrils, down to her lungs, and hopefully push it back out. I am amazed with my wife, and so thankful that I did not need to figure out how I would have managed on my own.

But they are inside now, and they have Agnes in their sights. One of them seems to be in charge of the others and is doing the most talking and assessing. He's a larger man, but extremely calm and has a great disposition about him. His hair is long in the back and tied in a ponytail. If he wasn't so calm, he would be incredibly intimidating. Thankfully, he seems to be well-versed in what it is he needs to do.

"What's her name? Agnes? Agnes, I'm Owen. I'm here to take care of you. Can you talk with me some Agnes?" he starts.

She doesn't respond, but I do not think he was really after a response as much as he was just letting her know she was in good hands. I'm watching from the background, away from them all so that they have space to work. Amanda is on the other side of where I am standing, just watching as they talk with Agnes. She finally looks like she is relieved that they are there and able to take over for her, even though I know she knows she did well.

"Okay Agnes, we are going to go for a short ride to the hospital so we can get you checked out and back home, okay? How does that sound Agnes?" Owen continues.

The second he gets that out of his mouth, he doesn't hesitate another second and is controlling the entire room like a fine-tuned orchestra conductor.

"Let's get the gurney over here, and we can lift her carefully and get her secured. Mom, dad, one of you is welcome to ride along with us and the other can follow along. Do you have any other children here that we need to figure out?"

In all the commotion, I forget that we do. Dot is here. She was napping upstairs when this started and is probably still very much asleep. Erik is at my parents' house, having a sleepover. The kids take turns sleeping over once a month, and this was his month.

I know Amanda is not going to let Agnes ride without her, so I don't even bother asking.

"Honey, I'll get Dot up and we will meet you at the hospital just as soon as we can," I say.

Amanda grabs her purse and watches as they place Agnes on the gurney and ready her to be transported to the hospital that's just about twelve minutes away from where we live. She looks around the room to make sure that she hasn't left anything on that needs to be turned off, and quickly follows the men outside to the waiting ambulance. No time for goodbyes, but it's a short trip so I get it.

I watch as they get into the back of the ambulance, and then head on up to get Dot up and ready. She's been asleep for a little over an hour now, so she should be pretty rested. She doesn't always take naps, but she's been pretty tired lately with all the running around she's been doing. I don't know where that one gets her energy, but I wish I could bottle it up and use it later.

She wakes easily, so there is no issue there. Thankfully. I just need this to go easy because I am sort of a wreck trying to ensure that I am doing all I am supposed to. When you have something such as this going on, it's easy to forget things.

Just as I am trying to rush to the car, I remember why I need to slow down some. I've left my car keys in the house and already have Dot loaded in and ready to go. No big deal, but those few extra minutes bother me. I want to be on top of this and get to where Agnes is. She needs me. I need to know she's okay, and I just wasted three valuable minutes of that time.

As a child, my father was always complaining about time. He would tell us that for each minute we lost because we weren't prepared, we altered the course of our lives tenfold. At the time, I had no idea of what he meant, but now I get it. He was saying that fate could adjust if we were not moving in the right direction, at the right time, in the right way. Here I was, all these years later, and I'm still tempting fate.

Okay, keys are in my hand, wallet is in my back pocket, and I have my phone with me. Dot is all set, and we are off. Finally. I really need to work on my time management skills more, and I absolutely need to find a way to stay focused when faced with adverse events. I suck at that, but I promise myself I'll get better with time.

Dot is asking a million questions while she is strapped securely in her car seat. She wants to know what happened to Agnes, and where mommy is. She's wondering if we will catch up to the ambulance and see the lights. Will the nurses and doctors take Agnes away, and are we allowed to run the red lights because we have an emergency. The things that children think of.

I'm trying to answer her as best I can because I know Dot. She will just continue to ask until she gets her answers. It's cute normally, but today, I am just trying to get there as quickly as I can. I know she doesn't mean any harm, but

I'm just terribly sidetracked.

We are within a few minutes of the hospital, and I tell Dot that we will not be catching up to the ambulance, because, unlike us, they are allowed to go through the red lights so that they can get her there as quickly as they can.

Only, I am not telling her the truth. But it's not my fault, I don't think. I am just not able to do what I said I was going to do. It's just not my fault. Sometimes we are faced with situations that alter our plans beyond our control, and we must accept what fate has in store. Even if it doesn't seem fair.

Chapter 16

Meeting Harold

* * *

Birds are interesting creatures. Not only do they travel in groups, switching off which one is leading, but they do so without question. Agnes knows this. She's always talking about them whenever we are driving anywhere. She loves to watch and explore and has such an appetite for learning that it even impresses me. She definitely is my child, even with her quirkiness. Amanda tells me this all the time.

Those trips her and I take together, are always filled with questions, and sometimes with fascinating facts. If she learned something particular in school that day, she was sure to tell us. I never had to ask how her day was, because Agnes would just tell me from the moment she first walked through the door.

"Pigeons can recognize a human face. Did you know that dad? They can. I learned that today. Mrs. Palmer said so. She told me when she was young, her brother had pigeons as pets, and he would tell her their names, and they would know to come to him when he called. She said they all knew his face. Isn't that great? Can we have pigeons? Before you say no, I would feed them all the time and take care of them. I promise. Can we?" Agnes said.

Of course we never got her the pigeons because, well, we just were not getting any pigeons. I didn't even have to ask Amanda that one. What I did though, was to surprise Agnes with a trip once. I had a client who raised pigeons and learned to race them. It was a strange thing in my mind, but he loved it.

I asked him if he would mind showing Agnes how that all worked, and he was more than happy to oblige.

That was some day. Before we arrived, I decided to not let her know what we were going to be doing that day. Instead, I told her we were heading on a secret adventure, and that only she and I could go. Usually, we all went to wherever we were off to, but this morning, this day, was all about Agnes and me.

When we arrived, she was so caught off guard. She had no idea we were going here, and the look on her face... well it was something out of a movie. Her exaggerated smile was enough for me. I could have gone home right then and been completely happy. But we had things to do, and I wanted her to experience everything.

Charlie, my client and friend, welcomed Agnes. He gave her a "pigeon taming" hat and told her all the young people had to wear it so that the pigeons knew they were there to train. I chuckled, but somehow Agnes bought it, and she was all too eager to wear that silly hat. Oh, I swear, Amanda is going to love these pictures. This is going to be hilarious, but special.

As she walked over to where the wooden and metal cages were, I saw Agnes running her hand along the outsides, looking into each cage with such a playful, but serious look. She was all about this, and I knew I had done something right by her.

"Agnes, now you come over here and I will set you right up. I think with a little training, I can get you sending these trained pigeons off, and with a little luck, they will fly back safely in your care in no time at all. What do you say?" Charlie said.

Agnes, she just stared at all the birds, and I could see her mind at work. She was either wondering what their names were, or which one she was going to beg me to let her take home. That was not going to happen though. But maybe she could guess at their names for the fun of it.

"So, do you see one or two you like more than the others, Agnes?" Charlie asked.

Agnes was still looking over all the neatly arranged cages as she ran her fingers through the tiny gaps, and over all the cooing those birds were doing, she said she felt as if one of them was asking her to be picked. She even said it had told her its name, so she was sure that was the one.

"Mr. Charlie, that one there. Harold. He told me his

name is Harold, and he's the one that I wish to set free," Agnes said.

Charlie laughed to himself and smiled. He opened the cage Harold was seated in and leaned in to fetch him. Somehow, with all those birds working themselves to the front where he had opened it up, he scooped out the exact bird that Agnes had selected.

"Harold, meet Agnes. She's going to work with you today, so you do me a favor and listen well, you hear?" Charlie said.

I was just sitting back observing this all. It fascinated me how people had hobbies such as this, even in today's world, and I never gave it a second thought. But I guess there are a lot of hobbies and careers that we never give a second thought to. Whenever the kids ask where the chicken we are having for dinner comes from, I tease them and tell them from the grocery store. They know that isn't true, but do they really want to know where it actually comes from? In fact, I realize I don't want to know those specifics either.

Charlie is good with handling this. He's a natural and has a ton of patience. I suppose one would need a lot to handle training birds to fly away and come back when you expected them to. Even when Charlie would mention his hobby while we were discussing business, I rarely asked him much about what it was that enticed him to get started. I felt bad that day for having never asked any questions until I wanted a favor. I wasn't certain that was fair of me, but Charlie was eager to oblige.

"Charlie, hey, listen. I just wanted to thank you for all of this again. I had no idea this was such a well-orchestrated operation. You certainly have this managed well," I say.

Charlie is showing Agnes how to place the bird on her hand, and how to pet Harold. She doesn't seem to have any fear at all, but if you place that bird on my hand, the first thought in my head would be is this thing going to bite me. Not Agnes though. She has complete trust in this tiny creature whom she has just met for the very first time. It's impressive.

"Jon, thank you. I'm just happy this one here is so interested. She's a natural at this and could be ready for her own set of trained carrier pigeons at some point," he said, knowing that I would not have anything to do with such an idea. But he laughs anyway. Maybe that is his way of reminding me that I never asked him about this, or maybe he doesn't care that I haven't. He doesn't do this hobby of his to impress me or anyone else. He does it because he gets an endless joy from it all.

Just as Agnes dances. She doesn't care that the moves aren't perfect. Nor does she care if those around her giggle or tease as she takes each step. She dances because it makes her pause in the realities of life and her mind wanders off to a place where she can be whomever she wishes to be, including a fairy dancing in a beautiful, flowered garden.

I know I've mentioned to Amanda about that before, and how I worry she may not mature as quickly as the other kids around her, but my wife tells me that that is a good thing. I know it is in some sense, but I worry she will get teased and fall into a depression.

Amanda has always been the voice of reason though. She just says,

"Our children are meant to be exactly who they are. We are here to not shape them, but to encourage them to shape themselves. They are not meant to be like you and me. They are meant to be exactly who they are. So, let's allow them that luxury. It's possibly the best gift we can give to them."

She's right, of course, but I still worry. I will probably never stop worrying, even long after I die. I will look down and worry about what the rest of their lives will be like, even if I cannot express that to them.

"Daddy! Look!" Agnes says.

She's holding the pigeon, and for a moment, it looks magnificent. The sun is allowing the colors that seemed mute a moment ago to shimmer in the light. This bird, this Harold as Agnes has either named it or as someone told her, is resting on her hand, waiting for her to tell it that it's time to go.

Charlie whispers to her something, and I see Agnes extend her arm, and with her fingers stretched out, she gives a slight upward nod, and the bird is off.

We all watch as Harold flies into the air, seemingly with a purpose beyond my comprehension, and with a note attached to his leg for someone on the other end.

"What does the note say?" I ask confused.

"Well, it's to inform a friend of mine that this is Admiral Agnes flying her maiden voyage, and to please return a note of gratitude," Charlie says.

Agnes is just staring at the mid-morning sky, through the bright sunrays and the fluffy clouds that are floating freely in the sky. Her attention is strict, and she is intent on finishing her mission. I am in awe, because what I thought would simply be a fun adventure for her, is so much more than that. It's not just a chance to do something different for Agnes, it's a chance for me to see, that she is capable of so much more if I just allow her to be exactly who she is.

Charlie has a small table set up, and on top of the table he has some different types of cheeses and wheat crackers, plus a few plastic champagne flutes with a bottle of sparkling water nearby.

"Well, Agnes. Should we celebrate or what?" he says.

This chapter in my life is one I know I will always look back on. Agnes feels like one of us, which is the inclusion that I always seem to want for her, but she also feels like an individual today. While Charlie gave her the details and direction, she didn't hesitate once. From the start, she knew which one she wanted, and followed all the rules well enough to set her bird off on her own. I'm extremely proud of her today and learned something truly valuable.

I need to not worry so much about the paths my children will take, because there is no telling what they can accomplish if I stop interfering in what I think they can do or should do.

We sat there and ate the snacks, while talking about all the other pigeons there with us. Charlie is laughing hysterically at all the names that Agnes is coming up with. She tells us that all the birds are letting her know what they wish to be called, and whenever we look confused by a name, she says,

"Hey, it's not my fault they picked that name. I'm just the messenger."

Charlie enjoys all of this. He never had children of his own, and now in his late 60s, I wonder if he wished he had. I've never asked him about that, and why he never did, but it doesn't matter I suppose. It's not my journey, it was his, and I am sure he has his reasons.

He's enjoying this, and for a moment I wonder if I should have been more of a friend while helping him with his investments. Work is important, but so is building a rapport with those people you come into contact with. I know so little about this man, but he is learning so much about us. And the funny part is, he's simply asking questions. Something I failed to do.

"Agnes, what do you think Harold is thinking as he flies through the air?" Charlie asks.

She barely hesitates, almost as if she had already thought about this prior to him asking the question.

"Well, Mr. Charlie, before he took off, he told me that he loves the feeling of being free and knowing that we trust him enough to let him be free. That's why he always returns. Because you love him enough to let him be exactly who he is. He will always return as a thank you," Agnes replies.

That child of mine. So understanding and intelligent. She seemingly knows exactly how I feel. That I have wanted to mold her, but struggle with knowing I don't need to. She will always be my child, and if I simply let her be free, she will always come back to me, exactly as intended.

We talked about this and that, and the weather and whatnot, passing the time on that porch. Charlie seems to need this just as much as Agnes. He's in his glory, answering non-stop questions from Agnes, and he never seems a bit bothered. I think it would bother him more if she stopped asking. This is his chance to share all that he has known over the forty plus years he has been doing this. It may be that most people never care about what he loves, but Agnes does.

After about an hour and a half, Charlie looks down at his phone nonchalantly and sees the time.

"Well, Agnes, you think Harold is just about finished his round-trip flight? What do you say we get ready for his return, and see if we can't catch him in time?" Charlie asks.

Agnes jumps up and with her hat still perched on top of her head and begins to walk over to the spot she released Harold from a little over an hour earlier.

Both Charlie and Agnes are talking to each other as Charlie peers through a set of binoculars he had laying on the table. He tells her, "Nothing yet, Agnes," until he sees in the distance, something that grabs his attention.

"Oh Agnes, I think I see our bird. He's on his way back.

Now, you just put your arm out like so, and extend your fingers like this...there you go. Now, just be relaxed, and stay still. Harold will do the rest," Charlie explains.

I watch in anticipation, and I can feel those butterflies in my belly. I'm more nervous than Agnes I think at this point because I want this to go perfectly for her. How great she must feel at this very moment, knowing she is about to show us, and herself, that she can do just about anything.

As the pigeon comes into my sights, I see Agnes stretch a broad smile across her face, then she puts it away and forces a serious look onto it. Perhaps she feels she needs to so that Harold knows she is all business. No idea, but she is totally still at this point, and not fidgeting an inch. That is surprising to me, because this kid never sits still. She fidgets in her sleep.

"That's it, Agnes, stand still and give him a good landing site. Steady. Here he comes..."

And just like that, Harold the pigeon, has landed safely onto Agnes' gloved hand, and on his leg is another note in a different color than the one they sent. This one is in pink, and Charlie comes over to help retrieve it for her.

"Well Agnes, you did it! Let's have you open this note up. It was sent just for you, so have at it," Charlie said.

As Agnes unrolls the note that had just been flying through the air, intended on reaching her at that very moment, that smile she had hidden a moment ago is back in full swing and the anticipation is killing me.

"Dear Admiral Agnes. Thank you for sending Harold

over to visit with me. You have now completed your mission. Consider yourself to be one of the lucky ones."

The very next time I had to deal with Charlie for work, I finally remembered to ask him some questions.

"Charlie, how did you arrange things so quickly for Agnes, and who had sent the other note?"

Charlie laughed for a moment.

"Well, I don't get a lot of company, so I wasn't going to waste this chance. That note came from a dear friend of mine who lives in another town not too far off. We met through a group that does this sort of thing, and the funny part is, I've never met her in real life. We just send messages back and forth and to me, that seems about as perfect as it should be. I told her I had a little friend over, and she was excited to help out. I'm glad you all had a good time," Charlie explained.

I was shocked that he had never met this woman, and wanted to press him as to the why, but it didn't matter. This was his journey, and his decision, and he was perfectly okay with that. Maybe he felt it was better to stay friends, or maybe he just enjoyed the mystery of it all.

Whatever the reason, it was his and I respected that.

He allowed Agnes to keep her hat, and she wore it from time to time over the next year. Anytime we were in the yard and saw a pigeon, I could see Agnes chatting with it, and when it left, she would say,

"Tell Harold to stop by and pay me a visit! He will know who I am. He can recognize my face!"

Chapter 17

My Place

* * *

I don't know exactly how or why I ended up here, but I am here regardless. The overhead lights are lighting up the entire area about me, and I can hear people speaking in a garbled tone, asking for different things but sounding as professionally as I ever heard people talking.

I know my legs hurt something awful. I feel that immense pain down to my toes just throbbing, but I just lay here for the moment. I'm afraid to say anything, and really have no idea of what I would say if I could talk.

But then I fall into a deep sleep, and I'm relaxed. I'm dreaming now and wondering if when I wake up, my legs will be good as new and all the people I heard talking just a few moments ago, won't be there any longer, as if they never really were there to begin with.

For some reason, I seem to have slight control over this

state of sleep, but not entirely. I hear no more voices, but I do hear the sound of nature not far off. The chirping of songful birds, and the buzzing of a playful bee hovering just overhead.

I'm not worried about this, though, because I have had many dreams over the course of my life that have animals and beautiful landscapes nearby. I think that all started when I was much younger. As a child, I would have horrible, vivid nightmares, and my mother would tell me to find a place that relaxed me like no other. She said if I could fall asleep thinking of gorgeous valleys or babbling brooks with birds singing wonderful songs high above where I stood, then I would surely find those in my dreams.

It worked, because after a few weeks, the nightmares ceased and the happiness of the places my mind created were so real, that I felt as if I could reach out and touch them.

Right now, I feel as if this is the perfect scenario for my mind to be playing in. I bet if I try hard enough, and focus my thoughts well enough, I can find Harold. It makes me laugh, even in my dreams, because for some reason I am able to think about Harold. I imagine that because I was on my way to see Agnes when this happened, I am thinking of her and all her cute adventures.

My mind is not allowing me to worry about all that now, so I just am going with the flow of this beautiful dream and allowing myself to relax for the moment. There will be plenty of time to worry later on, so why not take full advantage of this time while I can.

Maybe I should walk around and explore some, I think to myself. I mean, I can probably envision anything I choose to, but perhaps I can focus a little less on what I want to see here and see what my sleep wants me to see, as opposed to me trying to dictate that. Yea, I think I'll go with that. I'm going to shut off my brain for a few, and just look.

Wow, this is easier said than done. Or for me, easier thought than done. I keep feeling an urge to lay out the mountains and rivers to the left, and some high, swaying, brown grass-covered fields to the far right. Why, I have not a clue, but I'll allow it.

I feel the warmth of the bright sun, touching me just perfectly with its brilliance, and I feel like the temperature is a perfect seventy-five degrees, like that time we were in Cancun swimming in the crystal-clear blue ocean. Amanda loved that trip and we have plans on returning just as soon as the kids are a little older. I made that promise to her, so I need to remember that. She loves when I remember the things that are important to her, no matter how big or small they may be.

There is what appears to be a family of elk, just beyond the grassy fields, but I don't think they notice that I am here yet. If I am quiet, I bet I can sit here and watch them as they graze off the landscape I seemingly created for them out of nowhere. They have no idea this is a dream, so what difference does it make?

I find a good spot in the open to rest my legs, which for now, are not bothering me at all, and I softly sit myself down, so as not to disturb the animals. I have an urge to look at them and see as they walk around from one spot to another, as a family.

This brings me back to all the questions that Agnes asks non-stop as we drive from point A to point B. It doesn't matter how long or short the drive is. She finds something out of each window she peers through and has a million questions as to the "why" of creation.

I don't always have those answers, and in fact, I seldom do, but I try. I'm sure I have made a few up here and there to sound intelligent, but nothing like a terrible lie that she will get teased about. I wouldn't do that to her of course.

I'm so drawn to watching this simple, life moment. Animals eat all the time, so why is it that I am captivated by this small group doing what I have had the chance to see so many times when I am awake? I don't know, but I just am.

Maybe I should try to get a little closer to where they are. As I look around, I see no one else is there with me, and although I hear birds singing in rhythm somewhere close to me, I don't see a one. They are probably hiding in the tall grass, safely out of sight so they can sing in peace. I'm good with that because whatever they are singing seems like the most beautiful song I've ever heard.

Shimmying my way closer, I take small, muffled steps and watch carefully for any signs that they know I am approaching. But they eat as if they either do not sense me, or do not care that I am watching as they eat their food. Still, though, I want to be patient.

As I get within a few yards of these strong animals, I can see there are 5 in total. The larger ones that I assume are the mother and father, and 3 smaller ones that are in the middle, knowing their protection comes from the outside with the larger ones. They have a sense of peace, as they know they have nothing to fear with momma and daddy there watching out for them. At least that's how it appears to me.

After a while, I turn my attention elsewhere to see what else my dream state has conjured up. It's almost exciting for a time to see things so vividly. Much more so than most dreams I've experienced before this.

As I walk in a different direction, more towards the high merlot-color topped mountains that are just a little to the West, I no longer notice the music of the birds. Strangely they have stopped their song and I hadn't noticed while I was watching over the elk. Maybe my mind forgot and turned off the sound, because it's stone-quiet now as I look towards the bottom of the highest peak.

In walking towards them, I pause for a moment to inspect the elk, wondering if they are still feeding on that tall grass, but they too are now gone. Just vanished from the landscape I was sitting on a minute ago. Strange, I think to myself, because I created this space, so why would I just simply turn off so much that I was enjoying?

The base of the mountain is now at my feet, which for some reason have no shoes or socks, and I find this funny. I am never barefoot unless I am showering or at the beach.

I find shoes comfortable and honestly, I just don't enjoy being barefoot. So this is not something my subconscious would do without my permission.

The mountain is so high, but there are paths carved out within its large stones that make it appear as a manageable climb in sections. It doesn't seem all that bad, at least on the lower levels, so I decide to investigate further and take a few steps to test it all out. Maybe I will get a glimpse of the elk from a higher point, or stumble onto something else that I am unable to see from my current vantage point. I still have no idea of why my mind created such an interesting place in such grand, vivid detail.

Climbing is going well so far, but I don't really feel as if I am seeing much else yet. The path looks pretty basic, and each time I turn around to see more of the horizon, I seem to see the same views as I had down below. So, I continue my ascent and decide to not turn around as much. I want to gain some ground first, and then possibly when I turn, I will see a much different perspective.

When I feel as if I have been climbing for a good twenty minutes or so, I stop, and take a deep breath of the fresh, cool air that is encompassing me. The air feels so rewarding, but it's not cold enough to bother me. It's more refreshing than anything else.

I turn to look down, and realize I am certainly higher than when I started out. The landscape has changed a great deal, which is both strange and satisfying. The high grass seems to have left from one area, and in its place now stands a large black fence, with a swinging door. It's hard to make out what it says on the post, but I guess it doesn't really matter. It's more about the gate than anything else to me. It's open, but just barely. Like as if someone should have closed it tightly, but instead had a specific reason for leaving it cracked. Or maybe, it was simply laziness. I've done that many times.

After I study the new terrain, I wonder if I should climb higher up on this mountain or work my way back down. I'm standing there and trying to determine what should come next, or when I will wake up and realize that this amazing dream I somehow created for myself.

I feel fifty/fifty on which way to go and need to decide, but I don't have a massive sense of urgency. The first thing I do is reach into my pocket to see if I have a coin to flip. I rarely ever carry change anymore, so the likelihood of that is not strong. But there is something in my pocket, so I decide to pull it out and see if it's worth flipping.

In my hand I appear to have a medal. It's nothing I remember having at any time before, but it feels so familiar for some odd reason. I'm not sure how that is possible, but it doesn't matter, because it can be of use to me here, because I notice it has two different shapes on each side, making it perfect for flipping in the air. On one side, a large gate, with doors opened wide, and what appears to be a bright light on the inside, just beyond that gate. On the other, as I flip it around in my outstretched hand, a bird, that appears to be a pigeon, if I am not mistaken. Oh Agnes would get a kick out of this for sure.

Okay, we will call the gate heads, and the pigeon, or whatever bird it is meant to be, tails. Heads I climb higher, and tails I head back down lower to where that black fence is.

As I am literally a split second from tossing the coin into the air above me, my attention is removed from the coin, and placed to a figure down below, just on the inside of the fence. Then another, and another. I now see what appears to be three, no, four outlines of something. Maybe those elk have wandered back into the area to graze some more. But it's not. The outlines my eyes are seeing, are shaped differently. They are shaped like humans, but I cannot make out anything else, other than that.

As I think my mind is made up to head back down and investigate, I hear a bird's voice, just above where I am standing. It's the first noise I have heard since I left the high grass, and it's quite impressive. This isn't a song that I have heard before. In all my days sitting out in the backyard with the children and my wife, I have heard some pretty music, but this is brilliant. Like nothing I have ever laid ears to, and my body is feeling this. It's almost drawing me in with just its powerful song.

I'm struggling now, because I have such a curiosity for both directions, and I am certain I will wake soon. So, in my mind, I have just enough time to see one. But which is going to give me answers? Higher up into the mountain side, or back down to where I started this dream?

My head is starting to hurt some, which is the first real feeling I have experienced since I arrived here. For the most part, I have felt light, and amazingly well. No pain, and in fact, no anything. My legs don't feel tired from the climb, and my body doesn't seem to be responding to the temperatures around me.

Looking down I can now see for sure that the figures are people. There is a woman, and I guess her three children, as those others are small. Much too small to be other adults. One child seems to be further away from the other ones, and closer to the gate that is cracked open. She's probably female because her hair is much longer than the other children's. I assume, anyway. Boys can certainly have long hair, but something about this one makes me feel she's female for sure.

Again, I find my curiosity peaked and I decide to sit down on a nearby rock and just watch, as I had done with the elk earlier. I want to be careful to not disturb them and potentially scare them off. It may be fun to watch and see what it is they are doing here in my dream.

The mother appears to be confused. She's holding one in her arms, and another by the arm. She's reaching forward, as if she's trying to coax the other child back, but that one seems to be in her own little world. She's not looking back at all to this point and is playfully dancing towards the open gate. Funny, I swear when I left that place, there was not a sound in the air, but this child seems to have found her music regardless. It's fascinating just watching, but I can't help wondering why the mother seems to be in a panicked state.

I turn to listen a little, wondering if that bird is still above me, and it is. The music is still just as pretty as it was when I first heard it, and I close my eyes for a second to soak that song in. My soul feels so relaxed and at peace when this tiny bird is chirping away.

Then I look back down below, afraid to lose what I was watching. This dream is a little on the odd side, but I've learned that in turning away for just a moment, things can change in an instant, and I am not willing to lose this just yet.

I'm afraid I've lost sight though, because I see the mother at the gate that is now closed shut, and she's struggling with the handle, trying to pry it open once more. She seems panicked and upset, but she still has those two little ones with her, clutching them with all her strength, as she almost begs that gate to open. I wonder if that missing child somehow closed it and now it's locked from the inside. But where did she go, that third child?

Looking back down to the base of the mountain I spot her. She's looking down at her feet and seems to be in a state of confusion. Is she trying to climb this mountain as I have, or is she going to turn around and find her mother, and calm her fears? She has to know that her mom is struggling with the lock, so I can't understand why she is not helping with that. Somehow, she was able to get through with no issues, so she needs to help her mother out.

"Hey kid! Turn around," I say, as I am pointing to where her mother is.

"You need to go back and grab them. Don't leave them go. Kid, can you hear me?"

She is still just standing there, not moving up or down. I wonder if I am just too high for her to hear me, and maybe I am just the person she needs to convince her she needs to turn back. I wasn't sure which direction to go, but for now, I need to attempt to climb down to help her out. This poor child is either lost or stuck and what type of person would just let her stay there?

I start to walk back down the very path I have traveled, and as I do, I am calling out to her, letting her know to stay put. I will be there shortly to help. Eventually she will hear me and know I am on my way. It's just that I must be higher up than I thought.

When I am about a third of the way back down, I notice she is turned back around, staring in the direction of her mother and the other children. Looking back at the adult, I see her on her knees, as if she is begging this child to come back now. She doesn't appear angry. It's more of a sorrowful plea she is sending this child.

Now the child is looking sad, and she appears to be crying.

"Kid I am almost there. Hang in there. I'll get you back to your mom. Just stay there," I say.

Then I slip. The ground beneath me feels jagged all of a sudden, and I lose my footing. My head hits a log that is laying on the side of this mountain, and while I don't knock myself unconscious, I feel as if I need to slow down for a second.

"Hey, can you hear me? I fell. I hit my head, and I just need a second to gather myself. I'm coming. I promise, okay?" I tell her.

She looks in my direction, and her eyes are full of sadness. Her tears are flowing down her cheeks, and she quickly covers her face.

"Don't cry, honey. I'm okay. I just fell down a little. That's all. I'm coming to get you still. Stay there."

But she turns around and starts to walk back to where her mother is. I look over, and her mother is now off her knees, willing this child back into her arms. As she walks across the barren ground that now sits at the bottom of this peak, I see her with her head hung low, as if she feels like she failed at whatever she felt she needed to do.

Reaching the gate, she turns slowly towards me, waves my way, and somehow opens the locked gate that her mother could not seem to do. She slips on through, where her mother embraces her with a love I have yet to see in my life, and the four of them walk away and out of sight.

I am way too high to get their attention now, and I feel saddened by this. I had hoped to see what they were doing here, but it was just not meant to be. These people are so familiar to me, yet I have not a clue who they are. It's hard to focus on their faces, but I know that they have graced my life before, somehow.

I turn back around, knowing I should probably climb

back up, and find that bird. That gave me a feeling of peace that I need once again. At least until I wake from this dream and find my way home to where I belong.

Chapter 18

Not Ready to Climb

* * *

Seizures are scary, not only for those who experience them, but also for those that watch as someone else is experiencing one. When it's a small child, and you have never seen one of those before up close, it makes you want to vomit, just watching one of your children convulse, as their eyes roll back behind their lids. It's nothing I ever want to watch again.

I know that it's not any choice we have a say in, because sometimes in life, we don't see what is coming from below the horizon, but we know that many times we will need to fight through and help someone in need, despite the unknown on how to do it.

I take great lessons from Amanda's parents. When Andrew is sick, it's not like one of your kids having a common cold. His parents know when he's complaining, it's not a good sign. That's because for the most part, Andrew has a strange ability to ward off simple things like a cold or a small fever. He doesn't complain much, if at all, and so it becomes hard to tell when he isn't a hundred percent.

My kids usually let us know when they aren't well, even with a basic sniffle. Either that, or Amanda can see what I cannot. Maybe she has learned that skill watching her parents raise her younger brother, because she's truly gifted with knowing how to spot things I cannot seem to find.

When Agnes first showed signs of a strange headache that afternoon, it was Amanda who knew something was off. I would probably had just told her to sleep it off and she would feel more herself in a few hours' time. But not Amanda. She knew immediately that our child was not going to heal with just an afternoon nap and needed much more attention.

It's not that I am foolish, or that I don't see when my kids aren't acting as they normally do. I guess it's more of a maternal instinct my wife has, and I am envious of that. To feel something before anyone needs to tell you is a strange gift, and I'm full of gratitude that Amanda can recognize she has that gift.

When they first arrived at the emergency room entrance, and the ambulance folks assisted my wife and Agnes from the back of the van, the sky began to open up. Rain came from seemingly nowhere, and it poured down in buckets, causing a slight delay in pushing Agnes out of the rear, and through the entrance doors.

One of the men, the one who had been in charge of the crew, looked up to the sky and said,

"Rain is a sign that change is on the way, Agnes. My grandmother always told me when it pours down heavy from the sky, it signifies a great change is certain."

I think he was trying to just get her to focus on something other than her seizures, or the ambulance she was starting to wake up in. He probably has kids of his own, or if he does not, he should. He has a gentle way about himself, and with how calm he comes across, a child would learn so much from someone like that.

Amanda appreciates that everyone seems to be focused on our child, and no one seems to be uninterested in what it is they are there to do. This is not just a job for these people. They are not there simply for a paycheck, and that brings an understanding to her (as much as she will allow it to) that she has done all she can, because she still has that instinct that she needs to be doing more than she can. She's remained calm this entire time from the start of the seizure Agnes had, until they are about to wheel her from the doors of the ambulance. But it's not easy, and finally, Amanda starts to break down.

When strong people focus on a task at hand, they appear to be capable of just about anything, including not giving in to their emotions. But when those same strong people finally have a moment to settle in, a floodgate can open up, allowing a dump in emotions that no one sees coming.

This is how Amanda is feeling right at that moment. She

begins to break down and the warm tears are streaming down her cheekbones, onto the ground just below. The man closest to her explains that everything is going to be fine, and that they are ready to push through the rain and the front doors to get Agnes to a room where they can examine her much more closely.

But Amanda seems to feel there is more to this all. It's hard for her to understand herself, but something deep within her soul is telling her, that grandmother was right on with what she had told this man.

Change is coming, but what and how and, more importantly, when?

Once inside the entry way to the emergency room, Agnes starts to come out of her coma-like state and begins to vomit over and over. One of the nurses frantically rushes over to assist the people bringing her in, while another uses a badge to open the door to the rooms beyond the waiting area.

"Agnes, it's okay baby. Let it out. Mommy is right here, baby," Amanda tells her.

While she is focused on her child, she's forgotten that I am on my way with Dot, just a few minutes behind. It's as if it's only Agnes and Amanda in the world at the moment, because Amanda is laser-focused, just as I would expect her to be.

By the time they reach an open room, Agnes is crying. She's confused about where she is and why she is in a room that is unlike one she is familiar with. At first, she doesn't even notice her mother standing there holding her hand, while the nurses tend to her and insert an IV to start fluids.

"I'm not ready! I'm not, please!" Agnes yells.

She's screaming, still vomiting, and so confused about what is happening. The nurse is trying to talk to her over the screams, letting her know she's going to be fine.

"Agnes? It's okay Agnes. You are in good hands. Just take a deep breath for me, okay?" the nurse says to her.

"No, you don't understand! I am not ready! I don't want to go back, and I don't want to climb. Please, don't make me choose," Agnes cries.

The nurse looks over to Amanda and tells her that this is common when a child is coming out of a seizure. She's seen this before with the talking about things that do not seem to make sense, and most times, the children never remember what they were talking about. Amanda should not worry at all.

It's comforting to my wife, but still, she can't help but to wonder what Agnes is talking about, and if she's going to be okay. This has been a lot on the both of them, and she simply wants it to stop.

"Agnes are you starting to feel better?" the nurse says.

She's been there for about a half hour or so now, and the vomiting has stopped entirely. She has the IV in her arm, and the seizures are just a vague memory now. She's resting in the bed, and just starting to come around.

"Where am I? Mom? Dad? Where am I?" Agnes asks.

"Sweetie, you are in the ER. You had a seizure, and we

had to bring you here in an ambulance. Do you remember that?" Amanda asks.

Agnes looks around the room, and at first, doesn't speak a word. She's trying to figure out something, but she doesn't quite know what. Her mind is confused, and she's still feeling weak from the effects of being out as she was.

"What's a seizure mom? Where is dad?"

Amanda called me but my phone must have been on silent. I do that from time to time, especially when I am playing with the kids. I made a pact with myself to separate work from family whenever I could. There are days when I can hardly place my phone down before another call is coming behind the one I am just ending. So, on days where I catch small breaks, I place the ringer on silent, so I can focus on whatever the kids and I are going to do. It may just be for a few minutes, or an hour, but that time is so important to not only me, but to our kids.

"He's on the way. Dot was sleeping when we left, so maybe she was giving dad a hard time getting out of bed. You know how she falls into those deep sleeps," Amanda says with a nervous smile.

"I'm thirsty. Can I have something to drink?" Agnes asks.

The nurse has already placed a cup of ice and water onto a tray next to the bed. Amanda grabs the straw, removes the paper wrapping, and slides the straw into the water. She lifts it towards Agnes and holds it just so that she doesn't need to raise her head much at all.

Amanda is frustrated that I am running late, but it's

not my fault. I'm trying to get there. I want to be with them both, and I want to let Agnes know she cannot do this again. I don't have the calmness to go through something like this. Of course, I will be kidding with her, but it's just how I break the ice. I have a hard time being serious outside of work. I think it's just a nervous thing I do. Amanda loved it when we first got married, but there are times she would prefer I was a little more serious. Still, though, she knows I mean well.

The rain is still coming down, although not as hard as it was earlier when they first arrived. Amanda decides to call me again, and once again, it goes to my voicemail. She's trying to stay calm, but I know my wife. As sweet as she is, lately she's lost some patience with me. I think that just happens with a marriage over time. The things you tolerate for the first many years of a marriage, become the things you tend to notice more as time goes by. Sometimes, you overlook them and realize, it's just a part of the process. It's a test to see if you understand that it's not always going to be roses. Sometimes, you need to push through the hard times, and slowly get past the curves of doubt.

A few years ago, I was laying in our bed, and sleep was escaping me. It was a few nights of restlessness, and I felt as if I was falling into an unhappy stage of my life. My wife, whom I have always found to be beautiful, looked plain and unexciting. I had trouble just holding her at night, when normally, it's all I had wanted in life.

Strangely enough, as quickly as those feelings came,

they left just the same way. There was maybe a week, or a week and a half, where I struggled with the loss of feelings, and then one morning, I awoke, and the struggle was over. My feelings had come back, and in the craziest thoughts crossed my mind. I found Amanda to be just as tempting as the day I first set eyes on her.

It was as if God himself was testing me. I had not prayed much after we got married. Life was good and the kids were amazing and all doing well. Why pray when everything is going as planned? I answered that question myself though, eventually.

During that time of questioning, when I thought for a moment, I may not want to be married to this woman any longer, I prayed. Deeper than anytime I remember. I prayed as I struggled to sleep. I prayed as I first opened my eyes to the morning sun. I prayed in the shower as the water cascaded down my body. I prayed while driving to and from clients' homes. I just prayed.

I think God was reminding me that we don't just pray when things are going bad, but we pray also when things are going as we planned. It only takes one step left, or one step right, to change the course of our lives. A moment can alter the very existence we take for granted, without our input. I learned that the hard way.

Needless to say, I found my love once again, and ever since that day, I've never questioned my marriage again. I am totally content. Well, maybe that's not the proper word. I am not content. I am deeply in love with that woman, and

I cannot see myself with anyone else. I love that feeling.

Amanda, I'm sure, has had times where she's had to rely on her faith, just to get through a stage in her life. I don't like to think about that, but if I did, I am sure she did as well. I believe most, if not everyone married, has those thoughts. It's natural to wonder, and to feel, or not feel, a certain way. Marriage is long. It wasn't meant to be a quick, exciting thing, that only lasts for a short time. I married Amanda for "life plus one more," as I like to say.

Life plus one more, just means, I am with you until the day I die, and then I will be with you for one eternity. It's silly, I know, but it's what I hope happens. Life is short. Eternity is not. So if I am blessed to stay with the same woman for my short, entire time here on earth, and then get to spend the remainder of time, however long eternity may be for, I am a lucky man indeed.

All I know is, if I do not get past the traffic lights and to that ER, the plus one part? It may not happen. Amanda is not going to be happy, so I need to get a move on. But I do not have those devices the ambulances do to change the red lights to green, so I am at the mercy of the traffic, rain, and the ever-changing lights.

Chapter 19

Letting Go

* * *

It turns out that Agnes may have epilepsy, and the doctors see a need to do further testing to figure out why she is having these seizures and terrible headaches. One of the main doctors that is keeping a close eye on her while she is visiting his emergency room, seems to have a good deal of empathy, which helps us out well with what we know, and what we don't know.

He tells us delicately that he is going to order some blood test and an MRI and would like to do those sooner than later. Amanda, without any hesitation, agrees to all of it. She just wants to know what is going on and get our Agnes back to the daughter she is.

The torrential rain seems to have caused a lot of trouble on the local roads, because there are people coming in, ranging from slips and falls to car accidents of all degrees. At one point, while we are sitting with Agnes waiting for the woman to take Agnes over to her MRI check, a man is brought in, clearly unconscious and in bad shape.

I hear the nurses and doctors rushing in to tend to this poor guy, and all I can think of is that I am so glad I am out of that storm. It came from literally nowhere, and just wreaked havoc in its wake. I was lucky to only catch the tail end, as Dot and I were only a few short blocks away when it dumped from the dark sky onto our car like something biblical.

As I sit there watching Agnes rest, I am mentally and emotionally exhausted. This feels surreal being here. She's too young to have these types of things happen, and I hate it for her. I'm angry. I also am well aware of the worst-case scenario, even though the kind doctor has yet to give us what he believes it could be.

Amanda doesn't want to think about all of that. Besides, we are at the mercy of whatever it is, so worrying doesn't do her any good right now. She's more focused on Agnes being comfortable, and what the immediate fix for this is. Long term? We will deal with that if we must, but for now, she would rather focus on getting her baby relaxed.

The ghastly noise from two rooms away is creating a chaotic scene, and because the hospital is short staffed today, it probably seems worse than it is. But for that guy they brought in just a short time ago, I guess it doesn't. He's alone, and I can't help but to wonder if he's going to pull through or not. I need to refocus though, because for now, Agnes is my focus. That guy is no one I know, and although I feel bad for whatever it is he's dealing with, I have my own family to worry about at the present.

Amanda is just sitting there, just as she did that evening Agnes first complained her head was hurting. She's running her hand through our child's hair and rubbing her arm with the other. She's trying to keep Agnes comfortable, and her focus is fully on that task. She's good at that sort of thing when she needs to be. It's like when she bakes something. She knows all the ingredients she will need to bake the perfect cake and can follow her instincts perfectly. That is the same care she puts into her children, and it shows.

When the lady finally enters the room to take Agnes back for her MRI, Amanda tightens up. It's apparent, and the woman tells her not to worry. This is routine, and most times comes back as nothing at all. She's wheeled back a thousand children, so she should not worry about this at all. We are welcomed to walk back with her, just until she enters the area for testing, so we do so.

Once we head out of the room we have been sitting in for what seems like a few hours now, we are escorted to the right, and walk right past the room where the man who was badly injured is now. I don't want to be rude, but I have to at least peer through the doorway to just get a glimpse. I hate that I have this morbid curiosity, but I think it's there for most people.

Amanda looks in as well at almost the same time I do, and we can clearly see that the man lying there did not survive. He's covered up neatly, and the nurses are gathering his belongings and placing them in a bag somberly. His feet are hanging out just below the blanket, and his socks are stained blood red, almost entirely.

Amanda turns away quickly, and glances over to one of the people walking us back to the room where we are to leave Agnes, and says in a low tone,

"I'll never get used to that. Shame that is."

I can tell you this with utter certainty; I could never work in a setting with so much trauma happening. Nurses and doctors are extraordinary people, with an innate ability to shut things off so that they can focus on the task in front of them. When their job doesn't go as planned, they somehow need to find a way to push guilt and doubt aside and continue on with the very next task.

Thinking about the man that has now passed on from this life, I wonder which doctor will need to give that terrible news to people he has never met before, and how those words will be received by those who probably have no idea he's even here in the first place.

That man lying there under the sheets may have been on his way to pick something up for a birthday party, or maybe he was running into the office for a few hours, so that he could finish just one more deal before the quarter was over. Things such as this always make me wonder more than I would expect someone to. I've always had that curiosity though, about what people were doing when their time is up.

Outside the room where Agnes will have her MRI

completed, I lean down and kiss her on the top of her head, and whisper softly into her ear that I am here with her and will see her shortly. I don't want her to be afraid of this, so I try not to make a big deal out of any of that. I simply need her to know her father is right there with her and will be waiting for her when she comes back out.

Amanda does the same. She gives her a warm smile and lets her know that she's proud of her for handling this so well. You can see the pride my wife has for our child, just in how she looks at Agnes as she's wheeled through the doors. As they close behind her, I see my wife crying softly, and she turns away to hide those from others around us. It hurts me to watch my wife feeling so terrible right now, but I know she's going to just need to cry for a time. This is mentally exhausting on her.

I feel that in this moment I should hug my wife and comfort her, but strangely my mind is restraining me. Amanda doesn't seem as if she cares that I am here, and I don't want to stress her more than she already is. I find it better to just be here for her and Agnes, but not to put pressure on things as I sometimes tend to do.

I tell Amanda that I am going to step outside and get some air. Hospitals make me feel claustrophobic for some reason, and I feel as if the cool air left by the rainstorm will clear my head and relax me until we know the results of Agnes' testing. I cannot change the outcome of what is to come from that, but I can control my anxiety just a little bit to make hearing whatever we will, more manageable.

In the state I am right now, I'm only going to make this stressful on everyone.

The rain has finally died down, and the sky is clearing just enough that the sun is peering through the rainclouds that are moving slowly off to the north. A calming breeze was left behind, and I push my head up with my eyes closed, to allow the sun to grace me with its rays. As I take a deep long breath in, I smile to myself, because I have a feeling that everything is somehow going to be okay. Things are going to fall as they are intended to do, and that is the plan designed for us. I don't feel a desire to fight what is inevitable here, and it soothes me in a way I would not have expected.

My wife is inside, trying to understand why this is all happening, and usually, that is me. I am the one that questions everything, and she is the more accepting one. But the roles are changed here today, and I have a sense of just how she feels, knowing we have to sometimes relinquish control when we have nothing left to fight. I am not good with that most of the time, and here, I feel her patience and calmness slipping just a little.

My wife is growing to understand my panic. She's seeing that sometimes when we don't have control over the things happening around us, we have a hard time letting go. We feel this insane urge to say no to the things presented before us, and to scream and stamp our feet, as we know this can't be how this ends up. That's how I have lived my life for the most part. Never accepting things I don't wish to as others can. I always feel a desire to push a little more, or to argue just one last point. Neither have seemed to get me any further, but both seem to be within my makeup.

This moment, this feeling I am having right now, I don't want to let go of. It's crazy to know your child is being put through testing to find out what is causing their issues, and I want to stand right in this spot I stand in now, and take this all in. I don't feel the urge to worry and rush back in, or to fight and blame everyone around me. I don't feel an urge to ask a thousand questions to the good doctors and nurses. I, instead, feel a desire to allow them to do their jobs, and to understand that what is going to happen is going to happen, regardless of my desires.

Don't get me wrong. I want Agnes to have nothing more than an explanation for her seizures that has a quick treatment, so she never has to experience these again. I want her to come home with us and get back to those silly dances she performs for the family, and I want her to go on those long rides with me to nowhere in particular, asking all sorts of questions that I would never have thought of in two lifetimes. That is what I want, but I also know, nature has a way of changing things to better suit a bigger plan.

My grandfather told me once that over the decades and centuries and millenniums, change is happening, and most times, we don't know until it's way past the time that change started. For instance, he said that people probably have fingernails and toenails because at one point in history, they were needed. We probably used them for climbing trees and removing shells from the food we wanted to eat, and perhaps for fending off attacks by animals that saw us as food in return. But over the years, over the many years, our nails have become so thin, that using them for anything we once did, would cause them to pull from the body. They are useless compared to what they were intended for, and time has made it so. They are not needed as they were long ago, so nature made that adjustment.

He was a smart man, my grandfather. At our wedding, he came over to me and sat down next to my bride and me. He didn't look at me, but instead, he looked at my bride. He was talking to me but looking at her. Most people would have thought he was losing his mind, but he wasn't. He was trying to see me in her. He wanted to give me advice, but through Amanda. My grandfather thought that it was easy to give advice to anyone, but it was more useful to give it to someone that you truly loved. He was teaching me that I was not an individual any longer. I was one with my bride, and therefore needed to see things within her, and not because of her. That was a lesson I didn't understand until he passed away a few years back.

At his funeral, my grandmother told me how much he appreciated our talks. She said that he would always tell her that if anyone understood the greatness of being one, it was me. It took me losing him, to really gain from him. That was a sad way of learning something that was right in front of me, but I think he would appreciate more the fact that I figured it out because of him. Even if he was unable to hear it from me now.

Agnes was fond of him as well. She's fond of everyone, really, but she would always ask him to tell her stories, and he would not disappoint. Sometimes, he would make something up from a mixture of things around the room he was in, and sometimes he would give her a glimpse into his storied past, sharing tales that would otherwise be long gone.

I never asked him much about his life, and so I don't deserve the lessons from all he learned during his time here. My grandmother tells me that's hogwash, but I just feel like it's stealing. I had the chance to take what he had to pass down, and I did not do that. Maybe that's the lesson most learned by us all. If you don't open your eyes and hearts to those people that want to give you all the knowledge they have, you lose. Period. I don't know. I just know, Agnes doesn't need to steal anything. That child gains from every soul she encounters for sure.

After a little while, I realize I should be getting back in. They will wonder where I went, and Amanda seems to be off today anyway. I don't want to upset her, especially with all of this going on. She's fairly easy-going, but lately, I don't know. I feel she's just a little bit off.

So I head back in and walk past the front desk person who is busy typing away on her computer. I walk through the doors and past the room that they now have empty, where just a short time ago, a man expired, and a family was surely changed forever.

I walk back to the room where we first came to when we arrived, and Amanda is still not there. The room is empty, except for a purse on the floor, and the clothes Agnes had on before they changed her into that hospital garb that they put on you when you first arrive. She went with a rainbow patterned shirt with the words "Be Kind," written across the middle, and her light blue pixie skirt, as she refers to it.

I've talked with her a few times over the past year, asking her if maybe it was time to retire that old, tattered skirt, and others she has like it, for maybe something more age appropriate. I really never meant to offend her, but she's getting older, and I don't want to have her experience bullying like her uncle had to endure. I realize they are completely different people, but still, I want my kids to fit in.

Amanda tells me to let her go. That she will find herself in her own time, and when she is good and ready. Besides, she reminds me, she is not hurting anyone, so it should not hurt her. Let her be a kid for as long as she needs to be, she says.

When I pick up the skirt, I laugh to myself, because I know Amanda was right. I'm worried about a choice in dress my child is wearing, and she's being tested for God knows what in an emergency department at our local hospital. This is one of those times I realize, I need to stop worrying so much, and let life happen. It could be worse. It could be so much worse.

As I think that to myself, I am aware of a noise not too far off in the distance and know it's my Amanda. I can hear her crying, but I am not sure from where, or why just yet.

Walking out the door of the room, I quickly scan left and right, trying to gauge the direction for which she is in, but I don't see her at first. When I begin to look around more, and just as I am about to ask a nurse walking by if she knows where she is, I see her out of the corner of my eye.

She's maybe twenty yards away, just outside of the room they took Agnes to a short time ago. She's on her knees, with her phone tossed down in front of her, and she's being comforted by two people with light blue uniforms on. I call out her name, but I think she is so out of it, and that I am possibly too far for her to hear me at first.

I race over to where she is, dodging people who are now looking her way, and finally I reach her, and place my arm around my wife.

She's so sad and I have no idea of why or what just happened to make her this way, but I am now also in a panic.

"Baby," I say.

"Baby, what happened? Why are you crying? What is it!" I scream.

"Where's Agnes?"

Chapter 20

A Hidden Talent

* * *

A few weeks prior to Agnes falling ill and being rushed to the hospital, Andrew spent two nights with us so that his parents could get away to the Catskill Mountains for a weekend trip. It had been some time since they last had a trip alone, and although they felt bad, we assured them that he would have a great time with us.

Fred loved to fish, and this would be a few days to do so, while his wife, Christine, took some much-needed time to catch up on her reading. She always had some sort of book in her hands whenever she was resting.

Andrew was really good with our children, and they in turn always enjoyed chatting with him. I think sometimes they understood what he was saying better than we did, but maybe that was just something kids had that came with their age. They could relate to his mind that was far closer to that of a child's and we sometimes expected him to think more as an adult, which he was. Or maybe, they just didn't see his inability to communicate well as an issue at all.

That Friday night, just after he was dropped off to our home, Amanda decided to make his favorite dinner of angel hair spaghetti with chicken parmesan and a side of buttered peas. He could eat an entire bowl of those buttered peas, and so when I stopped off to grab the list of food needed, I purchased a few extra frozen bags so that he would have an ample supply while he stayed with us.

Erik was the only one who would not eat the chicken. Anything that was part of an animal started to repulse him over the last year or so, and so he would settle for the buttered peas and the spaghetti with just a little sauce and a sprinkling of parmesan cheese. Amanda's sauce wasn't half bad, either.

Agnes and Dot both agreed with Erik, that eating an animal seemed kind of gross to the both of them, and they felt bad for any animal that died so we could eat, but their thinking was that it was already dead at this point, so it would be worse to waste it. I didn't have the heart to tell them that if everyone stopped eating them, they would have no need to kill them for food, but I, too, loved my wife's chicken parmesan.

Andrew watched movies with the kids and laughed whenever Agnes would repeat a dance that anyone did in the movie. He wasn't being mean at all. It was a laugh of excitement and happiness. He loved watching her dance around the family room, with not a care in the world what anyone thought of her routine. For Agnes, it was more about being free than it was about being correct.

One thing that Amanda noticed though, was that her brother was more focused on his bag, and with doodling inside on the papers that were neatly placed in a binder. He has been saving those binders now for years in his room, and when one is filled, he starts another. I've always been curious as to what he either draws or writes on those pages, but he's very protective about that all and I don't want to upset him by asking. Maybe one of these days he will show me. I'd like that for certain, but if and when he is ready.

Agnes has seen them. She tells me that Andrew has a real talent for both drawing and writing, but I am not sure if she's just being her silly self, or if she is speaking truthfully. I don't know the extent of Andrew's writing abilities, but I imagine they are not nearly as good as she thinks they are. It's cute still though, because Agnes can spend hours just sitting with her uncle talking to him and watching him play with whatever he has with him. It's one of her marvelous gifts that she possesses. She can make anyone feel right at home, even Andrew, who sometimes struggles when he isn't in his familiar bedroom at his parents' place.

We set up a blanket fort for both Erik and Andrew to sleep in, because whenever they are together, they throw all the covers off the bed, steal the extras from the hall closet that we use whenever we have guests over, and they build. Books are used to hold the corners down, and chairs are placed just so, allowing the blankets to stay high in the air. Erik has become quite good at building these, but Andrew is a huge help. He's a strong person, so any heavy lifting is done by him.

The funny thing is, Amanda and I lay in bed and wait for it. We wait for the books to fall hard to the floor, because someone shifted inside the fort, causing the weight to shift enough to drop the hardbacks.

No one gets hurt, and both stay fast asleep through it all. We don't even bother to look in the room anymore to ensure they are okay. Our thought is that if anyone got hit and was in pain, they would absolutely tell us with a scream we would clearly hear.

Agnes usually sleeps alone, but whenever the boys are together, she seems to favor having Dot beside her. I get it. My brothers and I would often find our ways into one another's rooms. If one of us was having a sleepover out with a friend, the remaining two would sneak into the same room as the last brother and find ourselves having the craziest adventures in our own minds. I miss those days more than just about any others.

So naturally, I find it interesting whenever the girls head into the same room. Sometimes they ask us, and occasionally, they sneak in and think we don't know. But we do. It's just that we find this a good thing for the kids to bond and create their own lasting memories like I have.

There are times when Andrew has trouble sleeping and will wake up calling for Amanda. She's aware that being in a different home can create a little anxiety for him, so she's really understanding, even if she's dead exhausted. It's a part of being in Andrew's life that she understands and accepts.

Me? Not so much. When I am in a deep sleep, it's nearly impossible for me to get up out of bed. Amanda can hear a floorboard creek as the kids wake to use the bathroom at 1:28 in the morning. They would need to rip the board off the floor, bring it in to the bedroom and over to where I am sleeping, and hit me on the head with it before I would even notice they were up.

For some reason, though, I am having trouble sleeping, and so I find myself turning a few pages of the novel I've been trying to read for eight and a half months now, just to tire myself out some.

But I hear voices in the hallway, so I decide to tiptoe down the hall to investigate. I figure it's just the two boys fumbling around with some cars or something, or perhaps the girls talking through the late night about a dance Agnes swears she's going to make it big with.

Only, when I walk past the bedrooms, I don't hear them. I walk some more, slowly, quietly, down the stairs to the main floor, and there I see Andrew in the kitchen with some fruit chews on the counter, a bowl of dry cereal, and a tall glass of white milk next to them. Agnes is also chomping away at the banquet the kids have laid before them, looking over some of the notes and pictures Andrew has been working on.

I decide to sit on the bottom step, just out of view, and listen. Agnes is speaking softly, probably with the intention of not waking her mother or I up. I know how kids need to talk low, but as I get older, I realize our hearing becomes super sensitive to our children. I swear I can hear the kids talking clear through the walls and closed doors, knowing they are awake without having to venture out of my cozy bed.

"Uncle Dew, this is so good. You are really working hard on these. I can tell that much," Agnes says to him.

I'm smiling because here is my kid, aware her uncle has some issues, and she's encouraging him to keep doing whatever he has been, because she finds it truly great. I have no idea if she's just saying that, or truly believes what it is she is saying and seeing. The truth is it doesn't matter at all. It's not about the truth, but more about the act of kindness she is exhibiting. Being truthful is not always being kind and humane. But I also know, sometimes what I find to be well done, others may not, and what they see as true art, may baffle the hell out of me.

I've never understood Picasso, but millions of people get him in ways I never will. His art isn't dependent on me finding it meaningful. Honestly, even if he were alive, my opinion to him would be worthless, so to me, it makes no sense to judge what I can't find in something.

I try to lean into the room a little to get a better look, just as Agnes is paging through the binder of pictures, and I inadvertently slip down, banging my knee onto the floor, making my presence known to both Andrew and Agnes.

"Dad! What are you doing?" Agnes says with a laugh.

I'm laughing now, too, because my soft landing was anything but soft, and my knee truly hurts, only I cannot show them it does. But it does anyway.

"Me? I was just, um, coming to get a glass of water, and I tripped," I say.

I don't want Andrew to feel weird at all. And I don't want him to worry that I am prying into his personal drawings and words he has scribbled for some time now. He protects them so well, and allows no one to see them, except Agnes for some reason. Strange as it may be, I think it's a great thing for him to have someone he trusts well enough to critique his personal work. Not even Amanda has seen what he does in those.

Well, now that I have crashed their party, I ask if anyone wants me to make an ice cream float. Both of them look at each other, as if they are trying to time the words at the exact same time, smile at each other, and exclaim,

"Yea!" to my question.

I have no idea why I offered to do this, but it's not often I get to eat a root beer and banana float with my Agnes, or any of the kids for that matter. So this just seems as good a time as any. Especially because I am still not feeling an ounce of tiredness.

Andrew has already placed his things back in his "stowy" bag and Agnes clears the food off the table so that there will be plenty of room for the floats and for me to sit beside them.

I'm opening cabinets softly, trying to be mindful that Amanda is a light sleeper, and pulling out the oblong bowls I like to use for these floats. We bought a set of eight light blue bowls maybe three summers ago at a flea market, and I've only had the chance to use them one other time. So this is a nice reason to break them out tonight.

Carefully I place the scoops of vanilla bean ice cream across the bottom of the bowls, and then slice the banana's longways, laying them just on top. In the refrigerator I find some cherries, a bottle of chocolate sauce, and luckily, there's some whipped cream that hasn't gone bad. Lastly, the root bear soda I've been saving for just this.

Altogether, I've created a modern-day masterpiece, complete with chocolate sprinkles and a strawberry filled sauce topping. It almost looks too good to eat, but leaving it to melt would be an utter waste.

I place two bowls of heaven in front of the kids, and then I carry the last one over for me and sit next to Andrew. I realize I call him a kid more than an adult, but he doesn't know that I do, or doesn't care much. He's never seemed to have an issue with that or anything I say, really. I think he just knows that I respect him, and nothing I say or do is intentional.

Somehow, over the course of eating a bite at a time, Agnes and I bond more than we have lately. She's always easy going, but I sense she is maturing and with that, her attitude changes, as does the time she seems to want to spend with me. This moment is full of time, and I am enjoying every bit of that while I have it.

I don't recall how I was with my parents much, but if I thought hard about it, I am sure there was a time that I went from needing my parents to be there for every step I took, to one day when I just woke up and no longer felt that I needed it or wanted it. Funny how as kids we don't notice that transition, but as parents, we see it. We feel it. Clear as day we see that time and remember it too.

Agnes is being silly with her float, as she savors each and every bite she takes. Andrew, for his part, is eating as if it were his last meal here on earth and he has a time limit for which to eat the meal in. That's basically how he eats everything he tastes. Food goes into his mouth at a frantic pace, and into his stomach just as quick. His parents have warned him time and time again, that one of these days he's going to choke on his food, but he doesn't seem to care. His mind and body tell him to keep doing as he has, and so he does without a second thought.

Once they are finished, I move on to cleaning up the table, and then to the mess I made while creating these floats.

"Okay guys, it's time for bed. Let's get you two back upstairs and into your rooms so that tomorrow you will be nice and fresh," I say.

Andrew stops and turns around to face me. He reaches out his arms and swings them around my shoulders. He's as tall as I am, so he doesn't need to stretch at all. I'm not sure why he feels the need to do this at this moment, but something has made him think, and he reacts. He holds on tightly for several seconds, until I tell him it's alright. When I do, he pulls his head back from my shoulder, still holding on to me, and puts his head down some, before slowly letting his arms drop.

Then he turns away, and begins his ascent to the bedroom where Erik is sleeping.

I have no idea of what that was, as it was seriously out of character for Andrew, but I brush it out of my mind, knowing I am not going to get an explanation from him. Not tonight. Probably not ever.

By the time I get to the bedrooms, just after turning off the lights in the kitchen we were sitting in, Agnes is under her blankets, and her eyes are closed.

"Sweet dream, Agnes. Get some rest," I say.

She smiles, knowing I can see she is still awake, and then turns over without saying another word. She's tired, so I just turn down her lights and let her be.

Andrew is somehow already out like a light. In that short time it took me to finish up, he managed to pass out. He has a heavier snore than most people I know, but it's not obnoxious.

His bag is tucked under his left arm, and I think about moving it so he can be more comfortable while he sleeps, but I think better of it. I do not want to invade his space, and so I figure it's better to leave it be. He's probably slept with that bag many times over the years, so I'm sure he's comfortable with it now.

Amanda is still resting, and I wonder if she knows that I

had gotten out of bed to take care of the noise downstairs, or if she is oddly in a deep sleep, which is extremely rare for her. Either way, she looks so peaceful laying there, and I watch her for a few moments, smiling to myself before I too close my eyelids and get back to sleep.

That moment with Andrew was sweet, but odd. It haunts my dreams enough that my sleep is interrupted throughout the night, but I cannot remember all the details as vividly as they were in my dreams. I just remember waking up and feeling as if something big was missing, and Andrew was trying to let me know in his own way that he missed it. It's hard to explain, really.

Thankfully, though, I am wide awake, and my crazy mind doesn't need to relive those thoughts anymore. So I push them out of my head and get going with the new morning that has greeted me.

Chapter 21

Back to My Place

* * *

Agnes. My Sweet Agnes. You are home, my precious one. You are home again.

It's been six and a half weeks since that frightening day at the hospital. The one where my Agnes was rushed to the emergency room, where she was put through testing to figure out just what was going on with her body. The good and bad news is that they were able to figure things out.

I say good and bad because at least we now have an understanding of what our child is experiencing and why, which allows us to form a better plan to help her as best we can. That is the most important part of this all. Knowing what exactly we need to do, or try to do, is just as important as getting Agnes back to being the kid she is meant to be. That clumsy, quirky, full of the most passionate love for every stage of life, child of ours.

Agnes is up in her bedroom, laying down, on her belly, flat as can be, resting. She's been vomiting again, and her energy level is nonexistent. Her little body is fighting this as best as it knows how to, but her body is struggling. It's hitting times where it simply wants to give in and quit, but I beg Agnes to push on just a little longer. I beg her to remember this will all be a distant memory at some point in time, and she will look back and smile, knowing she overcame something on her own with such a fight as I've never seen.

Agnes has developed a tumor in her head, and this has given us the answers we were looking for, but hoping not to have. That's a tough position to be in. One where you beg for answers, and then get angry and upset when you get the answers you begged for. Going back to not knowing doesn't help at all, but I think back to before we knew what was going on, and remember being worried, but not like this. Not like we are now. We are so worried that we don't talk to each other. We barely glance in each other's direction, and that's not helping. It's hurting me deeply and I'm confused, but I must understand that Amanda needs time and space to figure her emotions out, so I want to give her those.

But I'm also feeling alone and abandoned through this. I feel as if I, too, need someone to tell me it's going to be alright and that we are doing all we can. I need someone to remind me that I am a good father, and that all my efforts to help Agnes through this are fruitful. I need that reassurance, but I am not getting it.

This worries me. Not because I think this will change us and how we continue on with our marriage, but because just prior to knowing this about Agnes, my marriage was good, but not as it had been. I don't know exactly what happened and when, but things shifted a little, and I didn't really notice that until recently. But now is not the time to bring that up to Amanda, so I just must believe we are okay.

For now, my attention needs to focus off me, and off the things I feel are a struggle in my life. My child is fighting a real life-or-death struggle, one where she needs to be stronger than I am, and have a no quit attitude, no matter how hard this gets.

Do you know how hard that is? I do. I know that whenever I catch the flu, and not that man cold flu people speak of, but the real flu? I beg to die. I lay on the cold tiled bathroom floor as it spins, and beg God to take me, because I don't have the energy to vomit another time. I don't have the energy to sip water because my body needs it, but my mind tells me it's just going to come back up and simply be a waste of effort.

So, I am watching my tiny Agnes fight this, and wondering to myself, what would I do if I was experiencing what she is? Could I push through all the fatigue and nasty vomiting? Could I will myself to continue when my body was telling me that it was time to stop fighting? That has nothing left to give to this battle I am losing? Or would I somehow find a strength I've never known existed within me, buried deep down where I've never had to explore before, and push on?

I think I would want to quit. Maybe that is why I am struggling so hard watching Agnes go through this. Because if it were me, I would probably quit and beg to die, and I don't want that for my Agnes. I can't even begin to imagine a life without my goofy dancer entertaining a room full of close family, making each person smile more than they expected to. She has a light about her that no one else I've ever met does. It's simply captivating, her personality is.

But seeing her laying like this, just limp and overwhelmed, hurts me to the core. It makes me want to lift her little body up and take her somewhere where she can be free. Free from all the pain and free from all the struggling she is going to experience. I want to just take her away, but I know I can't. She needs to push through this because her mother needs her. Her brother and sister need her to. I need her.

The next couple of weeks are going to tell us a lot about how she is handling the treatments, and what to hopefully expect in the near future. The radiation she's going through is going to shrink this tumor of hers and give my baby back her life. I have faith in that. But the doctors just don't know. They are, of course, optimistic, but I would assume that goes with the job. No one wants to believe that the child they are entrusted with is going to die on their watch. No matter how many years a doctor has done this, it must sting them some each time a child passes, and I thank God

I don't need to have that on my hands.

My parents and Amanda's are here much more lately. I know they are worried about Agnes, and they are offering all their time to ensure we are set with things. I guess they know that with all this going on, we still have two other children to tend to, and that can be difficult with all the appointments for Agnes we must go to. I feel as if I haven't seen Erik and Dot in a while, but my parents have been taking them on day trips to get them out of the house. They don't need to watch Agnes get sick all the time, and they don't need to watch their mother and father struggling with all this. They need to also have their own time to be kids.

Amanda is finally laying down in the bedroom, because she has not had a normal night's sleep since the day Agnes was first brought to the ER. Whenever possible, she gets in an hour here or there of rest, because her body is so worn down, and she knows she needs to be stronger for our child. Otherwise, she will be of little use, and that is not my wife. She is the strong one, no matter how she is feeling. She's the dependable one here, and I know that for certain.

I take this time to sit on the floor next to where Agnes is sleeping, and I talk with her. I am not sure that she hears me, depending on the level of her sleep, but I want to talk to her regardless. Maybe it's not just for her, but for me as well. I need this as much as she does, I think.

"Agnes. It's dad. I hope you are sleeping well, baby. I hope you are dreaming of all the wonderful things you will do when you get through this, and believe me, you will. Remember Mr. Charlie? I bet if I ask him, he'll bring Harold over for you to see. Harold would love that, you know. He would recognize you right away, remember?" I start to say.

She's still not moving around, but I continue, because I want to get things out to her that I feel I need to.

"Honey, listen. I want you to know that if I could take this from you, I would. I know you don't feel well right now, and who would? But I know you, Agnes. I know how strong, and caring, and creative, and wonderful you are. I know all the things that make you who you are, and I love them all. You have so much to give to this world, so God is going to make sure you get through this so you can continue to share that amazing gift. He knows this is hard on you, but he knows that you are strong enough to get through this. That I promise, honey. You are so strong, and I am so very proud of you. Even if I don't tell you that enough. Agnes, I am so proud of you," I continue.

Eventually I, myself, doze off into a sleep, and once again my mind goes off into a strange dreamlike state as it has before.

I'm back on that mountain I was climbing before, and there I sit upon a large, white and gray rock, overlooking the landscape below, full of lush green grass and fields filled with wildflowers flowing in the gentle breeze that has greeted me. I'm looking for a sign of anything, scanning my eyes from left to right, and back and forth. The motion and soft noise of the flowers swaying is calming and fills me with a relaxation I have never known.

I don't feel overwhelmed, or any need to see more than what is now present in this dream, and so I think I shall just sit here, and take this all in, because I know when I wake up, all the struggles will once again be there for me. I think that if I can use this time to simply collect myself and gain a sense of calmness, I will be better suited to help Agnes through her struggles, and help my Amanda feel stronger about our marriage.

When we married, there were of course tough times, and those arguments people experience over who continues to leave the cabinet door open, or who doesn't make the bed, despite being the last one out of it. Sometimes we argued over things that weren't there, like an item Amanda swore she asked me to pick up on my way home, but never did actually ask me. Then it would be that she asked me before I left that morning, and she was just as sure of it as I was that she had not.

It was hard, wanting to defend my point constantly, but struggling with the notion that if I continued to, this would escalate into something it never needed to. That is always my issue. I want to prove that I was right, more than she wanted to prove I was wrong. She would stop, and just go on about her day, but I could tell she was still disappointed. It's something I work on, but probably not hard enough. I do close that cabinet door more often now, but every now and again, well, I'm trying. I really am.

Above me, I hear those birds that I once heard before. I want to climb on up and feel this strange urge to see what type of birds they are, and how far above me they may be, but I also feel this incredible pull to stay where I am, as if I am waiting for something I am missing and need entirely.

I guess for now I will wait. This is my dream, and although dreams are strange and you usually have little to no control over how they transpire, I have a feeling that in this one, I have a choice. Not on everything here, but just enough that I can decide on where to go and when, so that part is both scary but exciting.

I don't really know how long I have been sleeping next to Agnes, because in my dreams, there is no sense of time it would seem, and no need for urgency. I can rest here as long as I desire, and nothing will be affected by that.

I remember my mother talking to me about the dreams we all have and how they happen over just a matter of seconds in real time, but can feel like hours, or days while we are in the dream. I don't know how people have determined that, and I am unsure if I believe that entirely, but I guess anything is possible. I struggle with answers that people come up with that can't be shown to me easily. I always have, and that has caused me to question my faith on more than one occasion, but my hopes generally rule in favor of my believing. I would rather believe there is something after death, and live a life in less fear, than to not believe, and not enjoy hope through my time on earth.

Here, lying next to Agnes, who is just trying to be a

child, and suffering from this nasty tumor that she had no say in, frustrates me to no end, and I want to be mad. At times I am struggling with the fact an all great and loving God would allow any of his creations to suffer like this, and it makes me question his existence. But then I find myself praying harder than ever, because I need him more than ever, and it just seems like I am being forced to trust him.

But I will believe because I must. Because I want to. Because I need help, and he is the only one that can provide that on the level I need it, and the level Agnes needs it. If I decide he doesn't exist, then what will I do with my time, instead of speaking to him, and praying to him? It's therapeutic to just talk with him in my own way, and I convince myself I am not crazy for doing so, but if I feel he doesn't exist, then I am plum crazy for doing so.

Every now and again the breeze picks up, and it catches my attention. I look around the fields, searching for anything, but still find nothing. It doesn't feel like a waste of time to look, because it's giving me a sense of hope looking for things I cannot yet see, and a sense of calmness, knowing I may not find anything for a long while. Nothing needs to be found, and perhaps nothing is really lost, and I try to make sense of that in my brain.

There's finally a small, red flower that seems to come out of nowhere, and it's garnering my undivided attention, causing my eyes to lock in on this pretty flower I have never seen before. It's not a rose, which is usually the red I see. It's unlike anything I can explain, but it feels so familiar. This could be one of those times I dream and have no control, so I am aware it could simply be my mind tricking me.

It doesn't sway with the breeze like the other ones do. It seems more deeply rooted, and sturdier than the other swaying wildflowers. It's clearly built differently and has a very different purpose here.

As I keep focused on this plant, a loud bird startles me as it lands just next to the rock I am seated on, and for a moment, I lose my focus, and when I look down again, the red flower that had caught my attention, is now gone. I stand on the rock, trying to locate it once again, but it's useless. That gorgeous, purposeful, red flower is no longer going to allow me to admire it, and I feel a sense of sadness, but still, happiness that I was able to enjoy it for that short moment.

The bird is a pigeon, who is cooing just a few yards from me, and I want to be angry with it for allowing me to lose my focus, but it, too, is calming. It's just resting there, almost as if it's going to wait for me to decide on where I am going next, and willing to go along for the ride. Strangely, I am happy this pigeon has decided to stay with me, because I no longer feel alone.

"You remind me of Harold," I say to the bird.

I'm at first being funny, but the more I look, the more I realize that I may actually have Harold in this dream with me, and anything goes when you are envisioning strange phenomena. So, why not? This is my dream, and my state of mind, so it can be Harold if I choose it to be.

This pigeon looks my way, as if it can understand me, but I am unable to understand it. That doesn't matter, though, because I still miss that red flower.

"Harold, why? Why did you distract me like that! You caused me to lose sight of the flower I was looking at. Why?" I ask.

Harold, or the bird, whomever it may be, just looks at me, cocking his head sideways, and then looks down below, and something has caught his attention. He coos again, as if trying to get me to look at whatever it is he is staring at below.

So, I turn my attention down below as well, and scan the area once more, but focusing more on the direction that Harold is focused on. There, I can see just beyond the tall fields of swaying grasses, the gate I had in my previous dream. It's opened slightly, and just to the outside of the gate, is the red flower. It's once again standing straight with no swaying but doesn't seem as deeply rooted as it was. If a strong wind were to come by, I imagine it would topple over, because the roots are exposed almost to the bottom of the plant.

Nothing is on the other side of the gate this time, but I can hear a soft cry come from somewhere not far off from the open gate. No words, only a cry that is more out of sadness than desperation. One less of begging, and more of forgiveness. It's hard to understand what is happening, but I feel an urge to wake up and check on my Agnes, only I am unable to yet. Something is keeping me in this place, and I begin to beg it to let me leave.

Harold flies off quickly, startling me for a moment, and heads down to where the gate is. As I collect myself from the split second I lost focus, I realize that again, the flower has disappeared, and I frantically search all over the landscape, hoping to find it once more. I cannot seem to, so I stand and begin to descend down the mountain from which I am on, slowly because I want to find this flower and not lose sight of it again.

Harold has reached the gate and comes to a complete stop. He turns to look at me, and slowly walks to the other side, showing me that the red wildflower is now safely rooted in a planter, away from the land I have created. I cannot see much of anything on the other side, but I know the flower is safe, and so I stop my climb, and find another perch to rest on. I feel tired and wonder if I should not have climbed in the first place, but I had to know this flower was going to be alright.

For the time, it seems to be. I expect Harold to stay with the plant, but instead he seemingly nods to the flower, turns towards me, and begins to ascend back to where I am seated. As he comes through the gate, it closes behind him softly, and I can no longer see the plant, but I know it is fine.

Harold lands back where I am and sits. He has decided to wait for me to decide where I belong, and which way I should travel. I think Harold likes me, or respects me, because he refuses to leave my side. I appreciate him and decide to wait until I know where I wish to go. I feel no sense of urgency, and besides, I have been dreaming long enough, that it's probably long overdue that I wake, and so I do.

I wake, and Agnes is right where I left her, safely in her bed, sleeping away. Amanda is still sleeping as well, and I feel calm, as if things are going to go exactly how they need to.

Chapter 22

She's Ready

* * *

One of the hardest moments I've had to witness in my life, was the morning Agnes was going to lose her long, wavy, brown hair.

We tried to find ways to make that easier on her, and if you think of all the things that could be more life altering, you would think we could somehow make this manageable. It was not. I slept horribly the night before, knowing that Agnes had to make this decision on her own, and it was one she was facing with her family close by, but still very much alone. I hate that I have to watch when all I want to do is take this from her. I hate that I am forced to accept when I want to change. I am angry that she cannot have a simple, easier life, like so many others around us, and that I cannot provide that for her.

That morning I hear Amanda's alarm go off, and I am dreading just the simple act of getting out of our bed. I feel dead alone in this, and I know Amanda is trying, but we are so distant anymore. I keep thinking about how our family is going to need therapy to cope with all the adjustments, but I can't seem to get motivated for it.

My wife turns off the alarm, and looks over to where I am laying, with my eyes up to the ceiling, in a daze. She doesn't mutter a word but lets out a sigh as if she is frustrated, angry, but more than that, she's hurt. She's hurting deep inside, and I get it. I just can't find the words to make this any better for the moment, so I just don't say anything. I know she understands, even if it's not ideal. We just need to find a way through this season of life, but for now, Agnes is our focus.

As Amanda heads down to start the coffee pot, I roll over to my side, and try to will myself to get moving. While I didn't sleep much at all, what little I did sleep was once again haunted by my crazy dreams which I have been unable to shake. A normal night's sleep has eluded me countless times, and now I realize how I took the simplest of things for granted far too many times. I miss that peaceful, resting sleep.

Agnes is in her room, with any luck, still not awake yet, because I need her to feel refreshed today. I know she's been also struggling throughout the nights, and her dreams seem to be just as crazy as mine. The medication she is using to push through her pain is hopefully helping her to fight this, but at the same time, it's changing her and her routine in obvious ways.

Just a few nights back I heard her just before midnight,

as I was sitting up trying to get myself tired for bed. When I went into her room to check on her, Amanda was over her, caressing her head, and listening to our child speak nonsense over and over. Instead of trying to wake her and stop what was going on, Amanda, for some reason, decided to listen to her as she spoke in patterns that seemed to have no direction whatsoever. It was making no sense what she was barking, but to Agnes, it seemed to flow perfectly in her head. I saw the frustration on her face as she was shouting odd scenarios out, but Amanda was having a hard time deciding what to do.

It was if she needed to hear what Agnes was saying and needed to feel what Agnes was. I wanted to interrupt, but I somehow felt Amanda had her reasons, and decided to let my wife do as she wished, as hard as it was to watch.

Fate would have it that Agnes did wake on her own, and in a turn of events, had no recollection of her dreams and strange phrases she was uttering. She was perfectly fine, well, as fine as a child fighting a tumor could be and was shocked to see her mother sitting next to her as she was sleeping. I had backed out from the doorway, so that Agnes would not worry too much that we were both there worried. She would struggle further if she knew everyone in the home was focused on her, when she could not recall the faintest of things from just a moment ago.

When I decide that my body and mind has had enough of struggling with the morning rising, I place my bare feet to the floor, and wipe my face with both my hands, feeling a speck of sun touching my face, as it tries to greet me with its warmth. The sun usually is a welcome sign for me, but I can't feel what it's trying to do right this second, because I am not wanting to. I have willed myself to lose some of the simple pleasures, maybe because I feel that Agnes has lost some of those without her permission. Why should I have something she cannot?

A crashing sound comes from the kitchen, and I quickly gather myself and run down to see what has happened.

Amanda had two coffee cups on a tray, with some cut grapes and a banana, ready to be brought up. She must have lost her footing, and that all crashed down to the ceramic tile flooring, shattering both cups, and tossing the fresh fruit all along the kitchen floor and underneath the refrigerator.

She's crying, and I can see this is harder on her than she had let on. I feel her exhaustion strangely, and God, I just want to make this all go away. I am so frustrated that I am the man of the house, the father and husband who these people rely on to fix things, and I have nothing to offer. I have no answers and no ability to understand this more than anyone else. It's not fair!

She drops the rest of what was in her hands and wipes her eyes, and she puts on a face that shows she's under control, when she is anything but. She's aware that Agnes needs to see her mother strong, or she will grow more concerned herself, and that does no good for anyone. This is where my wife does things I cannot. She can hide her emotions when absolutely necessary. I still struggle with that greatly.

I bend down to pick up the broken pieces, and Amanda walks past me, and heads to our daughter's room. She must act quick, because we are sure the noise has awakened the rest of the house, and she wants to do damage control quickly. It doesn't make it easier for me, as a simple touch of my shoulder, or a small, few words would have made me feel seen, but I get it. I know this isn't the time.

As she does get to the stairs, before she enters the room, I do hear my wife say downstairs to me,

"Jon, I know we are in this together. I just need more from you."

I am crushed. More? What more? I'm giving this all I can. All I have. For the love of God, what else do they want from me? I'm watching my child suffer, just as she is, and I am trying to hold it together, just as she is, but all she can see is not what I am doing, but what I am not doing? Does she even know how badly I want to give up and cry, night and day? Does she understand the feeling of helplessness I experience each time I close my eyes at night, and open them once again, first thing in the morning? Does she? I just want to scream, but it'll do no good, because she doesn't even see me lately. She has acted like I am secondary to everyone and everything else, and I hear her. I hear her.

When I finish picking up the pieces that dropped from her fingertips, I open the back door, walk out onto the patio, and drop to my knees. I just want to be away from here. I want to be back where I have a chance to create my own existence as I want it. A place where I have some control, but some surprises as well. My dreams seem to give me more understanding than my reality, and I need that. I need to know there are some things I have a say in, and that people understand my opinions, and know I am struggling as well to grasp things. I haven't slept in weeks, and neither has my wife. We are in this together, yet I am feeling so alone.

The yard needs a cut. The weeds that I pick each time the rain allows them to coexist with the flowers I purposefully planted, are invading my beds. The yard looks as if I haven't touched it in weeks and weeks, and I know that is so unlike me to let it get to this point. First thing tomorrow, I am getting out here and handling this. I'm ashamed I let it get this far to begin with, and perhaps this is part of Amanda's frustration. That I have let so much go. That, despite what we are dealing with, I have let go of so many things that brought us a sense of peace.

Damnit. I just…I just want a sense of my old world and life back, and here I am feeling so detached from what we have known for so many blissful years together. How did this happen so suddenly? How, when life was so normal and accepted, did everything change without my approval? Without my input into what I wanted, and what I needed for my family?

There is a sense of pride people have when they complete a task, whether the task be small, or something grander. There is a different sense of pride a man gets from being a father, and a different sense a woman gets from being a mother. Most times, nowadays, both parents take on similar roles, which is much different from the time my parents and their parents were raising children.

Today, my wife can easily cut the grass if she chose to, and I can prepare a dinner for the entire squad if I felt the desire to. We have some older traditional roles, but not because we feel that is how things need to operate. It's more because we gravitated that way from the time we first married. We took on those roles, and never questioned them, really. More often, we knew our place and accepted that, but within the past year or so, we've crossed over several times, to where we switch jobs without knowing it readily.

I'm feeling as if she is trying too hard. She's doing so many of the things I have done and blaming me for not doing more of what she has typically done. I struggle with that greatly. I know I do, but give me a break. Give me time to adapt. Give me time to find my level of acceptance with what Agnes is working through.

Agnes has decided on her own, that she will not lose her hair to the treatment. She will control that part of her life and remove her hair on her terms. When you talk about strong people, you think of body builders, or firemen, or nurses who see people suffer daily, and find a way to keep going back anyway. That's strength. You don't realize, until the moment hits you, that your children are so much more resilient than we give them credit for.

Had you asked me a year ago, how Agnes would handle the loss of her hair, I would have said terribly. I would have said she would have fought to keep those locks and looked to me for a solution in order to keep them.

Not now. She's not afraid, for some reason. She has handled this entire situation better than I would have been able to, and she's doing it with a determination I have seen from no one, ever.

As the moment approaches, and Agnes is seated in the plush chair where her mother is preparing to cut her hair from the top of her head, I am standing alone in a corner, turned away, because I am not sure I can watch this. To be honest, I am so glad no one asked me to do this. I don't know if I would be able to, and still keep things calm and playful, the way Agnes prefers it to be. In fact, I am sure I would not be able to.

My baby Agnes. My sweet, innocent, loving child. Why am I unable to take this from you? Why is it we don't get to decide who will take the burden on, and who will go free from that same burden? Because even though I know this would probably kill me, I would take it from her. I would without hesitation, take all this pain and uncertainty from my child, and suffer through this with a smile. Because that is what daddies do. At least, it's what we would do if we had any say.

"Mom, don't cry, okay? Remember, we are going to laugh when you are done, and pick out a wig in any color I chose, even if it's rainbow. You promised me that, remember?" Agnes says.

Amanda has the clippers in her hand, and Agnes has

asked that Andrew be there as well. She has a strong bond with Uncle Andy, so I get it. It makes sense to me that she would want his cheerful personality nearby. He probably doesn't understand why she's removing her hair, and that makes this perfect.

"Uncle Dew, come closer," Agnes says, reaching out for his hand.

Then, with little hesitation, Amanda gives a soft, warm smile to Agnes, tilts her head, closes her eyes for just a moment, and then turns on the clippers. The sound sends shivers up and down my spine because I am aware of what is happening. I know what to expect, but not how to expect to feel. There's a big difference in those. One allows you to prepare, and the other gives you butterflies, wondering what will transpire.

"Agnes, I love you. I love your spirit, and your strength. And I love that you teach me when I think I am teaching you. You are showing me in this moment, more than I have shown you in your life. Thank you. Thank you, my sweet Agnes," Amanda says.

The clippers touch her hair, and tiny locks start to drop to the floor below. I watch those pieces, more than I do the act of the removal. It's too much for me to bare, but the locks falling, symbolize a change in seasons for her. Her hair, just past the skin, is already dead. The falling strands remove the dead cells from her body, but not from her spirit. She's letting go of something that has let go already, despite what we feel.

Over and over, Amanda runs the blades back and forth, and up and down. She's gentle, but she's not allowing for time to affect her. If she hesitates, she breaks down. If she continues in motion, she knows she will finish this and not allow it to affect her until she has completed the task she's been given.

The moment she is finished, she places the clippers down to her side, and smiles at Agnes. Agnes has had her eyes closed the entire time. Partially to keep the hair from falling into her eyes, and partially because she wants to imagine in this moment that she is not here, but somewhere else, doing whatever it is she wishes.

She opens her eyes, and sees her mom smiling at her, with watery eyes she cannot hide any longer.

"Mom, how does it look? Does it look like I need a colorful wig? Because remember, you promised me any one I wanted!" Agnes says.

As I am watching, I'm becoming aware that Agnes is sensing her mother's struggle with this and creating a type of levity to help her mother through this moment. That's how she is. Worrying more about others than she does herself. It's making my eyes water, but I still have not looked her way. I am trying to let her concentrate on one broken parent at a time. If she sees me crying as well, it may set her back and make her feel ashamed.

Andrew is smiling and giddy. He's looking at Agnes, and the joy he has, for some strange reason, is energetic. I can't explain how I feel watching him, but I know I feel something truly special. He may not get this all, but he gets enough of this. That I am sure of.

His bag is held tightly to his chest, and slowly he opens his arms enough to pull something out.

He hands Agnes a figurine. It's blue in color, and features a man standing tall over a child, with a dress that seems to be about 3 sizes too big for her. The same figurine I purchased for Andrew years ago when I first met him, is now in his outstretched hand. I can't believe he still has that. It was just a simple thing he saw and wanted, and although it's interesting for sure, I never expected him to keep it. I figured he would break it over time, and his parents would toss it in the garbage when cleaning his room.

But it's here, and more magnificent and meaningful than I remember.

I finally muster the courage to look at my Agnes, and I can see a smile from ear to ear. Her hair is clean off, and she's not bothering with that at all. She's so consumed by this small statue her uncle is passing to her, and this moment in time has helped me accept what I could not.

"Uncle Dew, thank you! It's so pretty! Is this for me to keep?" Agnes asks.

Andrew nods in a silly way, but it's enough to tell her that yes, it is indeed for her.

She takes it from his hand, and places it against her body, holding it gently, but securely. I am poking my head out from the corner, trying to get a glimpse of this figure, as I remember it, although not well. I know it was of two people, but I did forget that those two people were of a man and child. That the child is looking up to her father, and the father is smiling, looking down on her.

It reminds me of Agnes and I, as she has always looked at me like her hero. In that instance, things changed. I felt relaxed and accepted, with no words needed to be spoken. Just a gesture, an acceptance, and an understanding were all I needed, and I saw it with my brother-in-law and daughter. It did not matter that it wasn't directed at me, because it was still about me. It's a lesson I learned that day. I am meaningful and I matter, even if you don't tell me I am. I still am.

Once that moment has passed, Agnes stands up, and walks over to the mirror in our foyer area. She wants to see what she looks like with no hair for the first time since birth.

When she arrives in front of the mirror, she hesitates only for a second, and then takes a deep breath in, and opens her eyes. As she stares with no expression on her face, I wonder what it is that is going through her head. Is she scared? Is she embarrassed? The waiting for her words is the worst. It's agonizing. Then she opens her mouth and speaks finally,

"Teal green. That is the color wig I shall have. It's settled," she said.

And just as she gets those words out of her mouth, she hears that familiar sound of those shears that moments ago cut her hair from the top of her head, and she turns to see why.

In the chair she was seated in, now sits Andrew. He has

asked his sister Amanda to cut his hair just the same way as she did to Agnes. Amanda is now crying, finally letting go of her emotions, but she's also so proud of her brother, and she agrees to do as she just had done to her daughter. Andrew is smiling and sitting very still. As her hair did, his falls too to the floor as his legs kick back and forth. He has not a care on his face and seems to be enjoying this moment quite well.

With each pass, I can see the sadness drain from Amanda's face. Her tears aren't of sadness. They are of pure joy, knowing that family has once again created a bond that is simply unbreakable. It came from a source no one would have expected, except maybe Agnes. She seems to know something about Andrew that the rest of us have still to figure out.

Chapter 23

Learning to Let Go

* * *

Once again, I find myself drifting off into a sleep, and I feel myself back on the ledge of the mountain that has become my home away from home. It's a place where I can think, and be alone, for the most part, anyway.

Sometimes I find that Harold is back to pay me a visit, and other times I see people coming through the gate below, but I rarely head back down to see who they are anymore. I figure that if they are looking for me, they will find me on that ledge. Otherwise, maybe they aren't there for me.

Gradually, I have come to accept that I will have an ability to see what I want, but not entirely. It's a balance here. I get a sense that there are things meant for me, and other things not meant for me, or maybe just not at the present time.

Time. It's something I seem to not worry about while

I dream, and that's fine by me. When I am awake, everything is constantly about time. There are appointments, and schedules to keep. Soccer games and stores that close before I've finished my shopping. My parents, who are now retired, still must worry somewhat about time. They are up bright and early, have their coffee, but before they can head out, they need to take a look at the time to see if the person or people they are visiting with will be up yet.

But here? Here, I am not concerned with that at all. I can sit here for as long as I like, and I don't feel that sudden pressure to look at my phone, or the pressure to finish up so that I may move on to the next thing I have on my list. Here, I am simply without the element of time, and for a change, it's extremely calming.

It's mostly sunny here in my dream, but occasionally, I notice a rain come through, which wets the area and then quickly heads off into a new direction, leaving no damage and no real change in temperature. It's warm here, with only a slight breeze from the east, which is just the way I like it. I imagine you don't ever feel cold or hot in your dreams. Of all the dreams I have had thus far, I cannot recall one where I felt temperature that made me feel uncomfortable or unsafe.

The birds that sing just above me never seem to sleep either, and it never grows dark, but I don't feel tired, so that's just fine with me. I remind myself that for every night I sleep, I probably have a hundred different dreams take place, but remember very few, if any. So this dream is probably happening over the course of twenty seconds at the most, but I don't notice. It's as if I am to forget time while I visit here, and focus on the moment, rather than the time in that moment.

Sometimes I catch myself hearing a new sound below, and I look towards the black gate to see if it's open or not. Harold never seems to visit unless the gate is cracked open at least a little, although I don't know why, because he could simply fly over the top of the gate, which is maybe four feet high, and it wouldn't seem odd at all. In fact, it's stranger that he needs the gate open to visit. I would ask him, but for as much as he seems to understand me, I have yet to learn to speak pigeon.

I do find that I am not anxious here, and I've learned each time that I visit to look around more at my surroundings. While I feel a draw to those birds singing still, it's not as intense as it once was. I am content sitting here and studying the grassy plains below. Sometimes I see a waterfall and hear the water as it hits the river below, and sometimes it's not there.

The thing that is a constant, though, is this mountain and that gate. They are here no matter what else is here or not here. Those two things are a staple and I'm glad, because one gives me a peace I have been yearning for, and the other, a sense of excitement and wonderment.

Lately, when I am visiting this curious place in my slumber, I try not to wake as I know I will eventually. The calmness and the serenity of my situation is almost too good to be true and sitting here is not like I am doing nothing at all, but I feel more as if I am accomplishing a goal that I had no idea existed within me, and the ledge seems to be providing the vehicle for that.

At some point in my dreams, I see high above the grass, a vision. It's coming into focus now, and I begin to see a doorway to my past. The clearer it becomes, the more I understand that my mind, my dreams, are sharing with me some of the most important times in my life. It has captured my undivided attention, and as I sit there, just allowing whatever to come across the screen, I'm sure I will be surprised as well by what my unconscious finds to be important.

There are moments when I was just a little boy, riding my dark, maroon bike through new neighborhoods, along with my two brothers. We ride as if we are a thousand miles from home, yet looking back now, I realize we were much closer than we realized. It wasn't the distance that was important, but the idea that we did this as brothers that was. I see that here and now, and a smile grows across my face. I am glad I spent those younger years chasing streets and neighborhoods, without realizing where we were. It allowed us to bond in ways kids today don't. I need to call my brothers when I wake and thank them for that.

Birthday parties are apparently strong memories for me as well, because I can see those as if I am right there again. Watching my mother work so hard to make the invites, and to ensure everyone feels welcomed, is something I missed while enjoying my time. I thought the party was about me, and celebrating my birthday, but it wasn't. I now understand that it was about what others saw in me and wanted for me, and the sacrifices they made to make sure I knew. My mother looks tired, but she never allowed me to see that. I would have never thought she was so run-down at times because she would never allow me to get that from her. How did I miss that?

My father and I are sitting on the rear steps to our house, and I am asking him if he's going to go to my ball game this time. He's missed so many events in my life, and I always tried to understand why, but felt hurt when he never made it to the stands. Then I see my father struggling with work, and he's pushing through a nasty mistake that he made, causing him to question his own life. There, I see him fighting back tears as he drops down, wondering if he is good enough. I never saw that side of my father. He was always the strong type that doesn't allow you in too close.

Then, I see my first date with Amanda. Wow, she looks so incredible and so full of flavor for life. Her smile shines through the entire time we are together, and although I am sure I noticed that at the time, I forgot so many of those simple smiles over the years.

I watch her as she is playing with her brother at a younger age, much before I met her. She's frustrated with him but trying her best to grasp that it's out of his control. I have only seen the side of her where she has the patience of a blooming flower that waits for the right time to pop.

But she struggled. A lot. She struggled. It makes me wonder now, how many times has she struggled with things and just never told anyone? Has she been struggling with me and just refusing to let me in on that?

I watch my children, Erik, Dot, and Agnes, playing around one afternoon, and Agnes is making Erik wear one of her princess dresses. He's laughing about it, as are Amanda and I, but I notice that when we aren't watching, and he has no eyes upon him, he's looking in the mirror, and he's feeling good about what he sees. This seems to confuse him, and he starts to fight with himself over how he is feeling now. I have never noticed a single time when Erik seemed confused by how he felt, but now, looking back and watching things as they were, I begin to think to myself about it. He has enjoyed the time with his sisters, where he can be whatever he wishes, and they have no judgement for him or for how he wishes to play. Did I simply overlook who my boy is?

I feel no need to judge either while I am sitting here. Nothing seems to be causing me pain, or anguish. I feel as if I am finding the small details in life I missed while awake and understand now that I need to pay much more attention to those things. More than I ever have. Life is moving at a pace that continues to speed up as we get older, and I am more worried about the things that do not define my journey, instead of allowing the things I miss to shape me as they should.

I know one thing for sure. I will not allow that to happen

again. I pray that I will be able to remember all of this when I wake and remember the feeling I have at this very moment, so that I carry that through the rest of my trip.

When I am thinking my vision is about to close, and the view is starting to fade, I see there is one last one waiting for me. It's of the night I walked in to make those root beer banana floats for the kids. The one where Andrew has spread out his papers on the counter where we eventually ate together.

Andrew, at least here in my thoughts, has a talent I have never known, nor would have guessed in a million years. I see sketches of figures and landscapes, that you would see a full-grown adult artist make. There are pages and pages of notes and stories, and here I had no idea he could even write more than his own name.

This vision allows me to see closer, and there is Agnes, looking through all those papers, smiling as if she knows some big secret, but knows that it is hers and Andrew's alone. It's as if she knows that Andrew does not want the added attention and prefers to keep this masterful secret all to himself, except for allowing Agnes into his world.

Agnes looks at one closer than the others, and she stares at it, trying to figure out what he has drawn. I lean in some as well to get a better view of what she's trying to see.

I almost fall off the ledge, as it comes into view. On the paper is a full-scale drawing of my place. Not the place I live, but the place I created here, and dream in. He has the strange, metal gate down below, and the grassy fields throughout the valley. The mountain is a spitting image of where I am seated now, and there, halfway up, is a silhouette of a man, perched on the ledge, looking down below. The man is watching as the gate is opened, and a figure has one hand out, but the rest of their body just to the other side.

The man has words above his head, and as I read them, I come out of my dream, and I am once again, sitting next to Agnes in her bedroom.

I look quickly to check on Agnes first, and when I see she is still sleeping a peacefully as possible, considering, I refocus my thoughts onto the dream, to see if I indeed took with me all I wanted to, and have it here with me now.

I run through the thoughts at the ledge and remember the gate down below. I can almost hear the song the birds were singing above, and I can smell the gentle air and tall grass around me and below me. The visions I had about my past, are there in my head still. I can remember watching myself as a child, and my parents as they tried to ensure I had what was needed, even if they didn't always understand what I needed.

I can see Amanda, just as she was all those years prior to having our three children, and how different our lives were, with pressure that really wasn't as much as we made it out to be. Struggling in my parents' basement seemed so different then, than it would now. But it was what we knew, and so to us, it was a difficult time.

I walked out of the room, and over to where our bedroom

is, and see my wife sleeping on the edge of the bed, with the sheet she is using to cover herself, stained with the tears she was crying just before she fell asleep. Next to her hands is our framed wedding photo that has sat on her nightstand for years. I look at it and remember that day well. How young we were, but how we felt like full grown adults because we were allowed to make these big decisions about the rest of our lives. I remember feeling as if things would never get better than that day, and a feeling that I had to enjoy each second of the wedding and reception, because it would be gone before we knew it.

I look so young there, and she? Well, she looks just as beautiful to me as she does now. I have always found my wife to be attractive. Mostly always. There was that short time where I felt I may have been questioning the whole being married thing, but that went by naturally, and I knew I still was in love with her.

She has music on lightly in the background, I'm sure to relax her, but it's turned down enough to also ensure she can still hear Agnes if she needs her. Although, I am here as well, so I can help when she needs me to, and Amanda can just sleep as long as she needs to sleep.

I touch her on the head gently and smile as I stand up, and head out of our bedroom and into the hallway once again. From here, I decide to walk into both of our other children's rooms.

Dot's room is full of dolls and small toys that have lost more parts than they now have left, and things are in order, but a bit chaotic, nonetheless. Her bed is nicely made, and a blanket that her mum-mum made for her lays across the middle. She rarely goes to bed without clutching her favorite blanket.

In Erik's room, there are cars and trucks and sports stickers on the wall, and I am wondering, are we pushing him to act as we expect him to act, or does he really enjoy the room he has? I feel as if I need to sit down with him at some point, and ask him, what is it that HE wants? Does he want all the sports and blue and cars and all of that in his room, or would he prefer something different? We have never asked him, and after my dream, I feel as if I have missed an opportunity to let him tell me who he is, not who I think he is.

The house is so quiet, and peaceful. I know it won't be for long, but for now it is, and I am soaking it in. I hardly ever take the time to ponder on the lives of my children, outside of what is readily known, but I am doing that now. I'm laughing to myself, because I have spent so much time trying to be the dad everyone thinks I should be, and little time being the dad I need to be. There is a massive difference, and I am so ready to be that father from this point on. My kids and my beautiful wife are going to see a different season of who I am, and I could not be more excited.

I also will view Andrew in a different light. One where I see him as so much more gifted than I have, and more capable of things that I understand now. If what I saw in my dreams is true and accurate, than Andrew is going to shock a lot of people if, and when, he is ever ready to share. For now though, I won't let on that I know his secret. I will just sit back and know he is so much better than I have given him credit for, but that will change. I'll give him the credit he deserves, and secretly wish he decides to share his talents with others.

Besides, if he has captured the exact place I have dreamt of several times without me ever muttering a word to anyone about it, there is something more to him than we could possibly understand. That is both a little scary, and a lot of a blessing.

His words that he carefully wrote above the photo are still with me. I still can see them plain as day, even though I am awake from that time.

I am going nowhere and will wait until you are ready. Take your time. I shall wait.

Chapter 24

Thank God for Chase

* * *

Watching children being treated for conditions like cancer, tumors, and anything that is life-altering, is terribly difficult. You see such small, beautiful souls fighting something they know so little about, if anything at all, and they are forced to accept their fate.

On our trips to the hospital, Agnes feels awkward at first, having her hair removed while all her friends around her still get to keep theirs, but eventually, she grows to see that there are so many other children who are just like her, and she gains an appreciation she did not expect to gain.

She's come to know the nurses well, and even some of the patients being treated for various illnesses as she is. Some of the kids are a lot younger than she is, and a few are older. Some have been going to treatments for only a few weeks, while others have been battling this for most of their young lives.

I watch these children as they smile through pain I could not imagine, and yet, they still have a zest for life like no other. It reminds me that those who seemingly have it all figured out, the ones who post non-stop about their happiness for everyone else to see, could learn from children like these. Just as the ones who complain incessantly about their day's problems, or the price of things going up, have yet to understand the true measure and value of life. It's not in finding the fault in the simple things around us, but in finding the positives in all the hurtful experiences we live through, and always looking forward.

Chase is one of those inspiring children. He's just a year older than Agnes, and at the age of thirteen, he's become somewhat of an ambassador to this place and those that pass through its anxious doors.

You can't walk the halls without knowing that Chase is something special and has a gift that he understands well. For those children that are just toddlers, he treats as if they are the only ones there, and guides them to a place of acceptance, even when he knows they should not accept this fate. Maybe he knows that the more they accept what it is they cannot change, the clearer they will see when things are right in front of them.

For those kids closer to his age, he never allows them to feel as if what they are going through is meant to be easy. Chase knows that each person is struggling in ways he cannot completely understand, despite the fact he is struggling as well.

"We all look at things from different perspectives, and we all feel pain and emotions at different levels, but that doesn't mean we aren't the same," he tells Agnes.

Agnes takes a liking to Chase and quickly seeks him out each time we bring her in for her treatment. It's like he was sent from God himself, to suffer as others are, but to teach like others need to be taught through his suffering. His balance in life is amazing, but he's still very sick indeed, and the nurses are growing more concerned as each passing day goes by, like the wind forcing its way through a storm.

If he were to leave, they know that the children in their care would find being so positive difficult beyond what they already feel. He brings them a sense of hope they need and have come to admire. Hope is something we all share, but don't all understand. If you know that hope exists for the purpose of granting you what it is you are after, and that it is truly possible, then hope is a blessing. For those, however, that want to believe their hope is real, but know that their struggle is coming to an end, and they will be moving on from here, hope is a shot in the dark. It's something they understand is real, but feel that for them, it is no longer valid. That shouldn't stop them from having some though.

For Agnes, she's still very new to this, so her hope level is off the charts. She doesn't feel she will get better. She knows she will. Having had little experience with death, she cannot grasp the idea of not being who she is, and not walking around as we do today. Her mindset is not on dying, but how long she will need to wait until her hair will grow back, or how many more times she will need to have nights where she vomits more than she doesn't. She cares about being "normal" again.

It's not about being afraid to die for her, but about being afraid to live.

These are the times where I want to pick her up, as I did when I carried her into the doctor's office when we first knew something was off, and not let her down until she is fully healed. I want to let her know that she isn't fighting this alone, and that whatever, literally whatever I need to do, I will.

The issue is, though, I have nothing to offer her. Can I tell my child that she's going to be just fine? Can I? How can I on one hand tell her to embrace this because it's temporary, when I don't know myself? This is new to all of us, and I am at a loss for where to begin helping her.

I see Amanda struggle like never before, and she's the stronger of the two of us, so what does that tell me? It tells me, I am not going to be good at this, so I should prepare myself for failure, not my child's failure, but my own. Where I will give her pep talks and try to not act concerned. The more concerned I act, the more Agnes is going to know my faith is waning. I can't have her see that from me, or else she will lose the faith she is going to need to fight this nasty disease.

Chase is going to be the spirit I need to lift me up enough so that I can be of use to my daughter. I'm going to watch him and learn from him as he navigates his own impending crisis with a style unlike any other I've seen. Most people that I have come across in my life are strong, until they have a reason to not be. Men who normally are cool and calm, find out they need a simple surgery, and they panic. Women who seem to defy the odds when sickness travels through an entire household, can get nervous for a multitude of reasons, and all are considered certainly good reasons for concern.

This child, though, Chase? I am not sure if he has given up and accepted his fate, and therefore wants to live out the remainder of his days enjoying life rather than fighting with it, or if he is simply not accepting what those around him are telling him his fate is. Maybe he just doesn't care what he's told, because he hasn't resolved to the fact that he is losing this battle.

Either way, I know Agnes could use Chase around her, especially now that I am struggling with what to tell her and what not to.

One of her nurses here, a woman named Pamela Dunking, is just as much a God-send as Chase. She's the one who is most involved with our Agnes, and she, too, has a sense of style unlike most. Her brightly colored outfits and her bright pink shaded hair, make her stand out, but that's not the reason Agnes enjoys her. She has such a gentle nature, while never allowing others to tell her that she needed to mature in the way others have. Her mindset is such that she believes she has matured just as much as others, but in her own, unique way. She enjoys a different view of the world than most see, but she doesn't see that as different. She sees it as the way she is intended to be.

Pamela can be found singing out of tune, or dancing from one station to the next most days we are here. In fact, I find myself hoping that she is on call when it's our time to visit. I get a joy out of watching her be exactly who she wants to be, and I learn from her. I learn that I need to allow Agnes, Erik, and Dot, to grow into the people they are meant to be, even if it's hard for me to watch. Even if I cannot begin to understand the why and how of it all, because I am certain they were not meant to be as I envisioned them to be.

Although Agnes is drained most days, she and Chase and Nurse Pamela have become somewhat of a group while here. The way Agnes doesn't allow others to alter her feelings, makes it so that she fits right in with them, and it's created an atmosphere of hope for not only Agnes, but for her mother and I as well.

Weeks go by and I've had the chance to visit my dreams on several occasions, and each time I do, I feel as if I am understanding it all much clearer than I had in the beginning. I'm getting a strange feeling that this is how things are supposed to play themselves out, and that while I struggle watching Agnes go through what she is dealing with, there is a reason beyond my understanding. I'm most likely never going to fully grasp that knowledge to accept it entirely, but I feel relaxed more than I normally would be.

Chase seems to have a strong mother, but his father is the one I find the interesting one to me. Him and I find ourselves talking during the visits over coffee, and we find that we have a lot more in common with each other than most people I've come across. He is further along than I am in the acceptance department and can clearly see that from his perspective. He offers me comforting words, even if he's a little rough around the edges. It's not how he says it that matters, but the strength behind what it is he says that stands out to me. His confidence is rock solid, and although he knows Chase is nearing the end of his battle, he's aware that a greater good is coming for his son. A plus one.

"Chase is a great kid. I can't thank you enough for sharing him with us and with Agnes especially. He's the reason that she stands a chance at pushing on, because she sees how well he handles everything," I say.

His father, Dominick, smiles as he takes another sip from his coffee cup, and looks over to where Agnes is lying, talking with one of the nurses.

"You have a beautiful child there, Jon. She's a fighter for sure. Chase would not have a gift if others didn't need what he has. We only gift what others are willing to take, so I thank you and your Agnes just the same," Dominick replies.

"Dominick, can I ask you a question?"

After a few weeks of chatting with this man, I notice a similarity in how we are here. He doesn't seem to speak with his wife much, and seems so disconnected at times, but he talks about her to me as if there is no one better suited for him. I begin to wonder if it's the situation that causes parents to pull away from each other, and maybe this will bring me some answers as to the why of how Amanda and I seem to be.

"I find myself seeing things from the outside in. What I mean to say is, I find that I am disconnected from things that once I played such a massive role in. It's as if I am afraid to offer help, maybe from fear. Fear of being wrong, fear of hurting someone's feelings, or fear of telling someone they are going to be okay when I honestly don't know..." I ask as my mind trails off.

Dominick laughs and pats me on the shoulder hard. He's a larger man, and I am not sure he understands his own strength, but he means well.

"Jon, if I can tell you one thing, it's this. Whatever we decide to say or not say, and whatever we mean with the words we eventually do speak, life is happening, and so is death. One we can manipulate enough to get us through, and the other we must learn to accept more than we would like to. Both, though, are blessings. You do the best you can, and when everything lands where it needs to, you will realize you understood more than you expected to," Dominick responds.

His words are hitting me hard, and although I understand what he is saying, I also feel that this man has accepted that his son is about to die, and he's okay with it. I don't quite understand how he can sit there and be okay with it, but I realize he is not living as I do, and maybe he just has no choice but to accept it.

Agnes is so new to this fight, and the thought of her dying is the furthest thing from my mind, because I cannot begin to think about that potential outcome. It's about holding on for me, by not letting go. Dominick has held on for years to the hope that his son would pull through and be the miracle he needed him to be. When things started to slip away from that reality, he was forced to accept something he never wanted to.

My wife and his wife have also become close friends while here, and I can tell you, Amanda needed this. She needed to know that other parents understood how she felt and why she was confused. She had to know that while she did not want anyone else to experience what she was, that there was a strange comfort in knowing she was not alone.

Dominick and I watch as the two women talk, laugh, and cry together. We don't interrupt because this is a bonding between these two mothers who were forced to be stronger than they should ever need to be, and they are embracing it together.

For us, we are bonding in a different way, but it's a bond between two fathers from different backgrounds, finding a common acceptance that we too, never imagined we would need to.

On my way out that one afternoon, just as Amanda is packing up the bag of things Agnes brought with her, and the items the nurses made with Agnes while there, Dominick pulls me aside and the look in his eyes seems pretty serious.

"Dominick, you okay?" I ask.

"Hey Jon. I'm fine. Listen, I wanted to talk with you about something, and I wanted to wait as long as I could, but now I am out of time, and this needs to happen today," he begins.

For a man so strong and serious, he has a look of both concern, but in a strange way, acceptance in his eyes. He continues as I pay close attention to his words,

"I'm going to stop coming to these appointments. It's time I do. I cannot explain it right now, Jon, but I need you to know, I am proud of you. I know this isn't easy, but I promise, you will find an understanding that you cannot find yet. I've enjoyed our chats, and wish you the very best, for both you and Amanda, as well as little Agnes. She's a tough kid, and no doubt, she's going to give this hell. That much I am sure of."

With that, he gives me a strong hug, and I watch as he leaves through the doorway, following out his wife and Chase, and just like that, they are gone.

I'm stunned for a few moments, trying to figure out what he meant by that all. Did he mean that he and his wife were separating and maybe she felt it best he not come anymore with her there? Did he mean to tell me that Chase was going to another hospital for treatment, but he somehow could not find the right words to tell me? Maybe he meant that for as strong and well as he seemingly handles this, that deep inside he was struggling just too much, and was unable to watch as Chase dissolved away, from the boy they had brought into this world and raised so lovingly?

Whatever it was, I was stunned and saddened. Dominick was an addition to this struggle that I needed, and now, he too, was gone. I felt as if I was slowly losing so much around me, and it saddened me.

But I know I still need to be strong and remain here for Agnes, and that even though my friend is not going to be there to encourage me to push on and give me words of wisdom that sometimes I understood, while other times I had to take those home with me and really see what he meant by them, I can do this. I can be strong for my family because that is my job.

As we leave, I turn around to look at this place that has felt like a second home, even though the time we have been here has been extremely short in comparison to that of, and I smile. I smile because this is a place for hope, and through all the struggles and pain and death and despair, it remains a place of hope for so many, including us. We have hope and that is not going to change.

Chapter 25

A Visitor

* * *

My place, the place I dream of so many times, over and over again, is growing. I find that sections where there once were the simplest of things, are changing each time I am back.

The grassy fields are still down below, but now there is a gentle river that flows through the valley, with a wooden bridge spanning from one side to the other, and stone covered banks on either side, with soft, rainbow blankets spread across the pebbles below. On the sand that divides the pebbles from the water, I see plates and cups, and a basket that resembles something you would take on a picnic.

The temperature still has not changed, but if I look hard enough, I can see snow falling far to the east, and I begin to wonder if that snow would feel cold, or just as it does here now. I cannot imagine snow being warm, but then again, I can't imagine how this place has come from just the thoughts I have when sleeping.

When I wander around the mountain more, first a little to the left, then some to the right, I realize there is a back to the area I am resting on. It appears as if I can journey in both directions and would then be able to see more off into the distance in other ways I cannot see from my current perspective.

I'm worried if I venture too far, though, I may miss something I am supposed to be waiting for. That sounds strange, but it's a strong feeling I have, that I am here waiting for a sign, or for something to share with me the meaning behind my dreams. So, I am weary, but curious at the same time.

I finally decide that maybe if I go just a short distance and then return, I won't miss anything important, and besides, I should be able to see for a good distance before I head too far out. But I need to figure out in which direction to travel first, left or right.

I hear some noise to the right and turn my head to investigate where it's coming from. There's a line of trees I need to navigate around, but it's not too bad. The trees are maybe a story and a half high, with the most beautiful, green leaves with a slight touch of red on the end of every branch. They look as if they have never been disturbed, and that perhaps a storm has never reached this area, because they are just perfectly there.

Behind the trees, I come in contact with some elk, and I think back to when I first arrived here and saw those creatures down below. They are now up where I am seated, and no longer eating the grass I saw them constantly chewing on before. They are standing there, looking down towards the same black gate I have admired for some time, and appear to be waiting as well.

When I look down below over the green, tall, swaying grass, and out to where the gate is, I notice that it is once again opened just a bit and I grow ever the more curious about the why behind that. It's been opened a few times for sure, but this time, I don't feel it calling me. I feel as if that gate doesn't need me to know if it's opened or closed, but because I see these animals watching, I sit down again and watch along with them.

They seem to not care that I am close by, but I still do my best not to disturb them while they wait. I shall just wait with them patiently, until they see what they are after, or move on from the ledge.

Because time doesn't seem to matter here, I am unaware of how much is going by, if any. I like that feeling of not being in a rush, because when I am awake, everything is rushed, and people always seem in a panic. Here? There is no rush and there is no panic. Only a sense that when something needs to happen, it precisely does.

The leaves on the trees start to dance a little, as a breeze comes in to disturb them just enough to catch their attention. I bet Agnes would ask a dozen or so questions about these leaves and why they are dancing as they are. She never seems to run out of her curiosity, and I love that about her.

I hear the largest of the elk make an odd noise at something below, and I quickly look down to see what is happening. Down below, I can see a smaller elk, just at the foot of the mountain, crying up to where we all are. This Elk is looking for a way up and begins to put one hoof in front of the other, until it finds a steady enough pace to calm it down. The other Elk are not moving, as if they know this little one needs to complete this journey on its own. It's fascinating, sitting there and watching this all take place in my dream, but it feels so incredibly real.

At some point, I see the creature lift its head just enough that the ones waiting are able to see. A tear forms in the corner of my eye, and I feel a sense of accomplishment, even though I had nothing to do with this. Maybe I am just feeling happy for this little guy, or girl, for having completed the journey to this point. The pride it must feel has to be enormous.

When they are all back together on that road leading around the entire mountain, they smell each other, and the entire bunch seem perfectly content, as if they were awaiting this exact moment for some time, and now, it's finally here.

Then, without notice, they all start to ascend again up the mountain, looking back only once to see if I am following, or staying put. I am surely not following, because I am not part of that journey. I am here where I belong, but they apparently have more searching to do, so I wave goodbye, realizing I am waving at wild animals, but they seem to understand regardless, and send a gentle nod back towards my way.

I feel a slight bit of loneliness when they are gone, even though I had been alone for the most part while here. Just something felt right about that act, and I feel as if I am missing something great. It's a struggle for sure, but I know when I wake up once again, I will be back home, with my wife and children, and this place will be just as it has been for me, a dream and nothing more.

There are options I still have though. I can walk back to where I have sat for the most part when I am here, or I can continue to walk some and explore the place a bit more. I decide, it's probably good to see what else I may find along the way. And so I continue on the path of perfectly placed trees.

As I walk, I am going through my head, thinking about all that has happened over the course of my life. The fun times with my brothers as a young boy, and the marriage I yearned for, and have had, for the last dozen or so years. There are memories of when I broke my arm and my father, who was not always the most sympathetic person, came to my aid, and actually shed a tear, knowing how much pain I was in. I think about my children, and the births of each, and how truly magnificent those times were for us all. I think about Agnes, with the struggle she has been dealing with, and the people whom we never would have known, aiding us to ensure we had all the support we would need.

These thoughts make me both happy and sad for the same reason. I love the fact that I have had all these experiences in my life and wonder what other experiences I will have as I continue that life. Will I ever stop visiting this place in my dreams? Will this place just cease from existence, and will I go back to dreams that mean nothing, or make no sense whatsoever? I hope that that does not happen. I've enjoyed this place in my subconscious and would be saddened to have that disappear forever.

A few hundred yards from where I began this walk, I turn around and see that below me, through the clouds that have formed just below the ledge, a figure staring up from the opened gate. The figure is hardly recognizable because of the distance away, but I can tell it's not a full-grown adult. The way in which it walks gives a lot away. It's walking with a strong purpose towards the base of the mountain, and once it arrives, I can see that this person is looking up, waving at something high above.

My eyes turn sharply around, but it's too hard to see around the many trees I have passed, so I have no idea as to what it is I am looking at, but it seems to be heading towards that spot. My spot.

As this figure starts the climb, I begin to walk back, slow and steady at first, then more briskly as I gain an excitement to see what is happening. I feel no fear, just excitement running through my veins the closer I get. But the trees are once more swaying in the wind, and my path is getting harder to navigate.

The figure below is now out of sight, just around a bend in the road leading to the first peak. I'm rushing as best I can, but I seem to keep stumbling as I work myself past the trees, as if the mountain doesn't want me advancing any quicker than I am.

Finally, I reach the spot where I saw the figure waving towards, but no one is there. No one is standing on the ledge, and no one is climbing the path, leading to the spot. Below, the gate is once again closed, and I see no one. Not a single soul out there, anywhere.

Again, I feel saddened and alone, wondering what I missed by having to be as curious as I was. If I had not been so, I could have seen what was coming and who was standing here, and possibly learned more about this place of mine. Or maybe it's not mine. Maybe this is someone else's dream and mine combined, and we crossed paths by mistake somehow. But now I will never know.

As I am collapsing to the ground in frustration, I hear the birds above singing up a storm. They are louder than before and seem to be quite excited for some reason. I don't wish to see why, because I am upset with myself now, but I decide what could I lose by looking to see? Well, other than a moment like I just lost. That is what I stand to lose, but at this point, I don't bother to care.

Above me, when I focus my eyes to the ledge, I see a man and a boy reaching the second peak, and when they do, they both turn and wave to me in a way that someone who knows you and is excited to see you waves. It's apparent they know me, but I cannot see them with the bright sun invading my eyes. I try to use my hand to block it out, but as I do, they are over the ledge, and onto wherever they are heading. They, too, are now gone.

I scream as loud as humanly possible, but no one replies. I am screaming at the top of my lungs, and there is no one there to hear me. It makes no difference how upset I am, and so I start to laugh. I laugh because I want to wake now and get back to Agnes. I laugh because I find it funny how I am feeling so down and out, and this is not even real. It's a dream, and so I laugh.

I begin to tell myself over and over to wake up. Just wake up. I am done with this place for today and want to go back to where I belong. After several attempts, and some serious concentration, I wake. I am back home, right where I left off, and my family is there. This. This is paradise for me. Not that silly place in my dreams that lately has been toying with my emotions. This place is my paradise.

Erik and Dot are running around in the rear yard of our home, and Agnes is sitting on the back steps leading out from the kitchen, watching her siblings enjoy the warmth of the afternoon. Amanda is in the kitchen, putting some items away in the lower cabinets, and I am just sitting there on the couch, admiring all of this. A time where time matters, seems to be where I need to be right now. Time is a funny thing. You either want it to move, want it to slow, or want it to stop. But when you experience all three, you realize, you just want time to be just as she is.

I want to check in on my new friend, Dominick, and

to also see how Chase is making out with his treatments, but I wonder if maybe those people just need some time to regroup during the hardest times of their lives. I can't help but think about how bad Chase appeared when we last saw him, and how difficult it looked for his mother, who seemed to not accept that her son was nearing his end.

Dominick, though, seemed to accept this more than his wife, and I wonder if he is simply forcing that onto himself so that it makes it a little easier to handle if, and when, that time arrives.

Just as I finish my thoughts, Amanda's cell goes off, and I hear her pick up.

I poke my head around the corner, and the shattered look upon her face tells me something terrible has happened, and she's trying to keep herself composed while talking.

"Gail, my God, Gail, I am so sorry," she begins to say.

"If there is anything I can do, please, anything, we are here."

She ends the call, and I see her look out through the window to the rear yard, where our children are unaware of anything, other than what they have right in front of them. I am about to ask Amanda who that was and what happened, when she turns to the back door, and starts to walk out to where Agnes is seated.

"Hey, honey. How are you feeling?' She asks.

Agnes is covered in the shade of the afternoon clouds, enjoying the sounds and sites of the yard around her. She pauses and looks at her mom, seemingly knowing more than I do, what is going on. How, I do not know, but she does regardless.

"Was that Chase's mother?" Agnes asks.

Amanda places her arm around Agnes to offer some comfort, and realizes that she doesn't need to say anymore, and honestly, it's for the best. Allowing those words to come from her breath would just cause a flood of emotions and tears that both are trying to contain.

Chase has lost his fight, and so many children and parents alike, who have benefited from his infectious personality, wit, and charm are now at a great loss. Those of us who have gained from this young soul, are now left here alone, hopefully able to take the lessons from which he gave, to get us through the stages of this entire exhausting process.

His mother, Gail, must be beside herself. Chase had no siblings, and the relationship between Dominick and Gail seemed already strained. I wonder if this allows for an abrupt turn, where they lean on each other for comfort and support, or if this becomes the straw that breaks the marriage into an unrepairable crisis, and they go separate ways. I hate to think about this now, but it's a true concern for me as well, that what Agnes is dealing with could cause my own family to suffer in ways I never imagined.

Dominick. Man, I need to talk to him. For as strong as he has seemed to me, the impact of the reality of this must create a void that is damaging to his very soul. Not even the strongest of men should ever have to say goodbye to a child for the final time. This just isn't right, and I need to make sure my friend is handling this okay.

I think about heading out to ask Amanda for more details, but the bond I see happening that moment is something that should not be disturbed. Agnes appears to feel something great within her, and she's adjusting her mindset back and forth, I'm sure. The struggle of a young child who is fighting such a nasty, heart-wrenching disease is difficult to watch, but I know she needs this. She needs to understand that life is fragile, and sometimes the fight we give is simply not enough. Death is full of sadness and regrets and learning that for the first time is confusing.

Here she was, watching this wonderful boy treat an incurable disease as if it was not going to alter who he was deep down, and then it just decides whenever it wanted, that it was going to end that beautiful journey for him. He had no say in the matter, and as hard as that is to understand, there's a valuable lesson hidden in there. Chase lived as if each day, each moment, was more important than the last. He lived knowing that eventually he would die, but instead of counting down the days until that day arrived, he counted the ones that he had lived.

I need Agnes to focus on that. She needs to know, that the days she is living are more important to not just her, but to those around her. They are important to me. I need her to enjoy each moment she is blessed with, but to know, things can turn when we aren't ready for them to. There are things within our control, and things that are not. But we cannot give up, and we certainly cannot give in. When they are not within our control, we must look beyond those moments, and have a hope that more is to come for us. We can control hope.

"Would it be alright if we have Chase's mom over for dinner one night, mom? Do you think it would be okay to ask her?" Agnes asks.

Amanda smiles at our daughter and lets out a sigh before answering,

"I think it would be wonderful, honey. I'm sure she would love to see you again. Let's give it a few weeks and check on her to see if she's ready for that, okay honey?" Amanda responds.

Rather than reach out to Dominick now, I figure we will be able to speak briefly in a few days. Once they have Chase's funeral, and they have a couple of days to figure out what their new normal will be like, him and I will have a beer or three and talk about everything, or nothing at all. I haven't a clue as to how to talk with him about this, so maybe talking about anything but that will be best for him.

Chapter 26

A Difficult Truth

***

The sky opens up early the morning that Chase is set to be laid to rest. I think back to the funerals I have been to over my life, and many times, it rains as one would see in a movie. My mother told me long ago that it was the angels crying down from heaven, but that they were not tears of sadness. Rather they were tears of joy, knowing they were about to welcome a wonderful person through the gates of heaven.

It's funny, that in this moment, I am thinking that exact thing. That this rain is from far above, and although science can explain it as the clouds releasing the water they have accumulated, I think maybe we aren't as smart as we think. Maybe it is something greater than we can see or understand, and maybe the angels are crying today, tears of happiness for Chase.

Agnes is sick this morning. Sick enough that Amanda

wonders if she should even attend, but Agnes is having none of it. She is positive she will attend and will not allow this horrid disease to dictate that. This, to her, is one of those times that life feels it has control, but Agnes knows, she does.

We are all dressed in our best suits and dresses, and ready to head out. I have a stop to make on the way, so I decide to drive myself and meet the family there. I just want to pick a small card up for Dominick, to let him know I am thinking of him. That we have bonded over something so vicious, so horrible, but we have bonded still.

The feeling of the cold, damp rain, on the top of my head is interesting to me. Here, awake and far from my place of dreams, I feel the temperature. I feel the tiny drops of rain and they are wet, cold, and real. In my dreams, I notice I have not felt any rain, nor much difference in temperature, and this makes me feel so much more alive than the place I have created.

It also reminds me that Agnes is very much alive. The fact that she is not feeling well today could be taken as a bad thing, but I decide it's a good one instead. She is feeling. She has a sense of pain, sickness, and uncomfortableness, but she has feelings, which means she is very much aware and alive.

As I arrive, I see that my family has already headed in and is walking in the long line to where Chase is laid out, and his mother is standing, crying, as one would expect.

I think about walking past everyone to catch up with

my family but think differently of that. It may come across as rude for those who are waiting patiently to pay their respects, and I can simply meet up with my family once we are all out of the line.

I don't see Dominick at first, but then just as I am about to enter the line, I see him seated at the rear of the church, in an out-cove that has a single, wooden bench seat, and plush, red cushions.

"Hey, Dominick, are you alright?" I ask.

I'm a little confused, because he should be up there with his wife, greeting all of these people that have come out in the rain, and next to his boy who is now no longer with him. I don't get it. Maybe he is just hurting bad and needs a break. Perhaps him and Gail are worse off today, and he just can't add to his stress any more than he already has.

Dominick looks up at me, and smiles. It's not what I am expecting at all, but he seems to be in better spirits than one would expect a parent to be at their child's funeral.

"Jon, it's nice to see you friend. Come. Sit. Let's talk," he says.

As I make my way over to where he is seated, I notice that although people are walking back and forth by him, no one else is saying a word to Dominick. No one has glanced in his direction, and no one seems to care. I am a bit confused, and probably a bit angry, too, that no one seems to understand this man is also in need of condolences. He is just as much a parent as Gail and has lost just as much as she has. I feel for Gail. I truly do, but he seems so alone and for whatever reason, he seems to accept that. I don't get it at all.

"Dominick, I don't, I guess what I am trying to say is," I start.

Before I can get the thought out of my head and mouth, Dominick puts his hand on mine, and pauses me.

"Jon, this isn't going to be easy for you to understand at all. There are no words I am going to say to you now that are going to make this make sense at the moment, but I promise you, you will understand much better when the time is right. You just have to trust me. Do you trust me, Jon? Will you let me explain what I need to, and will you have an open mind about this?" he asks.

I am starting to fidget in the seat next to him and wonder what is happening. I feel a strange sense that whatever he is about to tell me, and whatever I am about to hear, is going to be hard to accept, but true to the core. It's hard to explain, but I know in some strange way, Dominick is sincere in his words.

I just swallow hard, and look back at him, nod my head in agreement, and wait patiently for him to go on.

"Jon, my friend, I want to tell you a story, and I think when I do, you may grasp a greater understanding of many things around you. You will know why things seem so difficult in my marriage, why I am seemingly happy with all of this, when everyone else would be miserable, and why you have those dreams of yours and that place you created in your mind," he starts.

How does he know about my place? I have told no one, ever. Why would I? People would think I was crazy and look at me differently than they do now. I would never tell anyone about my dreams, but this man knows. How is this remotely possible?

He begins to tell me the story of his life over the past five years or so, and how those years were bound in happiness, sadness, frustration, and loss. I sit up in the chair, and am totally focused on each word he speaks, and the people who were around me, pacing back and forth through the back of the church, seem distant now.

"There was a time when things in my life were more complete, before all the changes that shrouded me from that happiness. When Chase was a young boy, we discovered he had a disease meant for anyone but him. Here I was, this father of the sweetest, most caring, carefree child, and I was being told that he would never reach the age of ten. Those words cursed me to a life different from what I was accustomed to, and I had to face the pain that my seasons were changing without my say," he began.

I listened as this man I have known for weeks, not the years it feels like at times, poured his heart out to me, in a way that almost felt as if he had to. Maybe he had no choice in the matter, but he seemed to understand that sometimes we have to face things we would rather not, and that we may not ever understand the reason behind it.

He went on, explaining that Chase never had a chance to understand death as an adult would. He would never have that same fear, because he did not have the time to build the panic we do when we know more about what death means to us.

When we are young, we hear about death, but we don't associate pain, or discomfort, or loss with that. In our minds, we go to this amazing place where angels sing with harps, and golden gates open with a man who sits there and inspects us, before letting us through. We picture fluffy, white, billowing clouds, and imagine that we are looking down on the world below us, enjoying the highlights of our loved one's lives, until their time comes to join us.

As an adult, we grow to fear the pain of death. How our heart gives out, and the struggle of our last breath, before we go to an unknown place, or maybe to nowhere. Even though we are taught about heaven, and eternal life after death, there is that "what-if," factor that enters our minds over and over. It's as if we want to believe, and we know we should believe, but do we trust it? Do we trust that life continues after we leave this place, and do we believe the ones we love most, will greet us once again when their final breath is drawn?

The issue for Dominick, was that he did understand his fears. He did suffer confusion and panic, but not for himself. He suffered those for his son, Chase. Dominick felt that he could not watch as his boy came closer to certain death and hated the fact that he was unsure of how that would be for everyone. He also suffered from a depression he carried with him his entire life, which did not help at all.

So, just over two and a half years ago, when Chase had

a close brush with death, Dominick decided he could no longer watch. He could no longer bare the prospect of losing his only son, and so he sat down one evening, and in a fit of frustration he had felt several times during the course of his sons' treatments, Dominick swallowed a large quantity of pills, fell asleep, and never woke again.

In his mind, he did not want his son to welcome him when it was his turn to die, and he did not want his son to wait for years and years, afraid and alone, so he beat him to it. It was his decision to be the one waiting for his son to arrive, and his decision to ensure, he would never be alone in death. That was a sacrifice Dominick begged to not have to make, but one he ultimately did.

Fortunately, at the time, Chase survived his scare. Somehow, someway, he was able to push through the pain and his mind and body refused to give in.

Things were hard for Chase and his mother, because they loved Dominick, and needed him to help with this fight. His wife became upset with her husband who she felt gave up for selfish reasons, even though his intent was far from selfish. His reasons were, in his mind, selfless. He wanted to do right by his son, and knew, he could not allow him to die alone.

As I am seated here, listening to this man talk about his life ending, I am in such a fog, a daze, that I stop hearing the words coming from his soul, and I can feel my body rise off the seat, and walk towards a window just to the front of the room.

Dominick walks over behind me, places a hand on my shoulder, drops his head, and continues to tell me the story.

"Jon, I know this is not what you expected, and I know this is extremely surprising to you, but I promise, it's about to make much more sense to you. You just need to trust me, Jon. I know more about you than you understand. I am here to help you, not scare you off. I'm here to make sure you understand this all."

My mind starts to go off in different directions, wondering if this man is sick, and perhaps that is why no one goes near him, or maybe I am the one sick, and I am seeing things that aren't there to begin with. Both of those make more sense to me than the story I am hearing. This makes absolutely no sense, because this man is telling me he is no longer alive, yet I somehow am standing here at a window, in a church, talking and listening to him. It's not even possible, but why am I feeling as if this is real?

Dominick knows I am utterly confused and disbelieving, and he gives me a moment to catch myself. He then continues, trying to ease this for me more still.

"My son, Chase, may not be here any longer, but he is far from dead. We understand death to be something it is not, and so when we speak about people dying, we think that it's over, and they are gone. In some sense, we are right, but in the most important senses, we are far from right. Death isn't the end, Jon. It's really just the beginning. Chase is fine. I met him on the ledge of the mountain and welcomed him with open arms. I saw you there, as you tried to scurry over to greet us, but I knew you were not ready for us. You were not ready to understand that, and so we moved on from there."

I peek out into the main part of the church where Chase is laid out, and people are crying and struggling with the loss of this boy, and see my family up at the front, comforting Gail, as they smile at each other. It's as if they are bonded for more than one reason, and I am beginning to understand that now, here.

"Dominick, I don't understand. If I am able to see you and talk with you, does that mean…?" I ask but stop before I say more.

"There was a storm, where the rain came down in heavy amounts as you and Dot were rushing to meet up with your Agnes and Amanda, remember?" he says.

I think back to the time when Agnes had her seizures, and how the ambulance only had room for one adult, and I would just need to get Dot together and meet my wife at the ER as soon as possible. I remember that clearly, and things start to fall into place.

"Jon, you ran a light. You were so worried about Agnes and had the thoughts of your marriage that was being tested, and things were getting hard for you. It's not that you intended to go through the light. Sometimes these things happen. With or without our input."

My mind is racing, and I am seeing that crash. I am able to see how the truck hit us, and I was thrown into the windshield, as Dot, thankfully, was tightly secured in the back in her harnessed car seat. I had secured her well, and for that I am grateful. She was uninjured with the exception of a few bruises from the straps.

Dominick turns me towards him, and I am now looking right at my friend.

"You were brought to the emergency room, and they tried like hell to save you, but they were unable to, because it wasn't within their control. Just a few rooms away from where they had Agnes, they worked on you and pumped your heart over and over again. Amanda had no idea of any of that, until they took Agnes to get tested. Once she was back there, a doctor pulled Amanda aside, and gave her the news. She was devastated, Jon. Her lover was gone, and she was still in a midst of uncertainty about what was going on with her Agnes. She was struggling. It wasn't that she didn't want to be around you, Jon. She couldn't because you had moved on."

"I died? Dominick, are you telling me I am no longer alive?" I ask confused.

"You are very much alive, just not in the way you were. We don't die, Jon. Not like you think. You moved on. It's a different journey in your life, and one where you have choices to make. You can continue on to a new place, where we don't know what to expect exactly, where all our questions can be answered, or you can wait. You can wait until you have whatever it is you want, and then move on. Either way, Jon, things are going to be as they are going to be. I chose to wait for Chase. His time was coming, and I didn't want him to be alone, so I waited, and he is now with me as we go further up the mountain to a new beginning. I know what you are thinking. Why aren't you waiting for Gail? I know Gail is young still, and she will find love once again. She will find someone who can give her much more than I ever could, and I am okay with that. He will be there waiting for her when it is her time. For now, though, I have Chase, and we have decided to see what is out there. I want to know, Jon, what beauty lies ahead for us, and we are ready to see."

Suddenly, things are making sense that had not just days before. My wife had not spoken to me and in fact, walked around as if I did not exist, and she had reason for that. I was no longer there for her, and so she was struggling with that harder than I would have thought. She felt abandoned, even though she knew I never meant to leave her. She loved me more than I knew, despite what I had thought.

Marriages all have troubled times, but true love doesn't just go away. It may get lost for a short time, or hidden beneath a barrier we don't intend to move, but then with time, with patience, and with a full heart, we let that love back in. Amanda had never lost love for me. She was having some troubles in her life, and when Agnes started to get sick, she simply shifted her focus onto her. It wasn't about forgetting me, but more about moving that focus. She knew Agnes needed her more than I did, and she had full intentions of finding that love for me once she had a moment to breathe.

She just never got that chance.

I turn around to look out at the rain as it drops onto the warm earth below, and the night of the crash comes back to me even more. I start to remember how Agnes cried and blamed herself for what happened, and how Amanda had to remind her over and over, that it had nothing to do with what we could control. It was out of our hands, and even though we could not understand it, it was destiny. Amanda believed that. She did not like it, and she did not understand it, but she knew she needed to accept it.

The weeks after my burial, the kids slowly began to build their love for life back. Kids are resilient. They bounce back from broken bones, illnesses, and even death. They are the lucky ones, I suppose.

Amanda has a long road ahead of her. She is nowhere ready to sit down and figure this all out. For now, she has to raise our three children, and ensure that Agnes continues on with her fight, even through the hardest, most challenging of days. She has to live her life as she had once intended, and build a future without me, even if she doesn't know where to begin.

For me, I know I have a lot to learn, and I have all the time in the world in which to learn it from. Do I wait, or do I travel on to the unknown and find a peace and happiness I could not even dream of? For now, I am not in a rush. I think I will wait some and see how things pan out here first.

When I turn back to thank Dominick for explaining things to me, he is no longer there. I look around, and for a brief moment I see him standing next to his wife. He's leaning in, placing his hand and head on her shoulder, and resting for a moment. He's offering her a comfort she desperately needs, and perhaps, saying goodbye for the time being, until she makes that journey through the gates, and up the mountain for herself.

He notices me staring from the back of the church and smiles my way. He squeezes his wife one last time, and then, he's gone.

I can see Gail has a change in her stance, as if she knows now, all is somehow going to be okay, even on the worst of her days.

Chapter 27

Dancing With Her Daddy

* * *

"My favorite thing to do, is to stand outside on a warm summer day, barefoot on the silky grass, in a perfect rainbow-colored, fairy princess dress with a sparkling silver tiara on the top of my head, stretching up to the endless sky, as the sun pours its warmth onto my face," she said.

It's been a year since I left this place I knew as home, but I am here, now, watching my Agnes twist around in the backyard, with the sun dancing across her tiara, and I am sure, all is going to be okay.

Amanda stares in the direction of Agnes, as if she is still unsure of where this is all going to go. She's still lost, and in a state of disbelief, but I know, it's temporary. She's going to find a strength even she didn't know she had, and she going to live out the remainder of her days here, full of love, and hope. That much, I know.

For me, I think I will go out and dance with my Agnes one more time. I think she has struggled with this cancer, and battled like a true warrior, and she deserves a break. She has done what her mother and I never imagined she would need to do, and she has helped people without ever knowing. She will continue to help others, long after her time stops here.

I walk over to where she is, and I take her hand, and spin her around and around, comforting her from a different place, just as Dominick had done with his wife. Agnes could use this touch, and besides, I had never danced with her, despite all the dancing she had done, and I feel it is long overdue.

We spin in the bright sun and laugh and smile through the warm summer's day. It's strange, but somehow I know, Agnes can sense I am here with her. She knows that she is not alone, and it doesn't give her any fear. It gives her a great sense of calm, knowing her father is once again by her side. She turns to where I am standing, and whispers to me,

"Thank you for dancing with me, daddy. I cannot wait for our plus one, so you can dance with me for always."

Amanda stands up, and she walks over to where Agnes and I are, and she has a confused look on her face.

"Agnes, who are you talking with?" she asks.

Agnes just laughs and throws her head back.

"I am dancing with daddy, mom. He wanted his one dance."

Amanda smiles, either in disbelief, or in a strange sense that her child is telling the truth. I don't know, but it doesn't matter. Amanda has smiled, and that is more than I could ask for.

This next year or so is going to be hard for Amanda, and I feel as if she is aware. I think for the most part, she is trying to cope with the loss of her husband, and the fact that she may, indeed, lose her Agnes. It's not about dying for her, it's about living. She's trying to soak up each adventure and savor every word that Agnes speaks to her. She writes down phrases in a notebook that she wishes to remember for always, so that Agnes will never be too far from her mind.

I want to tell Amanda that it's all going to be okay. I want to share with her all I am learning from my time on the mountain, but I know, she needs to find that for herself. It's no longer about my journey. It's about hers. She will find that peace when her time comes, and until then, she can imagine what that wondrous place is going to be like. It's part of the process. We all must push through and live. If we all knew that the place we are heading to was so much more amazing than the one we were in, what would keep us here? That's the test of faith we struggle with. We want to know, but we are not allowed to.

It'll be several months before I stand at the ledge, and look down, to find the black iron gate open once again. But when it does open, I will be ready. I will wave from up above to down below and watch as my Agnes makes the ascent up to where I stand. Then, and only then, will we decide together if we should stay there, or to move higher up the mountain and discover what is truly waiting for us, just as Dominick and Chase decided.

I promise both Erik and Dot that they will have an exceptional life, full of excitement and fulfillment. I promise Andrew that when his time comes, he will not be afraid, but that he has a long way to go. He should share his gift of writing and art with more people when he is ready, and I hope he does. I truly hope he does.

As the days go by, and the leaves begin to fall from the only home they have ever known, I am sitting on the ledge, admiring the perfect trees of my new home. The ones who never need to shed a leaf. They start to rustle a little, and I train my eyes down below, and notice the gate is opened just slightly. A small, familiar bird comes through the gate first, and I can see it is Harold, coming to keep me company once again.

He sits on the ground, and I watch curiously, wondering why he has not flown to me yet as he always does each time he has visited with me. But then I discover the reason why.

There, about ten feet behind Harold, is a small, frail child, with long, beautiful hair, wearing a cute rainbow skirt, and an unmatching top and tiara. As she comes through the gate, it closes gently behind her, and I can see my beautiful, perfect Agnes is here. She's just the way she always intended to be, and for that, I am happy beyond my wildest dreams.

"Agnes, hello! Up here! Welcome home, honey. Welcome home."

Agnes smiles excitedly. The look on her face is one of total acceptance and immense happiness. Almost as if she had been waiting for this moment.

"Shall we dance, Daddy?"

I waited for this moment for certain. My smile says more than my words could ever convey, but I respond anyway,

"Yes, let's dance, my Agnes. I've been waiting for you."

And we dance. It's perfect.

The end

If you enjoyed this story, be sure to check out the Authors other novels, available on eBook, paperback, and hardback.

When the Dandelions Sing

"When The Dandelions Sing," is a warm, heartfelt story about a young boy named Ronnie Jefferson McFarland Jr., who is trying to understand the meaning of the word "purpose", and what his purpose is in life.

His grammy, who nicknames him Jasper for some reason known only to her, and his grandad, give him valuable lessons through their own eyes, and a window to the past that sometimes gets overshadowed by bigger things in life, but never truly forgotten.

While Ronnie's momma struggles with her life, he leans on others around him to gain perspective and a sense of understanding. He learns that even after people leave his world, their impact remains, and he never stops learning from them. As it turns out, some of the best lessons in life come from those who seemingly have nothing left to give.

Ronnie learns that a family is not always conventional, but oftentimes made up of the people you choose for yourself, and who choose you in return. He discovers that joy can be found in the smallest of things and the simplest of moments...for even among a field of perfect flowers, the simple dandelion can sing.

"Everything has purpose, and everything, a meaning beyond what we are even meant to understand. That's just the way it is. Purpose is not what we want it to be. It's simply what is meant to be."

Phoebe's Heart of Stone

In 1919, an unthinkable tragedy struck the blue-collar town of Alliance Ohio, and one particular family, the Bradway family, found themselves at the center of its terrible wrath. In the wake of disaster, Carl, a father of six, was forced to make a decision that would affect both himself and those he loved for the rest of their lives.

Carl and his beloved wife, Phoebe, had worked tirelessly to build a life of love and contentment for themselves and their six young children. Though determined and deeply in love, the young family could not escape the horrible black cloud that haunted their family, seemingly hell-bent on taking all they had built together.

This story follows the shocking true-life events of a family who wished for the simple things in life, but instead faced a path riddled with misfortune that altered the course of each of their lives forever.

Made in the USA
Middletown, DE
06 August 2022

70713984R00182